"A winning fantasy . . . [a] satirical, rollicking adventure."   —*Publishers Weekly*

"*Stuff of Legends* rips the back out of the fantasy genre in a good-natured and loving way, taking on tropes and familiar elements of epic fantasy that deliver a killer comic debut."   —Anton Strout, author of *Dead Matter*

"For the reader tired of cookie-cutter adventures, here's a lighthearted saga with an original twist . . . [a] fantasy world where a hero is a real hero; a press agent is a necessity, then a nuisance; and where wishes are the greatest danger of all. If *Con_____* et *Entourage*, you'd ge_____d."

_____ of *Myth-Chief*

The bubble in the glass was swelling up like an overnight pimple, black-headed and greasy. It grew rounder and fuller until it had become a perfect sphere the size of a large melon, perched weightlessly on the card. Then, with a final chime, it pulled free and drifted upward until it hung in front of Eliott at the level of his wide-eyed stare. The surface of the bubble had gone opaque, like the black glass of the card, so that all he could see as he looked into it was his own distorted reflection looking back. It floated there like a soap bubble's evil twin. Waiting.

Eliott's curiosity could have killed the three-headed cat-beast of Mount Oblivion, if Jordan hadn't already done so. He poked the sphere.

It gave a gentle, contented sigh and swallowed his head.

STUFF OF
LEGENDS

IAN GIBSON

ACE BOOKS, NEW YORK

THE BERKLEY PUBLISHING GROUP
Published by the Penguin Group
Penguin Group (USA) Inc.
375 Hudson Street, New York, New York 10014, USA

Penguin Group (Canada), 90 Eglinton Avenue East, Suite 700, Toronto, Ontario M4P 2Y3, Canada
(a division of Pearson Penguin Canada Inc.)
Penguin Books Ltd., 80 Strand, London WC2R 0RL, England
Penguin Group Ireland, 25 St. Stephen's Green, Dublin 2, Ireland (a division of Penguin Books Ltd.)
Penguin Group (Australia), 250 Camberwell Road, Camberwell, Victoria 3124, Australia
(a division of Pearson Australia Group Pty. Ltd.)
Penguin Books India Pvt. Ltd., 11 Community Centre, Panchsheel Park, New Delhi—110 017, India
Penguin Group (NZ), 67 Apollo Drive, Rosedale, North Shore 0632, New Zealand
(a division of Pearson New Zealand Ltd.)
Penguin Books (South Africa) (Pty.) Ltd., 24 Sturdee Avenue, Rosebank, Johannesburg 2196,
South Africa

Penguin Books Ltd., Registered Offices: 80 Strand, London WC2R 0RL, England

This is a work of fiction. Names, characters, places, and incidents either are the product of the author's imagination or are used fictitiously, and any resemblance to actual persons, living or dead, business establishments, events, or locales is entirely coincidental. The publisher does not have any control over and does not assume any responsibility for author or third-party websites or their content.

STUFF OF LEGENDS

An Ace Book / published by arrangement with the author

PRINTING HISTORY
Ace mass-market edition / August 2010

Copyright © 2010 by Ian Gibson.
Cover art by Brandon Dorman.
Interior text design by Kristin del Rosario.

ISBN: 978-0-441-01930-4

ACE
Ace Books are published by The Berkley Publishing Group,
a division of Penguin Group (USA) Inc.,
375 Hudson Street, New York, New York 10014.
ACE and the "A" design are trademarks of Penguin Group (USA) Inc.

PRINTED IN THE UNITED STATES OF AMERICA

10 9 8 7 6 5 4 3 2 1

To my parents, my wife, and my librarian—
thanks for all the books

PROLOGUE

AFTER THE HOWL of battle died away, and the last of the monsters guarding the innermost sanctum at the heart of the glacier lay fallen on the ice, and the Witch Queen herself went fleeing into the frozen wastes, the conquering hero strode into the throne room of his enemy . . .

The throne was magnificent, in an artisan-evil way. The iron spikes had skulls impaled on them, and the skulls were carved with baleful runes. The seat was formed from broken swords and twisted spears, and upholstered with chips of bone. Jags of ice and spines of frost encrusted it from the floor up, while artfully drizzled coagulate gore dripped down from the cup holder in the arm. This was a throne that declared: Tremble and despair. And whatever you do, don't try to sit down.

Jordan the Red planted his boot against the unholy throne, braced his broad shoulders against the wall, and with one mighty shove sent it crashing down from the dais.

"The ice demons rule no more," he shouted, and the vast dome of the chamber echoed his victory. "Their armies have been defeated. This land is free!"

A blast of arctic wind swept through the throne room, blowing back his long, fiery hair and billowing his wolf-skin cloak dramatically behind him. He raised his sword and saluted the heavens.

Then, out of the corner of his mouth, he added, "You got all that?"

At the foot of the dais, Jordan's bard, Shango, glanced up from his furious note taking. "Got the kick, working on the pose right now. Hold still and keep flourishing that blade while I find a way to fit 'o'erthrown' in. Y'know, for the pun. Very popular right now, puns."

"Hurry up; I'm freezing in this loincloth." Jordan shifted his weight from foot to foot. "You sure I can't wear pants?"

"Ceremonial," Shango answered, flashing him a grin with two missing front teeth. "Glister worked it all out. Good luck finding a barbarian tribe who'd let you kill their demon foes in pants. Who's this so-called hero with no knees, they'd say. Look at him, not freezing his nether-bits off."

"Fine, sure," said Jordan, too cold to argue. "How soon can we get back to the tribe, anyway? I need a sandwich. A hot pig sandwich, and some of Thorving's spiced wine . . . Hell, I'm looking forward to seeing that ugly son of a bear's face again. When I tell him and the Brothers about that last fight, when that thing with the horns came out of the wall— What?"

Shango said nothing, but it was an all-too-familiar nothing, a focused silence that bard after bard had used to avoid mentioning unpleasant details.

Jordan lowered his sword. "Thorving's dead, isn't he?"

"I really can't say."

"How 'bout the Brothers. Are they dead, too?"

"Jordan . . ."

"Is anyone still alive out there? Damn it, who'd I free this land for if they're all dead!"

The bard stopped immortalizing Jordan's feats of valor. "All right, off the record. They're doing the Clash of Armies thing against the ice demons out on the tundra right now. Outnumbered but unwavering, you know? It'll be very dramatic, very moving, when you find their bodies. Don't look at me like that. Jordan, we're creating an epic, not some cheap tavern anecdote. You can't make history without breaking eggs—or, in this case, barbarians. Shall we get back to work?"

"History. Got it." With a stiffness in his limbs that he forced himself to blame on the cold, Jordan resumed his heroic pose. After six years in the business, he could have struck that pose in his sleep—and did, if he could believe what giggling barmaids told him. Better to think about those times than to dwell on a battle he was already too late to join, or what he would find in its aftermath.

"Perfect. That's perfect," his bard kept repeating. "Best stuff I've ever written. I tell you, this one's going to take you to the top. They'll know your name across the continent— hell, they'll know it on lost continents. I can feel it. This story's going to be told for years."

"Great," said Jordan. "Years. Can't wait to hear it all again when I'm old and dead."

"A THOUSAND ICE demons flung themselves against the shields of the barbarian army, cracking the defenders' line with frost-barbed claws and the howling fury of an arctic wind. Hardened Northmen fell and died, were torn apart and left on the frozen mountainside, and the jagged cliffs and crevasses echoed the mad cries of the demons in their victory.

"But the demons knew not that their doom was at hand, for in the frozen heart of their citadel, Jordan the Red— Hey! Hey, I'm trying to perform here!"

A bottle smashed against the wall behind the stage, and Cyral immediately regretted drawing attention from the bar fight at the other end of the tavern. He grabbed his hat and ducked behind the ragged curtain as broken glass rained down.

The tavern was called the Ugly Crowd, and the bards who performed there were the kind who couldn't get work anywhere else—the incompetents, the drunks, and the desperately unknown. Cyral had a good voice and no money to buy even the cheapest gin, but he was beginning to think he had a death wish.

He shot through a rapid breathing exercise. This was the good part, the climactic confrontation between Jordan the Red and the Witch Queen of Hellsbrogdt, where he toppled her throne and drove her into the arctic desolation where only madness grew. If this couldn't capture their attention, then he had no business standing on this stage.

Steeling his nerve, he stepped out from behind the curtain.

The audience was waiting for him. They had taken the time to aim.

He plunged ahead anyway. "In . . . in the heart of the frozen citadel, Jordan the Red came upon the unholy queen—"

It must have been something in his inflection, thought Cyral, as they threw him out the back door. The phrase had taken a wrong turn somewhere.

"Illiterate rabble," he swore back at them, when the door was solidly shut.

Then he limped away, going over the approved litanies of self-pity—why him, it wasn't fair, alas and ouch—before settling on one he could believe in: this wasn't right. By all the laws of narrative, this evening should have been his big break, not the minor sprain it felt like.

He had worked for this. He had pinched and scratched his way through an apprenticeship at the Guild of Actors and Orators, and done his journeyman time heralding an unsung nobleman. A month ago, he had appeared before the Panel of Celebrity Judges and earned the right to perform his own compositions and those of the famous bards who had gone before. He had saved every dollar and bought the license to this performance of "Jordan the Red and the Ice Demons of Brok."

As he left the alley, a taverner coming out the front door of the Ugly Crowd saw him and swaggered over, chuckling. "You know what your problem is?"

Cyral, who had a fairly educated guess, shook his head. "No, sir. What's my problem?"

"You're boring! No, listen to me. You. Were. Boring."

". . . I was telling a saga of Jordan the Red. It's got everything. Bravery, sacrifice, swordfights, monsters, an evil queen—how can that be boring?"

The taverner looked at him skeptically, as if no one could genuinely be so slow at understanding a simple concept. "We've heard it. Heard it all way too many times before."

"It's a classic," said Cyral.

"It's old. Maybe it had some punch when it got written, but today, it's old, boring crap. Only kids still think Jordan the Red is hot stuff. Find something new, or find another audience."

Delighted at the wit and candor of his own artistic criticism, the taverner strolled cheerfully away into the thronged streets of Palace Hills. Cyral stared after him, choking back indignation and disbelief.

"Jordan the Red is not just a children's hero. His adventures are among the finest heroic sagas of our age. I'll show you something new." To his own astonishment, he was shouting. "I'll come back with the greatest adventure story you've ever heard!"

Seizing the unexpected opportunity and cue for passion, he tore off one of his boots and flung it down the street in defiance of all critics, fates, and muses. He would find a hero and they would create an epic to stand with the canon of Jordan the Red's finest bards. All he needed to do was connect with a willing adventurer, and somewhere in this city was a talent agent to provide him with one.

Firm of purpose and destined for fame, Cyral set out.

Then he limped back and retrieved his boot, because the cobbled streets were wet and muddy, and he had no second pair.

ONE

ELIOTT, LYING FLAT on his back, could see nothing but bleached blue sky and dragonflies. He was attempting an impossible feat of endurance and resolution: keeping his body completely still. It wasn't easy. He could feel Kess's fingertips brushing his neck, tracing the ends of lines she had begun above his temples and trickled down the sides of his face. If she had cracked an egg on his forehead, it would have felt exactly like this.

"Kess? Is it done yet?"

"Don't talk. I'll mess up your throat." Kess leaned over and gave him a pixie smile. "Almost done."

"Okay," he said, trying not to move anything but his lips. Out of the corner of his eye, he watched Kess; she was a lot more interesting than dragonflies. She looked eighteen, and always had, but lately Eliott felt like he was catching up.

"It's looking good," Kess carried on, dragging a delicate nail up behind his ear. With every touch, Eliott could feel Elvish magic painting his skin. "Really barbarian. You'll look just like one of the Eagle Berserkers of Skyld. I'm seeing you with a giant, double-headed axe. I know the saga says they used swords, but an axe seems more barbarian to me."

She drew an idle spiral and purred at the back of her throat. "Did I ever tell you I knew a barbarian? Rulph. Loved big weapons, anything that took both hands to hold. I don't think he did anything with just one hand."

Eliott's toes twitched. He couldn't have stopped them if he had tried.

But after a ticklish minute, he realized Kess wasn't going to give him any more details this time. Sometimes, she would go on for hours, telling him about fur-clad barbarians, cavalier young swordsmen, all-night dance parties with satyrs and dryads in moon-hazed forests, and Eliott would imagine himself there with her. Elves went where they pleased and did what they wanted, which sounded like the perfect life to him. But they loved stories more than anything else, and would steal bards and children for their imaginations. On rare occasions, Kess had explained once, an elf would take a job with humans to balance things out, telling stories to the children of the household and sharing their games of make-believe as payment instead of theft. That was how Kess had come to be Eliott's babysitter, until he had grown too old to be sat on. Now, she worked around the estate of his parents, Lord and Lady Symphata, as a general hanger-on and associated retainer, which appeared to involve doing no work at all.

Eliott had grown up with Kess's stories. She told him about her life—in more exciting detail now that he was a teenager, and her friend rather than her responsibility—

and she had told him all the old fairy tales. Best of all, she had told him his first Jordan the Red story.

Jordan the Red, they both agreed, was the greatest hero ever. He had the best weapons, the sharpest quips, and could send an evil vizier hurtling down a five-hundred-foot tower to be neatly impaled on the fangs of the giant serpent that he had killed on his way up. Kess and Eliott had sat through the telling of every Jordan the Red saga ever written.

A dragonfly landed on Eliott's nose. He heard Elvish laughter and realized that Kess had finished.

"Is it done?" He scrambled to his knees. The dragonfly took off petulantly. "Can I see it? What color is it?"

Kess stretched out on the grass and grinned. "Pink."

"You can't—!" Eliott slapped his own cheek. "Kess! There's nothing barbarian about a pink tattoo!"

"Tell that to Drog Steelshanks. His woad had glitter on it, too. We could do that."

Eliott rubbed his now-sore cheek. "I still say that bard got it wrong. Meant to be 'ink-painted was his rippling chest,' or something. Kess, how am I supposed to go to my stupid birthday party with a pink tattoo? All my friends will see."

"I thought all the guests were going to be—what'd you call them?—cardboard morons your parents had hired to be there."

"Well, yeah . . ."

"So, who cares what they think of your . . . very cute . . . tattoo?"

"Kess!"

She laughed again, a sound nothing at all like the tinkling of bells and more like a rabbit snorting. Her long ears twitched. "Relax. It's magic."

Before he could stop her, even if there had been a conceivable universe in which he would have wanted to, Kess pressed her hand across his forehead at the spot where she had begun the tattoo. He had one perfect moment's look up her sleeve at the pale, soft skin from her biceps to her armpit, then felt a coldness wash down his face and neck.

"There." Kess drew her hand away. "Now it's blue. Like you have sapphires embedded in your skin."

"It looks cool?"

She nodded. "It looks cool."

"I've got to see. Race you to the pond!"

"Winner gets thrown in!"

"No!"

Kess let him win anyway. She always did. The only time Eliott had seen her really run, he had been twelve; a basilisk had gotten into the garden and fallen asleep sunning itself on a rock. Somehow, between when he had shouted for Kess to come see what he had found and when he went to poke it with a stick, she had covered the fifty yards between them and knocked him away. It had happened in seconds. The basilisk had yawned, looked around, turned a squirrel to stone, and gone back to sleep. When she wanted to, Kess could outrun the wind.

When she reached the pond, at a casual jog, Eliott was on his knees looking at his reflection. The tattoo was everything Kess had promised: glinting blue whorls and jags from the peak of his peach blond hair all the way down to his collarbone. It looked like something off the skin of the northern barbarian tribesmen Jordan the Red had befriended on his way to defeat the demon at the crown of the world. It even hid the rogue spots of acne that had been showing up lately like marauding subdermal trolls. Eliott touched it lovingly, wishing that the rest of his face looked heroic enough to match it. Especially his ears.

"Hey, Kess? Wanna change the color of my hair, too?"

A pebble splashed into his reflection, turning his face into rippling rings. "Not today. But I've got something else for you . . . a birthday present."

Something in her voice made his heart race. She was smiling at him, not with her usual playfulness but in a mysterious way he had never seen before. His imagination sped forward into strange and exotic territory; he barely managed to reel it back before it went too far. "What is it?"

"If you could wish for anything in the world—"

"Eliott! Eliott, this isn't where you're supposed to be! Get up here right now, young man!"

All his private fantasies died like evil viziers thrown from towers. He rolled his eyes. "Mom," he muttered, summing up in one syllable his frustration, his boredom, and how much he would rather stay down at the pond with Kess.

Kess ruffled his hair. "I'll be back for your party. I'll give you your present then."

She stood and bowed gracefully, a gentleman's bow, just as Lady Symphata came around the rhododendron bushes. "Starlight shine on Your Ladyship. Your son is here; I've kept him out of trouble."

Eliott chucked a stone across the pond. He didn't dare look around at Kess, or she would wink at him, and then he would laugh, and his mother would know what a joke Kess was making with her formal manners.

"I'm so glad," said Lady Symphata. "You always could manage the impossible, couldn't you? Eliott, your father has gone down to the theaters to find a bard to perform your Jordan the Rogue saga. I expect you to be there to greet him when he returns, and to thank him for going to the extra effort. Now, go and get changed before the guests start showing up—we've only hired them for six hours."

"The Red," said Eliott, not quietly enough.

"I beg your pardon?"

"Not the Rogue. Jordan the Red," Kess supplied help-fully. "But Eliott would be happy with a saga of Drog Steelshanks instead. Wouldn't he?"

Eliott spun around and made a face at her before she could slip away.

His mother's mouth fell open. He had forgotten about the tattoo.

"Eliott Miles Symphata—what have you done?! Go wash that off right now before anyone sees!"

Her shouts chased him all the way back to the manor.

DRAGONFLIES GAVE WAY to fireflies, and the pleasant, early-autumn afternoon in which Eliott had been a tat-tooed barbarian with a beautiful Elvish companion gave way to a perfume-scented evening in which he was a child being put on display for his noble parents' friends and a few dozen rented guests. His parents had gone so far as to lay out an outfit for him: a pale green tunic with a frilled shoulder cape, tight white hose, and soft shoes that curled up to points at the tips. The cuffs of his jacket had lace on them. He figured it was his parents' way of saying they wanted him to become a court jester.

He rubbed at his neck where his tattoo had been. To his mother's great relief, it had faded away at sundown. He had asked if he could get a real one, but Lady Symphata had only stared at him as if he had asked for permission to grow a third eye.

The only good part of the evening so far had been the gifts. Amazingly, his parents had given their guests a good idea of what interested Eliott: woodcuts and tapestries of Jordan the Red's most famous battles; bronze miniatures of Jordan the Red's preferred weapons and armor; and one wooden triumph of craftsmanship, a fully articulated Jordan the Red action figure that could be posed in dozens of monster-slaying positions.

Eliott fiddled with its arms. If he had had anywhere else to go, he would have snuck away. No one would notice. Everyone else was dancing or drinking or pillaging the buffet; his parents, confident that his spirit had been broken by the outfit and their instructions that he was personally responsible for everyone having a good time, had retreated to the manor. If he was lucky, he wouldn't see them again before they left in the morning for their week at the court.

"Anyone sitting here?"

Without waiting for an answer, Kess swung herself onto the bench beside him. "Great party. People are really pretending they're having fun. Is it somebody's birthday?"

She smiled, and the party got better.

"Yeah, and somebody got this great tapestry of Jordan killing the dragon from the 'Skarbolg Saga,'" said Eliott. "Check it out!"

"Speared through the eye. Nice." Kess waved down two glasses of wine. "When's the saga?"

"Whenever we want it. I was waiting for you."

"Thanks. I was getting your present ready. Here."

She handed him a brown paper sack. It felt practically weightless. Nervously, eagerly, he opened it.

". . . You got me popcorn."

"That's for the saga." She grinned, ears twitching. "I'll give you your present afterward. Thought about what I asked you earlier?" Eliott tried to remember what she had asked, but Kess was already calling for the Master of the Entertainment to start the saga.

The curtain went up. Eliott leaned forward, his imagination dancing ahead to the best parts, where Jordan the Red would smash the tedium with a spiky club. The bard stamped a worn boot on the plank stage, struck a hollow chord on his six-stringed harp, and stretched out a hand to the crowd.

"Harken," he began, in a hoarse voice that wheezed out through the gap where his two front teeth should have been. "Hear now the story of Jordan the Red / How he fought bravely / Fiercely / Against the Ice Demons of Brot."

Eliott frowned. "Brok," he corrected, under his breath.

"Now word came," the bard declared, "of the demon armies / To the warriors of Hyjenac / To the brothers of Hyrame / Who sheltered Jordan then / And he was the mightiest among them."

Eliott glanced at Kess. "Did he just . . . ?"

"Yeah. I know."

"He skipped the prologue!" Eliott felt the wine in his stomach turn sour. "He isn't explaining about the ice house at all—'In the early days of the ice-shield kings . . .'"

"Maybe he's rearranged it."

"Maybe . . ."

The bard droned on, unaware that he was being given the benefit of the doubt. Stanzas passed, and with every absent line, every mispronounced name along Jordan's journey north, Eliott squirmed. Against all possibility, the bard was managing to take the meat of the adventure, flay it of excitement, and dry it over his voice until nothing was left but a flavorless jerky. The first battle sounded like a math lesson.

Eliott slumped. His parents had screwed this up, too. They had managed to find the one bard in all the world who could tell a Jordan the Red saga badly. Worst of all, nobody else seemed to notice. They laughed and gasped and applauded at the appropriate moments, just like they'd been paid to do.

Jordan the Red, thought Eliott, would have roundhouse kicked the bard right off the stage.

Kess nudged him in the ribs. "Let's get out of here."

"Yeah . . ."

No one tried to stop them leaving, which struck Eliott as one more disappointment. When the guest of honor wanted to escape his own birthday party, it ought to require more flash and cunning, or at least some magical trickery. But no one seemed to care. One of the waiters even winked as they slipped away into the dark.

They ended up at the stables. Every stall was filled. The warm chestnut reek of hay and horses felt like a blanket of protection against both the chill of the evening and the glare of the party. Kess wandered among the animals, absently stroking noses, while Eliott traded his hated pointy shoes for a pair of proper boots with cracked soles and scuffed leather. He wiggled his feet into them and felt like a real adventurer, ready to kick some trolls.

"Okay, good to go. Let's do something— Hey, could you put a curse on that stupid bard?"

"Like turn him into a frog?" said Kess idly. "Give him the head of a donkey?"

"Yeah, exactly."

"Nope. Sorry. He's a bard." She swayed, as if listening to music only she could hear. "Bards and storytellers get a free pass. Even bad ones."

"Then what do you want to do?" said Eliott.

"That depends." Kess held out a closed fist. Her eyes had a gleam of mischief, and her long, brown hair danced like fire as she shook back her head. "Are you ready for your birthday present?"

Eliott tried to swallow his libido. He stared at her fist. There might have been nothing in it at all. "I'm ready."

"Come here and hold out your hands. And close your eyes."

He did. There was the slightest brush of her fingers over his sweating palms, and then he was holding . . .

something. Something small. Almost weightless, with a slightly feathery end. He wondered for a moment if she had given him a woolly caterpillar, which made him begin to dream up reasons why. Before his imagination got too far, he asked, "Can I look?"

"Okay."

He peered at the thing resting in his hands. It was four inches of thick, soft thread, braided in three colors: gold, white, and silver. The silver and gold threads sparkled like real metal, and the white one looked as if it had never heard the word "dirt." Eliott turned it over. Other than look beautiful, it didn't seem to do anything. It might have been the world's most expensive, and simplest, friendship bracelet.

"Um . . . thank you? What is it?"

"It's a Braid."

"Yeah, I can see. Three threads. Like you made me do with your hair—"

Kess laughed. "Braid with a capital *B*. It's magical. Really strong magic, too."

She knelt down, scratching in the dirt, and Eliott squatted beside her. "It's traditional. At fifteen, an elf child is grown-up. You're a man now," she told him, with almost no teasing in her voice. "And when that happens, you get a Braid. Each thread . . . gives you a wish."

She drew three lines.

"Gold. Silver. And the white thread. That's the strongest of them all, because it sets everything right. You make your wish, and then you snap a thread. It's sort of a test, to see what you'd do with Ultimate Cosmic Power."

"Wow . . ." Eliott held the Braid up to catch the light of the rising moon. "I get three wishes!"

"Two. The white thread—"

"Oh, yeah. So how does that work? It undoes everything the other two did? Will I remember my wishes coming true?"

"Definitely. And so will I, because I'm special." Kess gave him a look that suggested she could read his thoughts, even the ones he hadn't had yet. "It puts the world back as close as it can to where things would have been if you hadn't made any wishes. Like, say you wished you had all the money in Palace Hills. You'd get it, but there'd suddenly be a lot of poor people there who'd be mad at you. The white thread would give them all their money back, and if they tracked you down and beat you up, it'd send them home. They'd be confused for a bit, and then they'd forget and get on with their lives."

"Cool!" Eliott paused, the feathered tips of the threads pinched between his fingertips. "So what would happen if I wished for something that got somebody killed?"

"Then they'd be dead," said Kess, "until you broke the white thread. And I'd kick your ass."

"Yeah, okay. But what if I got killed?" asked Eliott, hunting cheerfully for the devil in the details. He had no worries about his own mortality—he knew, secretly, that he was going to live forever—but he'd heard enough three-wish stories to know there was always a hidden catch.

Kess squeezed his arm impatiently. "If you die, then the white thread breaks itself."

"And I'd be alive again?"

"I don't know. Maybe? It's elf magic, and we're immortal. It should work the same way for humans, but I don't think we've ever let a human have a Braid before. But it doesn't matter. You"—she tapped her fingers up the buttons of his jacket—"aren't going to need to find out, because you"—tap—"aren't going to die. Come on, this is supposed to be fun."

"Wow, I'm the first human?"

"You might be. Or there could have been some old, dead wizards. I stopped paying attention halfway through when my grandmother was explaining it to me. You should have heard her. She was like an instruction manual. 'Step one, concentrate with all your heart and mind on the wish. Grasp the thread between thumb and forefinger.' She went on forever before she let me make a wish."

"Well, I've got one."

"Oh!" Kess got to her feet, looking genuinely excited. "Let's do it, then. If I get to hear it. You don't have to tell me what your wish is."

Eliott scrunched up his face, working out the exact words to use. The wish had come to him suddenly, out of the blue, but it was right. It was perfect. And it would be perfect for both of them.

"Of course I'm going to tell you! You're coming along." He pinched the gold thread. "I wish that you and I could go to wherever Jordan the Red is—the real Jordan the Red—right now, and have an adventure with him!"

He snapped the thread.

TWO

FAR AWAY AND beyond the borders of the lands Eliott
knew, where the sun had not yet decided to go down, Jordan the Red squinted against the dying afternoon light and
reflected on the downfall of kings. He was in a bad spot;
his own fault, but nothing to do about past mistakes now.
Focus. He wasn't beaten yet. He could move. Admittedly,
not to anywhere that would let him escape defeat, but he
still had the option.

No surrender.

He flexed his stiff fingers. He moved.

"Ten to six, Sam. All up to you."

On the other side of the checkerboard, Sam laughed
softly and bounced one of his kings lightly over two of
Jordan's pieces. "You ready to call it a game yet?"

"Nope."

They had been skirmishing all afternoon over their

little battlefield, in the shade of the high stone wall that
separated the road out of the village from acres of corn
and pumpkins. From time to time, a passing farmer would
stop to inspect their game, nod approvingly, and carry on
with his business. This was what passed for riveting entertainment in the neighborhood of that village, which was
called Cheese.

"You're not going to win by waiting for me to get tired
of chasing your last piece," Sam pointed out. "Call this a
draw and we can start a new game. One where you don't
make such an awful first couple moves, maybe?"

"Nope. Six to one. Crown him."

"It's your funeral."

Jordan tapped the board impatiently. "Yeah, but hell if
it won't be a pyre."

"Hah!" Sam snorted with laughter. The crows in the field
beyond the wall took flight, protesting loudly. "You're playing to your legend today, old man. Sure your piece wants a
crown, not a broadsword?"

"No idea what you mean." Jordan smirked with the tini-
est corner of his mouth and pushed back the wiry gray
shock of hair falling across his eyes, giving himself the
look of a freshly unhelmed soldier returning from the battlefield. "No legends here. Just plain you and me. Right?"

"I know, I know. How long've I been keeping your
secret?"

"Good. Now, hurry up and move your king into my
cunning trap."

Jordan took a long drink from his beer mug and settled
back to play out his valiant, but inevitably doomed, last
stand. At this rate, Sam could only beat him another three
or four times before it got too dark to play.

"You don't think they've given up yet?" asked Sam conversationally, as he made his move.

"Who d'you mean?"

"Glister and his search parties. Hasn't been one in years, but you still get edgy when anyone new comes to town."

Jordan shrugged. "How many good reasons can you think of for anyone to come to Cheese?"

"Other than trying to find a retired warrior hero?" Behind his milky cataracts, Sam's eyes twinkled. He waved a hand toward the village, grasping for possibilities. "Historical dairy enthusiasts, maybe? Or maybe for the same reason you did."

"I only came here because nobody else does."

Sam cracked a smile. "Sometimes seems like paranoia to me, is all."

A thump on the other side of the wall made both men turn toward it. Something scrabbled at the ancient stones. Jordan reached for his sword, which he hadn't carried for twenty years and was in fact currently packed away in the bottom of a trunk back in the village. He swore under his breath and gave the wall a pointed glare, which seemed to stop it making any more noise.

"Paranoia. Right."

A face appeared at the top of the wall. It was a long, thin face with big eyes, big ears, and a lot of wavy blond hair—very much a boy's face, and at the moment a very red face, too, as it seemed to be trying to lift itself over the wall by its chin. It made a sound somewhere between a grunt and a squeal and uncannily like the cry of a primordial swamp beast beaching itself.

Jordan stared at it. "What the . . ."

The face pulled the rest of a body up behind it, proving that it was at least nominally human, in the awkward way of boys whose bodies have yet to figure out the right length for all their limbs. The boy perched on the wall, mouth gasping and gulping, like a primordial swamp beast figuring out how to form words.

Jordan kept staring. "You want something, kid?"

The boy nodded wildly, before finally blurting out, "You're . . . you're Jordan the Red! I want to be just like you!"

And he fell backward off the wall.

ELIOTT SAT UP shakily. His head hurt. He rubbed the back of his skull and felt a fresh lump. Someone had propped him up against a pumpkin. He didn't remember that. He remembered the wish, and a wall, and hearing Jordan the Red—

He scrambled to his feet. "Kess! Where is he? Is he still here? I knew he wasn't dead—Jordan could kick the ass of a crocodile god any day. Where're we going? Did you tell him—"

Kess put her arm around his shoulders. This, Eliott had figured out long ago, was her way of signaling him to talk slower, or maybe even not talk at all for a bit. Lately, it was mostly effective because it started his pulse racing too quickly for him to think about words. "Hey, Eliott. This is Sam. He's a friend of Jordan's."

She poked him, and he stuck out his hand to a short, wrinkled man with a fringe of a beard and a tiny, puzzled smile. "Hi. I'm Eliott. That's with one *L*, two *T*s . . . I've never heard of you. Are you in any of the sagas? Because that's pretty cool. I didn't know Jordan had any friends. Living friends, I mean."

Sam found his hand and shook it. "A pleasure to meet you, Eliott. And no, I'm not in any of the stories. Jordan and me, all we ever did together was go fishing."

Eliott tried to make space for this in his mind. The notion of Jordan the Red fishing, unless it involved massive harpoons and giant squid on stormy seas, didn't fit. It was like trying to imagine Jordan going to the toilet, or brushing his teeth. Of course he would, but until now, Eliott had never considered it.

"Your friend was about to tell me how you managed to drop in on us like this," said Sam. "People've been trying to find Jordan for twenty years, and yet here you are . . ."

Eliott opened his mouth to answer, but Kess was quicker. "Magic," she said flatly, as if that was the end of the explanation.

"Ah. That would do it. He's not going to be happy about that, either, you know. Not fond of wizards."

"I'm going to go adventuring with him," said Eliott, bringing the conversation back to the point.

Sam chuckled. "That'll be a thing to hear about. You see, Jordan, he doesn't have adventures these days. I'm sorry, son. He's retired."

Again, Eliott's head tried to make room for the impossible. "No, I mean Jordan the Red. The famous hero. He kills seven-headed monsters when he gets bored. That's his life!"

He glanced at Kess, who shrugged.

"Hey, can I meet him now?"

"I should think he's still close by," said Sam. "Trying to decide what to make of you. You're the first fan he's had to deal with in a long, long time."

Eliott hurried off, pushing through the rows of corn as if they were an army arrayed against him. This wasn't how he had pictured meeting Jordan—there were fewer decapitated goblins, for one thing—but he was here, and it was happening. He'd made his wish, and he was going to get his adventure. Jordan was somewhere close.

The corn opened abruptly. In the open field beyond, a scarecrow loomed against the nearly extinguished sunset. It was an old, shabby construction, ignored by the local birds, but Eliott approached it cautiously. His adventure could start at any moment, and scarecrows coming to life was a classic device of the sagas. The only question was whether this one would spring knives from its empty sleeves and attack, or do a funny dance at him. Either way, there was a good chance it would go after his brain.

Eliott picked up a stone and took aim at the straw head.

"That's one of Farmer Wormick's old shirts," said a voice behind him. "His wife stitched the head. I watched her put the straw in myself. It ain't coming alive."

The stone tumbled out of Eliott's hand. Jordan the Red edged stiffly out of the corn beside him.

"Wormick'd give you a smack just for thinking of knocking it down," Jordan added, patting the tattered shirt affectionately.

Eliott opened his mouth a few times, but nothing came out. He wasn't sure if he was trying to talk or throw up from nervousness.

"I was waiting for you back by the gate," said Jordan. "Heard you talking to Sam. Look, kid—can you quit gawking?"

Eliott stammered. He couldn't manage real words. He had an idea that he should drop to one knee, or salute, or recite the "Skarbolg Saga." Something. Anything! The moment was slipping away. Humiliation set fire to his face.

"Yeah, this is going to go great." Jordan put a guiding hand on Eliott's shoulder, steering him back the way they had come. "You and your girl head back home and forget you found me, all right? I'm happy you remember me, but I'm out of the business. Got it? Good."

Against his screaming inner voice, Eliott nodded like a puppet. His hands sank into his pockets in defeat.

His fingers brushed the two remaining threads of the Braid.

And suddenly, the heat, the humiliation, the paralysis,

all went away. He remembered how to speak. He gripped the Braid tightly, like a talisman of courage.

"No."

Jordan blinked. "What?"

"I'm not going home," said Eliott. "Not yet. I'm talking to Jordan the Red! This is the coolest thing that's ever happened to me! You're amazing. You're—you're my hero! I know all your sagas. And I'm going to go on an adventure with you."

Jordan halted, staring off at a silhouetted ear of corn so intently that Eliott wondered if it was some sort of shape-shifted monster waiting for them. When Jordan spoke, his voice was thin and forced. "Ain't happening, kid."

"I won't get in the way! I promise. Just let me be there to watch. Watch and learn. I'd be like your apprentice!"

"You think I need an apprentice, huh?"

"You don't need anything. You've taken on armies by yourself. You killed twelve ogres in the 'Ashgrit Frontier Saga.'"

Jordan rubbed his left arm. "Yeah, and I still feel it when the weather gets damp. Twelve? I'd forgotten it was twelve."

"I could do those verses for you. Right now. Can I?"

"Last thing I need is to hear any of that bardic impshit again. No, thank you." Jordan grimaced. "Kid, the only thing I could teach you is how to get old and die. Find yourself another hero. Because I'm retired."

"But—"

"Trust me. Nothing exciting happens to me anymore. And that's how I like it."

Jordan pushed open the gate to the road and went through, but he left it open for Eliott to follow. Ahead, the village of Cheese was lighting up with a soft, domestic glow. Candles shone through decoratively carved shutters.

Chimneys rising from thatched roofs puffed out woolly smoke. If an evil warlord had wanted to prove just how evil and heartless he was, this was exactly the kind of village he would have ordered his rampaging hordes to destroy.

Eliott had to jog to catch up with Jordan, who was striding along at a good pace. "I don't believe it."

"What?"

"That you've stopped having adventures. Okay, there haven't been any new sagas for a while—"

"Twenty blissful years."

"—for twenty years, okay, and you've given up the bards and the glamour and the golden banquet halls—"

This drew a short, violent rattle out of Jordan's throat. Since he didn't follow it up by spitting out a lump of gravel, Eliott assumed it was a laugh.

"—but I don't believe you're having a dull life," Eliott carried on. "You just don't want anyone to know. So I'm going to be here, and when something happens, I'm . . . going to be here," he finished weakly.

"Kid, this is Cheese. People don't have a lot of problems here. And y'know what? They don't need a hero to deal with any that do come up. So unless you want to help me chase a stray sheep out of someone's garden, you're going to get pretty damn bored."

Eliott thought about this.

"A zombie sheep?"

"A— What? No, nobody here raises zombie sheep. Where the hell did you get that from?"

"'Skulp Saga.' The entire village got turned into zombies, including the—"

"Right, I get it. No. There are no zombies here. There will never be any zombies here. It's a zombie-free zone."

"Because it's got a hero to defend it."

Jordan spun around. "No! It doesn't. I'm nobody here.

I'm an just old man living in a little town where the name Jordan the Red means nothing. Got that?"

Eliott scuffed the toe of his boot into the dirt. He'd been yelled at before, on rare occasions, but this was the first time he'd felt someone actually getting angry at him. It gave him a strange, trembly sort of feeling. It had to be a warrior hero thing; Jordan could probably demoralize a legion of bloodthirsty marauders with his voice.

"I won't tell anyone your secret identity," Eliott said meekly.

Jordan stared at him. "My secret . . . Kid, I'm not doing my heroics in a mask after dark either."

They walked along the road together in silence as dusk gathered around them. A plump housewife came out with a bowl of table scraps for an equally plump cat. She gave Jordan a friendly, disinterested wave and a smile, the kind she might have given to anybody. When she went back inside, Jordan nodded with satisfaction.

"See? Nothing special. I can walk down this street, anytime of day, and nobody looks twice. Nobody stares; nobody asks me for an autograph."

Eliott perked up. "Hey, do you think I could—"

Jordan ignored him. "It's been twenty years since I've had any young twerps come at me wanting to prove themselves in a duel. Smacking them down got old, real fast. Right, we're here."

"Here" turned out to be a slightly run-down cottage set back from the road by a short path through a weedy garden. One wall supported, or was supported by, a large stack of firewood. In front of it sat a badly fractured chopping block, well on its way to joining the stack. The thatched roof was sagging, but free of moss, with several neat, fresh patches where the thatch had been carefully repaired. A sign over the door simply said DUN.

"This is . . . where you live?" Eliott ventured. He peered

around for the massive iron ramparts, the trophy weapons displaying the heads of Jordan's defeated enemies, the coffers of gold and jewels. The yard was unthinkably devoid of statues to the glory of Jordan the Red.

"Yep. And it's where I say good-bye. Inn's just up the road. Trout and Truncheon, you can't miss it. Stick around until you get bored. Or don't. I don't care." Jordan swung the gate closed between them. "As long as you leave my past alone."

Eliott watched him walk up the path, into the gloom of the gathering night, to the door of the cottage, without accepting anything Jordan had said. Of course Jordan the Red was still having adventures. Even if he had, as Eliott was forced to admit, gotten old, it was impossible to imagine that he could be living a boring life. Any moment now, goblins would leap at him, or a farm boy would bring him news of a princess in mortal danger. The world would behave as Eliott knew it should, the way the bards promised. If not, if someone could choose a measly country cottage over a life full of adventure and romance and battle, then nothing made sense.

In the doorway, Jordan turned around and looked back. "You waiting for something?"

Eliott shrugged. "Goblin assassins?"

Jordan shook his head and shut the door behind him.

A less devout believer might have been discouraged, but Eliott had absolute faith. He swung himself up onto the fence and hooked his feet through the rails. His wish would come true. All he needed to do was wait.

"BUT NOTHING HAPPENED! He never came out and he never got attacked and nobody came needing his help."

Eliott flopped backward onto the second-best bed in the Trout and Truncheon, where Kess had brought him after finding him still perched on Jordan's fence, his jacket soaked with evening dew. Great seas of gaudy rag-quilts swelled up around him, infuriatingly soft and comfortable. He wanted them to be prickly and unyielding, so he had a reason to feel as irritated as he did. The pillows were equally unsatisfying, giving him no cause to pummel them. He settled for a deep, frustrated sigh.

"Someone will need him," said Kess, sitting on the edge of the bed and unlacing her boots. "And he'll help them. He's still Jordan."

"He's gotten old."

"Yeah. People do that."

"Well, they shouldn't. They shouldn't get old and they shouldn't retire and they shouldn't have stupid birthdays."

"You still got to meet him," said Kess. "I didn't get to say anything to him. You'd better get me his autograph, or I'm going to paint your nails while you're asleep."

Normally, Eliott would have let her cheer him up with her teasing, laughed off his sullenness, and perhaps thrown a pillow at her, but tonight he felt perversely attached to his bad mood. He wanted to tell the universe what a bad job it was doing, and how it should straighten itself out right now. It was a childish thought, one that he knew he ought to have grown out of by turning fifteen, but knowing this only made his mood worse.

He rolled over onto his stomach. "Kess? I'm going to get my adventure, right?"

"You wished for it. Of course you are."

"Okay. Because that's what I want to do. I don't want to go to the court; I don't want to get old in some dull village and be in bed by dark. I want to be one of the people who does things. Real things. Stuff worth hearing about."

Kess smiled, and for a moment, he thought she was going to hug him. Instead, she went to the window and put her heel up on the varnished oak frame, stretching like a dancer. "Then that's what you'll get. We'll stay here until you do. It'll be a vacation."

"Yeah, not like anyone back home will miss me," Eliott muttered into the quilts. He kicked himself off the bed. "You really think he's retired? Like, not just from doing sagas, but from all of it?"

"Maybe he thinks so, but I know he'd still kill a giant fire-breathing scorpion if it came here."

"Yeah. Yeah! He's just . . . keeping himself in reserve right now. Resting up."

"Saving his strength."

"Like a coiled spring, compressing his awesome power."

"He still looks like he's in great shape."

"Training."

"For when the scorpions attack."

In Eliott's mind, the streets of Cheese swarmed with enormous, deadly insects, held back only by Jordan the Red. How quickly, he realized, the Jordan of his imagination had changed shape, becoming an old man but still a warrior. This Jordan was a weathered veteran, a grizzled survivor of not only a thousand battles but also of decades skirmishing with age. Eliott rolled the image around, looking at it from all angles, and decided he liked it. He added more bugs and put himself into the scene, and Kess, too; the three of them standing together against the swarm.

"This is gonna be great."

Kess gave his head a playful push. "We'll get our adventure with him. Have faith."

"Yeah," said Eliott. "I know. I do."

But when Kess had gone to her room, Eliott lay awake for a long time, counting the knots in the ceiling and imagining things that would force Jordan to stop pretending and leap into action. A wandering giant. An army of zombies. Some fantastical beast in need of a warrior hero to train it for battle against an evil emperor. Anything that would make the story hurry up and begin.

Eliott frowned thoughtfully. Having faith was easy. What he needed was a plan.

ON THE OTHER side of the village, Jordan was having trouble sleeping, too. A mug of warm milk with a little brandy in it before bed had done nothing. Neither had a rather larger mug of warm brandy with a drop of milk in it. He blamed the boy. Whenever the old memories got dredged up, his chance of a restful night went straight to hell—coincidentally, the same place some of his worst memories came from.

He twisted involuntarily under the blankets. It all came back so easily—the demon bats of Phorbis, that gate in the Boneyard of D'loom.

But only memories. Soon enough, the boy would be gone, and the memories would sink back into the muck at the bottom of his brain like so many weapons dropped into a turbid river. Tonight, he would face them, one more time; break their lines and fight through into dreamless sleep.

No surrender.

Jordan's eyes shut like portcullises as he steeled himself to make it through the night.

THREE

"SO I'VE FIGURED out what we need to do."

A perfect, golden, autumn apple arced across the cloudless sky like a second sun. Eliott swung, and three feet of maple branch met the apple with a satisfying, juicy crunch that sent it bouncing into the bushes on the other side of the stream, just barely missing the holly tree that was worth twenty points. A crow, worth fifty points, hopped down and pecked at it.

"At least, I've got the start of it," Eliott continued, beating the weeds with his bat. "I'm still working on the details."

Kess paused in her search for another apple. "What've you got in mind?"

"Well, y'know how you said if a monster showed up, Jordan would have to fight it? We need to find a monster."

They both looked around at a landscape of such bucolic blandness that dragons would have written it off on their maps as "Here There Be Tedium." The most monstrous thing anyone was likely to come across was a temperamental bull.

"A monster," repeated Eliott. "Or a secret coven of witches. Some old dead god sleeping under one of those hills. This place has to have something we can stir up."

"We might be able to find a wasp's nest," said Kess. She picked up a half-rotten, insect-ravaged apple and blew softly on it until it became a perfect piece of throwing fruit. "Nothing feels occult here. I tried talking to some of the farmers this morning—I've had easier conversations with trees." She patted the trunk of the apple tree convivially. "Anyway, there's never even been a war around Cheese. People settled here thousands of years ago, and have gone along peacefully with any king who's wanted to claim them since."

She lobbed the apple to Eliott, who caught it.

"If they've been here for that long, they must have had priests or druids or something at some point, right? And gods were pretty bloodthirsty back then . . . Maybe there's an old temple buried here." Eliott kicked the apple back and forth between his boots as the idea bounced around his head. The village didn't have much, but he was sure it had a shovel.

"Maybe. Probably all they had was a mother goddess." Kess shaped a fat, female body in the air with her hands, then brushed it away dismissively. "Dairy farming tribes don't need much from the Elder Gods of Eternal Horror and Mystery. But it can't hurt to look," she added.

"Yeah, but where you've got cows, you've got bulls, right?"

"If you want to have more cows," Kess agreed.

"And if you've got bulls, you know what you'll end up with."

". . . Men in very small jackets and big red capes taunting them?"

"Minotaurs. Wouldn't this be the perfect place for a temple built around a minotaur? There could be an underground labyrinth here, and nobody would suspect it."

"Okay. So, a long time ago—"

"Centuries."

"—centuries ago, all the cows attracted a really bull-headed man, and the villagers started worshipping him?"

"Of course."

Kess smiled encouragingly, as she always did when Eliott's imagination started to run wild. She turned her face toward his fantasies as if they were a pleasant scent on a summer breeze. "So why would they hide his temple in a maze and then bury it?"

Eliott thought about it. "The cows."

"Bovine revolution?"

"They started giving birth to freaky monster calves. Because, y'know, the minotaur liked to—"

"—go cow tipping. Okay."

"That's where your mother goddess comes in!" Eliott bounced the apple triumphantly off his knee. "She got her followers to trap the minotaur in his own temple, seal it all up, and then made them swear never to speak of it again! Bam—sleepy little farming village with a dark secret underneath. Now all we have to do is find it!"

"Sounds like fun," said Kess. "Where do we start?"

Eliott beamed at her. Once again, he had the incandescent feeling that she was going along with his idea, wild as it was. "We've got to get underground. We can go through the sewers."

"Gross. No."

"Come on. Jordan always found the entrance to secret lairs and ancient ruins by going through the sewers. Oh! You know what we need to do?"

"Find the village historian?"

"No! We need to bring Jordan along. I bet if he came

into the sewers with us, I'd lean on a hidden latch—totally by accident—and fall into a secret tunnel. Or we'd say there was no way we were going to find the entrance, and the ground would give way under us."

They both looked at their feet. The autumn-dried earth beneath remained uncooperatively solid.

"Okay," said Kess, "but Jordan won't come with us unless we find something he has to face. That's the whole problem. It's the chicken and the egg."

"Oh . . . right."

Eliott rubbed pensively at the two remaining threads of the Braid, currently pinned to his shirt like a prize ribbon. "I could make another wish, I guess. Wish for a monster. Do you think I should?"

"Up to you."

One wish left, he thought, and then only the white thread to take everything back to normal. But wouldn't it be worth it?

". . . No," he said at last. "I'll save it for something really special. Something good. We can still make this work."

"What's the plan?"

"Well . . . Jordan isn't the only one who always finds the monster's lair. The bad guys always manage to get there, too, right? So we'll think like villains!"

Inspiration launched Eliott off the ground, swinging him up into the branches of the apple tree in a flurry of limbs and leaves. He wedged himself into a comfortable crook, spat on his hands, and rubbed them together in a ritual of mental focus. He closed his eyes.

"Okay . . . okay, I'm a bad guy. Black cloak, bad teeth . . . We're like one of those duo acts—a short guy and a tall, hairy guy . . ."

"Which one are you?"

Eliott opened one eye. "The short one. He's always the brains. Remember Rinzini and Mister Thud, from 'The Last of the Merovians'? Or Nickel and Dime from the 'Rotwood Saga'?"

"Right, of course."

Kess leaned back against the trunk of the tree below him, lounging in a manner that completely shattered any notion Eliott had of her being the tall, hairy one. He pulled himself back into his state of deductive concentration.

"I'm coming to Cheese . . . Nobody's seen me because I'm not staying in the village. I'm camping somewhere and sneaking around at night, trying to find the monster's lair . . . I'm breaking into cellars. I'm stealing from the church . . . in the church . . . under the church . . . I'm getting into the crypts! And I've got a partner keeping an eye on Jordan . . . No. Keeping an eye out for anybody who might sound an alarm, because . . . I've got no idea that Jordan's here. I'm going to be totally caught off guard when he jumps in and thwarts my evil schemes—it's going to be awesome, Kess. I'm totally not going to see it coming. I can't wait to watch!"

"You're blurring characters. Come on, you're in the crypts. What's your scheme?"

"I . . . I dunno. But I've got to warn Jordan! He's got to stop these guys before they wake up the minotaur!"

Fueled by raw excitement and inspiration, he bolted down the road, picking up details of his scenario along the way. Kess grinned and followed after.

They found Jordan sitting on his front steps, carving a turnip. He didn't appear to be carving it into anything except a small heap of vegetable chips, but Eliott assumed he had a good reason. It was probably an evil turnip. Eliott vaulted the gate and flailed to a dusty halt in front of him. Jordan's eyes narrowed.

"So. You're still around," he said, chewing the idea over as Eliott caught his breath. "Not bored yet?"

"We've been finding stuff," Eliott managed.

"Here? Really? Well, as long as you keep it to your-selves."

"No, but it's stuff you should know about! It's impor-tant. There's this villain—I think he's part of one of those Egyptian death cults—and he's trying to break into the old sewers under the village!"

Jordan stared at him from under skeptical eyebrows. "Into the sewers."

"Yeah, he's digging down through the crypt."

". . . Why?"

Eliott blinked. He had assumed that Jordan the Red would leap into action at the first hint of the rumor. "Oh. Because that's how he's going to get into the minotaur's lair, where a thousand years ago—"

Jordan sank his carving knife into the dirt and looked at Eliott wearily. "Couple of problems with all this, kid. First, nobody's getting into the sewers through the crypt, be-cause Cheese doesn't have any crypts. And second, Cheese doesn't have any sewers."

"It doesn't?"

"No."

Eliott tried to mentally readjust for this. He glanced back at Kess, who shrugged. "Are you sure? Because every place you went in the sagas, there was a sewer."

"Yeah, I'm pretty sure I know where all the shit ends up around here. There are no sewers."

"Oh." Eliott shifted awkwardly. "How about any old, abandoned mines? Because the death cult might be hiding out down there . . ."

Jordan pressed his fingers to the bridge of his nose. "Sto-ries. Why do you have to tell stories? This is Cheese, kid. It has no sewers, no crypts, no dungeons, barrows, or ruins of any kind—and no evil cultists creeping around. Sagas do not happen here. So quit trying to make things up."

Again, the unfairness of the world reared up and snarled at Eliott like a wild troll. He hadn't been making things up. If the world were behaving itself properly, there would have been a minotaur under the village and a villain plotting its release. All Eliott had done was say what should have been true. Nevertheless, in the face of Jordan's basilisk stare, he nodded. "I guess . . . I got carried away."

Something like sympathy passed across Jordan's face. "You're young. When you're older, you'll be happy if you've had a boring life. Trust me."

Eliott nodded in automatic agreement. "Sure, absolutely."

He hopped back over the gate, his thoughts escaping as swiftly as they could from the concept of a boring life. His imagination rebelled—he had met Jordan the Red; how could his life ever be boring again?—and rushed out into wild adventure. He had a plan; he simply needed to stick to it and not get ahead of himself.

"So what's next?" asked Kess.

"Let's hit the forest," said Eliott. "See if we can find a witch. This looks like the right sort of country for gingerbread."

"Sounds good to me."

"Okay," he called back to Jordan. "We'll come back and see you again when we've got a witch!"

"What? Oh, forget that!" Jordan threw up his hands. "You two are going to get yourselves lost or eaten by bears or into some sort of trouble and I'll be damned if it's any fault of mine."

For an old man, his stride was impressive as he caught up with them. "Look, how long am I going to have to put up with you?" he demanded.

Kess put her arm across Eliott's shoulders before he

could answer. "Until the end of the week," she said. "Then we'll leave and leave you alone."

She caught Eliott's eye and winked. Trust me, she was saying silently, so as always, he did.

"Five days . . ." Jordan pushed a hand through his hair and squinted at the dark line of the forest on the horizon. "Fine. I'll make you a deal, both of you. Stay out of trouble until you go, swear you won't tell anyone you found me, and you can come back here tomorrow and read my journals. They're not bardic and they're not pretty, but there's stuff in there even you won't have heard before. You'll learn something."

He held out his hand to Eliott.

"We got a deal?"

"Oh, wow. Deal!"

They shook on it. Eliott swore he would never wash that hand again. Then Jordan turned and walked away, leaving Kess and Eliott to stare at each other and grin and massage the feeling back into their crushed fingers.

JORDAN'S GATE WAS open when Kess and Eliott arrived early the next day to take him up on his offer.

"We should have brought him something," said Eliott. "Like a ham. To say thank you."

Kess knocked on the door. A shuffling and a general low-grade muttering from within suggested either that warrior heroes were not morning people, or that a particularly unenthusiastic zombie had gotten loose inside. The door opened.

"Hey, Sam," said Kess. "Is Jordan in?"

Sam smiled and held the door open for them. "No, he's out back in the shed putting together our fishing poles. He said you were to come in and make yourselves comfortable. His books are on the little table under the window, and on the bed."

"Jordan's going fishing?" said Eliott. "He's not going to be here?"

Sam nodded, and the feathers and beaded flashers hooked to his fishing hat danced cheerfully. "He said you'd probably rather not have him lurking around, hovering and getting self-conscious while you read through all his things."

"Did he really say that?" asked Kess.

"No. But I took his meaning from what he did say."

"What was that?"

"That I'm damned if I'm going to stick around to be ogled," said Jordan. He reached past Kess and pressed a white cane fishing pole into Sam's hands. "You two knock yourselves out with those books. But not literally," he added, with a glance at Eliott. "I'll be back before it gets dark. Make yourselves at home until then."

"Hey! Thank you," Eliott called out, as Jordan vanished down the lane. "Catch some good fish! Or, you know, evil ones!"

Kess dragged him back toward the door. "Books," she said, with an inspired gleam in her eye.

They went inside.

The house had a sullen air to it, as though it resented having unfamiliar visitors. There was only one room, comprising kitchen, bedroom, sitting room, and pantry in what seemed to Eliott to be a phenomenal compression of space. A faint, musty smell permeated the house that should have belonged to a room left locked and unoccupied for a long stretch of years, a smell Eliott knew from the highest attics of his parents' manor, where furniture that had yet to go from old to antique was kept under dusty canvas sheets. The only signs that any sort of living

went on here were the stack of unscrubbed dishes by the
fireplace and the man-shaped hollow in the bed.

Eliott took in every detail. He felt like a pilgrim at a
holy shrine. The dirty dishes, the wool blankets, the crudely
carved wooden ornaments were all sacred relics of his hero's
daily life. Of Jordan's past, there were no tokens or trophies
on display at all, but Eliott was coming to accept that Jordan
was keeping those to himself. The Sword of Empire, the
Ring of Princess Amariah, the Teeth of the Chimera—those
would be hidden away somewhere safe, in case they fell into
the wrong hands.

A sudden urge to check for hidden compartments under
the floorboards crept over Eliott. There was nothing wrong
with his hands, after all . . .

"These must be them," said Kess.

Eliott looked up guiltily. Kess, who approached holy
shrines as places to dance and sing and sprawl on the grass
with vine leaves in her hair, had made herself comfortable
at the table with her legs tucked up under her and a stack
of leather-bound books in front of her. There were at least
a dozen, most no thicker than Eliott's thumb, but a few at
the bottom were fat and bulging with promise.

Kess took one off the top. "No titles. Guess we get to
be surprised."

Eliott lifted it from her hands. "I can't believe we're
going to see his actual handwriting. Do you think any of
these are written in blood?"

"Let's find out."

Holding Jordan's journal reverentially, Eliott settled
himself on the floor at the foot of Jordan's bed. He could
feel the blanket, Jordan's blanket, on the other side of his
shirt sending woolly prickles up his spine, infusing him
with the essence of the warrior hero. This was going to be
the most epic act of reading ever.

He turned to the first page.

* * *

"WHAT HAPPENED TO hiding your legend under a rock?" asked Sam.

Jordan shrugged. It was a near-perfect day to be out at the pond: perch were basking in easy reach of his fishing line, a light breeze was blowing down from the mountains, and Sam's home-brewed moonshine was giving everything a peach-colored bearability.

"A change of tactics," he answered. "Won't do any harm for them to read about me, and it'll keep them busy for a couple of days. You know me, Sam. Long as there's an end in sight, I can get there."

"You sure you can trust them?"

"They're not from Glister. Annoying and nosy as they are, they're up front about it. His goons are sneaky."

"I meant, can you trust them not to tell anyone they found you?"

"I think so. Definitely the boy. Nothing's better than having a secret at his age. The elf . . . I'm taking a chance. You know elves."

"And what if word does get back to Glister?"

The breeze died for a moment. Jordan glanced sideways at his friend. Once upon a time, when stories still began that way, he and Sam had been boys together, playing with wooden swords and working the boats out of Whale Harbor and, in their free time, hunting fantastic beasts that never existed. Then Jordan had met a talent agent and gone on to fame, while Sam had taken his earnings and moved to Cheese, and for thirty years, they had had no contact with each other. It took a special kind of friendship to pick up again after all that.

Some answers, you could give only to that kind of friend.

"If Glister tries to rope me back in, I'll deal with him,"

said Jordan grimly. "He never hires people who can't be bought, and if their price is too high . . . well, I'll deal with them, too."

They sank into silence, ostensibly to lull the fish back into once again forgetting that crickets rarely went swimming with barbed metal piercings, not even rebellious teenage crickets. Jordan rolled down his sleeves against a sudden chill.

"All that said," Sam ventured, "I think you're doing a nice thing for that boy."

"We'll see."

"Seems to me he's got a good spirit. Too much imagination, I'll grant you. Maybe more than any world could live up to. Or any man. But a good spirit."

"We come here to talk or fish?" asked Jordan, casting his line out emphatically.

Sam chuckled. "I'm along for the waters." He patted the case of moonshine beside him.

They opened another bottle. Jordan looked back toward the village.

"I wonder how they're liking the undecorated truth."

"'DAY 102. STILL snowing. Somewhere in Brok, no signposts. No villages. Occasional demon. Must talk to G. on return about better furs, not going to freeze like this again if he wants more north stories. Must have enough saved by now. Ponies ate bad oats and are farting half the night, will tie them downwind tonight or by Shango's tent if he doesn't stop whistling that stupid ballad . . .' Whistling. Whistling and farting, that's what he was writing about while he was hunting the Ice Demons of Brok." Kess slumped forward onto her arms, her ears drooping. She stared at the page as if changing her distance might bring a more dramatic version of the journal entry into focus.

"I guess that's what he was thinking about," said Eliott, who was having a similar experience with Jordan's version of what had to be the "Timebreaker Saga," in which Jordan had filled three pages with scribbled attempts at understanding the Tinkers' Guild's explanation of how a clock worked.

"I can't read any more," said Kess, sounding equally disappointed and surprised with herself. "I can't."

They had been poring over Jordan's journals for hours. From the first entry, it had been clear that these were not the original manuscripts of the heart-stopping, spine-chilling sagas Eliott and Kess knew, but there had been glimmers, or so Eliott had insisted. For him, the holy pilgrimage had become an archaeological expedition, sifting through the paper ruins of an ancient age, Jordan's youth, to find the buried relics of the glories Eliott knew had been there. If he could decipher the words, he was sure he would find the gold of a lost adventure, or at least the silver of a good fight scene.

"You want me to read to you?"

This did nothing to perk Kess up. "Not if you want me to stay awake."

"Kess! Don't even joke about— We're getting to read real history here!"

"And you always fall asleep in history," said Kess. "Besides, this is worse than kings and dates and battles. He skims over the battles."

"But it's still his own words. Jordan the Red, in his own words!"

A knot twisted under Eliott's ribs. He had argued with Kess before, even once or twice seriously, but never over anything relating to Jordan. Their one absolute, unshakable common ground had always been their hero, his adventures, and their shared belief that if Jordan was not in fact a god, he could at least give a solid kicking to any god he came across.

"Yes, he's Jordan the Red," Kess agreed. "Warrior Hero! Weapons Master! Unrivaled when it comes to stopping demons! Oh, and the world's dullest writer. Listen to this: 'Something in water. Killed it. Tentacles taste like sardines.' No wonder he had a bard with him." She let the journal fall back on top of the others.

"Okay, so it's kinda dry . . ."

"This whole house is dry. Dry and dusty and stale. How can he breathe? There's no life in here!"

"We haven't looked at all of them yet. I bet they get better!" Eliott shuffled through the journals, searching for anything that looked promising.

"I need air. My skin's crawling."

"We'll skip ahead to the good parts. This one looks like a scrapbook—that's got to be better, right? Hey, yeah, here's a poster for Jordan. WANTED DEAD OR ALIVE. Right next to this one where he's proclaimed a Defender of the Crown. It says—"

"You keep reading. I'm going for a run."

Before Eliott could offer any further arguments, Kess was through the door, shaking out her hair and picking up speed.

"Yeah, okay. Sure. I'll stay here. If I find anything cool, I'll let you know," he called after her. "Maybe."

He picked up the scrapbook by one cover, letting its pages splay open carelessly. Glimpses of clumsy sketches and old bloodstains flopped past, barely registering.

Something fell out and hit the floor with a glassy clink.

Eliott picked it up. It was an oblong of black glass, the size and shape of a tarot card, with silver writing etched into the surface. On one side, it had the image of a man prying open the jaws of a lion, under the caption, "The Star."

Which was wrong. Eliott, who had played with Kess's tarot deck, frowned at it. That was the picture of Strength.

The other side of the card had a name and an address: Glister Starmacher, Cherub Street, Palace Hills. Beside the name, the card bulged, as if an air bubble were trapped between the front and the back. Eliott pushed at it with his thumb, to see if the bubble would move or dent, but it felt solid as glass.

And then, from everywhere and nowhere, he heard a soft, chiming sound, almost musical. It snuck into his head without using his ears, through some secret passage in the back of his skull, and filled him with nervous excitement, as if he was about to be caught doing something forbidden. It was the sound he imagined signaled the arrival of angels and the start of holy quests. He looked swiftly around and, when the room remained angel free, felt vaguely cheated.

Then he looked back at the card.

The bubble in the glass was swelling up like an overnight pimple, black-headed and greasy. It grew rounder and fuller until it had become a perfect sphere the size of a large melon, perched weightlessly on the card. Then, with a final chime, it pulled free and drifted upward until it hung in front of Eliott at the level of his wide-eyed stare. The surface of the bubble had gone opaque, like the black glass of the card, so that all he could see as he looked into it was his own distorted reflection looking back. It floated there like a soap bubble's evil twin. Waiting.

Eliott's curiosity could have killed the three-headed cat-beast of Mount Oblivion, if Jordan hadn't already done so. He poked the sphere.

It gave a gentle, contented sigh and swallowed his head.

FOUR

IN THE LUXURIOUS privacy of his office, Glister Starmacher leaned back in his leather chair with his feet up on his desk. He had just discovered, to his amusement, that with a gentle nudge of his thumb, he could spin the crystal ball he had balanced on his fingertips. It didn't seem to make a difference to the image. Inside the crystal, the worried face of the Duke de Quiche stayed where it was, looking into Glister's sincere, focused smile.

"I know. I know. It's a pain, but it's for the good of the story, Your Lordship. Trust me. In ten years' time, everybody is going to have heard of the Duke de Quiche." Another nudge. He wondered how fast he could get it going. "Think of it as an investment in your future reputation."

"But what am I supposed to do—" the Duke began, only to be drowned out by screaming gulls.

"You'll be fine. Start writing your memoirs. Keep a

journal. It'll be over in no time. You want to be famous, don't you? Of course you do. It'll be just the way we talked about. Besides, you like birds—I've got it right here on your contract: 'I love birds.'"

"Yes, but I didn't expect to be imprisoned on an island with them for the next ten years!"

"Think of it as a holiday," said Glister. "Now, listen, we've got a comically stupid jailer and an enigmatic old prisoner being transferred out there to keep you company. Take full advantage of them! And one of my very best bards will be out twice a month to get the latest account of what you're going through. When it's all over, you'll be a literary classic!"

"Couldn't we skip over this? I could—"

But what the Duke de Quiche could do was again muted, this time by a gentle chiming tune from the crystal ball itself. Glister's perfectly barbered eyebrows went up.

"Sure, sure. Of course. Listen, Your Lordship, hate to do this to you, but I've got to go. You're going to be great—you're already great. We'll talk!"

The crystal ball went dark. Glister put it down carefully on its stand, an expensive little gold statue of three naked women. One of his bards had declared they were Muses, which meant it was an actual piece of art, but as far as Glister was concerned, it was three naked women.

He peered into it curiously, looking for the face. Only a very select tier of the talent he represented had direct access to him this way, and even fewer could interrupt him when he was on another ley line.

"Hello . . . ?" he ventured. "You've reached the star-maker. Who's out there?"

One of the barbarians, Glister guessed. No matter how many times he explained to them how the crystal balls and crystal cards worked, Ungk the Destroyer still kept using his card to pick his teeth. That had been a bad call. Glister hadn't been able to eat tongue for a month.

An unfamiliar face swam into focus. It had the biggest eyes he had ever seen on a human.

"Whoa," it said. "Where am I?"

"No idea. Wherever you were before, you're still there. But, hey, I've got a better question—who are you, and what the hell are you doing in my crystal ball?"

The eyes managed to get wider. "I'm in a crystal ball?"

"In a ball, in my office, in beautiful downtown Palace Hills." Glister was beginning to get annoyed, and his words were sharper and more clipped for it. "Magic! How about that. Now, since you clearly don't know anything about the cards and balls, how did you reach me? Whose card are you using?"

"Oh . . . I guess it's Jordan's . . ."

"Hold on! Jordan? Jordan the Red?" Suddenly, the face in the ball had his full attention. "Where'd you get his card?"

"He, um, he gave it to me. Because I'm . . . his apprentice. Yeah, I'm Jordan the Red's apprentice."

"That old devil! Taking an apprentice without telling me. He's told you who I am, right?"

"Not . . . exactly. You're Glister Starmacher?"

"Right in one. Glister Starmacher, talent agent to the stars. You must like the Jordan stories—of course you do; all boys do. You're talking to the man who made them all happen."

Glister grinned, flashing a gold tooth that had been responsible for some of the most thrilling adventures of all time, or more precisely, the 87 percent market share those adventures pulled in.

"Cool!" said the face. "I'm Eliott. One *L*, two *T*s."

"Sure, great. So, Eliott . . . where is the old devil these days? You two must be gallivanting all over the world, him teaching you everything he knows . . . Been any place interesting lately?"

Eliott rolled his eyes. "Nah. We're in this boring little nowhere called Cheese."

Out of the crystal ball's line of sight, Glister very calmly jotted this down. There would be time for a victory dance later. "Cheese . . . that's out beyond the Squamata Plains, right? Up by the mountains? Who'd have ever thought to look for Jordan the Red there."

"It's boring," Eliott repeated. "There's nothing going on here. Nothing you could make a saga out of; that's for sure."

"Hey, don't count me out so fast, boy! Let me shake a little of the old Starmacher magic on the story. I'll get you an audience. People love 'Where Are They Now?'— doesn't matter if they're nowhere."

Glister scribbled out a few more notes to himself: *Focus on apprentice. Jordan the Red Adventures, Next Generation?*

"Besides," he continued, "I bet Jordan's been doing a great job, getting you ready to be a star of your own. How 'bout it? You want to sign up for your own adventures?"

"Wow, really? I mean, sure! Jordan and I are ready to go adventuring anytime!"

Glister's pencil snapped.

"You . . . and Jordan? Jordan and . . . Together?"

He could feel the back of his neck start to sweat. It was like someone was blowing softly, delicately, on his wallet.

"Well, yeah," said Eliott. "Jordan's not going anywhere without me. I've—we've been waiting for something to happen."

"I think," said Glister, barely containing his gold-studded grin, "that I can make something happen. Standard contract, of course. Eliott . . . Eliott, baby, you have made my day. A brand-new Jordan the Red adventure. This is going to be big. This is going to be huge—the hugest thing since *Arthur II: Revenge of the King*. It's going to be a record breaker!"

"Wow—we're in! We're definitely, definitely in. Wait until I tell Jordan! This is going to be awesome!"

"Hey, hang on. Let's not spoil the essential spontaneous quality of this. Realism! I mean, Jordan always loved having his adventures start unexpectedly—he knew that's how you keep an audience hooked! They can smell a phony a mile away. And if that's good enough for Jordan, well . . . You want to do this the right way, don't you?"

"Yeah, of course—"

"Then don't tell Jordan anything. Not yet. Let me get some wheels in motion, okay? Okay. I owe Jordan the full treatment, after all these years." Glister smiled into the crystal ball, filling it with warm sincerity that had taken him years to learn how to fake.

"Sure. Okay, I won't tell Jordan, if you're sure that's how he'd want it."

"Definitely. Trust me."

"But I've got to tell Kess!"

Glister flipped through the index cards of his mind, searching for the name among the known associates of Jordan the Red. "Now, hold your horses, my boy. I thought we'd agreed, we're going to keep this between you and me while I get things together. Do you know how gossip starts? One person tells one person tells one person and—bam—spoilers everywhere, and I can't hire someone to bring Jordan a drink who doesn't know he's going to get attacked by a hydra at the end of Act Three. You see what I'm saying?"

"Sort of. But I know Kess would never say anything to anyone—she keeps all my secrets."

"Eliott, Eliott. Do you want to be a part of this opportunity or not?"

Eliott's face in the crystal ball wobbled. Glister assumed the boy was nodding.

"Great. I knew you were a smart one—Jordan would only train the best, am I right? Now, we're going to enter into a sort of a verbal agreement right now—don't think of it as a, ha, magically binding contract of some sort, just an arrangement between talent and management. You won't say anything about what we're planning, and I'll put my best resources into giving you and Jordan the saga you deserve. Say yes?"

"Um . . . yes?"

"Great. I'll look after all the production, distribution, finances, and marketing, and you'll get total creative freedom in your performance. Sound fair to you?"

"Yes, definitely!"

The gleam in Glister's smile ranked up another ten karats.

"Eliott, I love you. You are absolutely the perfect apprentice for Jordan the Red. You just sit tight, keep practicing your moves, and keep this conversation between you and me. I'll set everything up for Jordan's big comeback—and I'll make you a star right up there with him!"

"I can't wait! Thank you!"

"Don't mention it, Eliott. It's what I do."

There was a pregnant pause as they stared at each other, mutually grinning. Glister waited. The pause went into labor.

". . . If there's something else, kid, don't keep me guessing," he prompted. "Fine print? Catering clause? If you're wanting a stunt double, you'll have to hire him for yourself."

"No. No, I . . ." Eliott's face pivoted within the crystal. ". . . Um, how do I stop talking to you?"

Glister laughed. "Slap your ears."

"What, like—"

There was a soft pop, and a very faint "ow," and the crystal ball went dark.

FIVE

GLISTER STARMACHER THREW a black handkerchief over the crystal ball and sat back, fingers steepled in front of his lips. A new saga. A classic hero, one everybody loved hearing about. This had to be handled with care. Delicacy. And style—most important, with style. The last saga had seen Jordan tumbling off a waterfall with the Crocodile God Zebek in a death grip . . . Could they say that he had become a king between then and now, ruling a lost jungle kingdom? Now, at last, his crown weighing heavy on his head, he has returned to stop the evil . . . which?

Witch. Warlock. Wizard!

Glister stuck his head out of his office and shouted at his secretary, "Winnie! Send a monkey down to the wizards at Central Casting. I need someone who can chuck fireballs or turn people into sheep, someone who's got a grudge against Jordan the Red! And I need him in here ten minutes ago, babe. We've got a legend to make!"

He grinned, flashing his gold tooth. Just saying the name had caused a stir in the waiting room, where half a dozen hopeful bards, minstrels, and scribes were gathered. Everyone with their portfolios and their nervous, eager smiles, wanting to show off their talent and maybe get a shot at writing for one of Glister's big names. Well, boys, today one of you gets your heart's desire. Who's it going to be?

Glister's beady eyes went around the room like a roulette ball. No; too old. No; too opinionated, that piece in the *Duke of Yorker*, terrible. No; ye gods, what is that, a gorilla in motley? It's chewing on its lute! No. No.

He zeroed in on a young man standing next to the water barrel with a paper cup. Every detail flashed past Glister's mental adjudication committee. Old-fashioned suit, not too flashy, except for the terrible feathered hat. Patched elbows. Good face, shame about the mustache. Looks a bit like a young Jeff Chaucer, who also had a thing for bad hats . . .

Glister turned his back to the room and leaned over his secretary's desk. "Who's thirsty boy, and what has he done?" he murmured.

His secretary checked her files discreetly. "Cyral Gideon," she answered, without looking up. "*Druid Today* last March, temped as a herald to Sir Boise, performed *The Murder of Monteverde* for the Earl of Fernwood. One encore on that. Seven original songs officially registered. He licensed 'The Ice Demons of Brok' last month."

"Give me what you've got on him and I'll see him in . . . two minutes."

Exactly two minutes and six frantic seconds later, Cyral Gideon was standing on the other side of Glister's desk, trying to bow, flatter the decor, and fumblingly present his portfolio all at the same time. Glister cut him off mid-introduction.

"Yes, yes, great to meet you, loved your column in *Druid Today*; I never knew the migration of giant toads could be so interesting—sit down; take your hat off. Tell me, Cyral, have you ever trailed anybody?"

"Nice to— Thank you, I— Trailed?"

"Rode with, shadowed, written up adventures as they were happening. Field work!"

"A—a bit, sir. I have a partial ode if you'd like to see it . . ."

Cyral started to untie his portfolio. Glister waved it away with a glinting smile that said it was entirely unnecessary to actually see or hear the piece to judge its quality; when that smile looked at you, you knew exactly how great you were, and boy, were you great. In fact, you were so great that you wouldn't need to read over the contract the smile was about to hand you. Faced with that smile, Cyral retreated into his chair and let Glister carry on.

"Cyral, I took one look at you, and I said to myself, There's a boy with promise. A boy who's willing to go out and get the job done. Not afraid to get his feet wet. Am I right? Of course I am. You're exactly what I need to bring back the first new Jordan the Red saga in two decades." Glister laced his hands behind his head and let this sink in.

Various expressions of shock and awe wrestled for Cyral's face, until an openmouthed, gulping stare staggered victorious out of the fray. "Me, sir? You want me to write for Jordan the Red? I mean, of course, Mr. Starmacher, I'd be honored! He's a legend. I've even had some ideas for modernizing his story, just passing thoughts, you know . . ."

"Right, right. You've thought about—just sign here—writing a Jordan saga before?"

"Who hasn't, sir? You listen to one of the best ones,

say, 'The Ice Demons of Brok' or 'Doctor Novay's Monster,' and it bounces around in your head all night."

"Ah, the greats. Please let this saga be another 'Doctor Novay,' I always say, and not another 'Thundersphere.' I'm counting on you not to let me down."

"I'll do my very best, sir! Will I be working with Jordan directly on this project?"

"Of course! You'll be right there with him."

"But I thought that nobody's seen Jordan in years."

"We've had a lucky break there," said Glister gleefully. "His apprentice tipped me off. Seems they're ready for a comeback special."

Cyral shuffled his hat around in his hands. "May I ask, who will Jordan be fighting this time? Is there a synopsis yet? A working title?"

"Cyral, kiddo, you're not getting this. Jordan is the artist. He'll be making it up as he goes along. You're there to follow in his footsteps. Go along with whatever he tells you, and it'll turn out golden. Trust me."

"Yes, but still, if I could have something to work with, a rough idea of what to expect . . ."

Glister took on a pained look and threw up his hands as if Cyral had asked for a cash advance. "All right, twist my arm. Lose some of the spontaneity. I'm seeing revenge. I'm seeing old grudges, giant battles, magic tricks. Call it . . . working title . . . 'Jordan the Red versus Some Schmuck Wizard We Don't Really Care About.'"

At that there was a crack of thunder and a puff of smoke. Glister's office, by its nature intended for intimate, one-to-one negotiations, was suddenly forced to make room for a wizard in billowing robes, who by nature took up the space of three people. Cyral dodged out of his chair and barely managed to catch an award statuette knocked off the desk by the wizard's staff. The wizard, who had been gifted with a nose meant to be looked down, fixed him with a haughty stare and took his seat.

"From my contemplation of the universe and manipulation of the raw power of the cosmos, you have summoned me, Glister Starmacher," said the wizard. "So this had better be good. What's this about Jordan the Red?"

Glister recovered quickly.

"Oh, are you in for a treat. He's back."

"Back? Back from where? Isn't he dead? Eaten by a jungle crocodile or something? Fell over a waterfall? I had a little party when I heard."

"Nah, that was just our way of keeping the stakes high. Trade secret," said Glister, with a wink.

"Intentional ambiguity," added Cyral, who felt that if he made a contribution, he might be entitled to unwedge himself from the corner.

"Exactly. Worked like a charm, didn't it? The old cliffhanger ending."

"So he hung on to the cliff, did he? Damn," said the wizard.

"Right. Exactly. We left his fate up in the air. Makes his fans more eager to hear what happens in the next saga. It just happened that this time, the next saga was a bit longer coming than we expected." Glister coughed. "By about twenty years."

The wizard scowled, stroking his long, white beard. It was such a perfect beard that Cyral couldn't help wondering if it was a chin wig. The white was definitely powdered on. "Too bad about him still being alive. Although hanging from a cliff for twenty years serves him right. So what—"

"I take it you're not a fan," said Cyral.

This must have been the first time anyone had ever interrupted the wizard. Anger rose in his eyes and vexation quivered in his beard.

"Not a fan! Not a fan? You might very well say that. Indeed, even your minuscule, unenlightened mind might be capable of perceiving the loathing I feel for Jordan the Red," he growled. "Who might you be?"

"Cyral Gideon, at your service."

"Oh, yes? And are you anyone important?"

"Not . . . not really, sir."

"Good."

The wizard flicked his wrist dismissively. There was another small thunder crack. Cyral found himself suspended from the ceiling, unable to move.

"That's much better. Now we have room," said the wizard. "Go on, Starmacher. You have my attention."

Glister stared up at the magically pinned bard. "Okay, I'm impressed. Full marks for show. Really, really great stuff, but can you bring him down? We're going to need him for the saga."

"What saga?"

"Yours, my friend! Your big break. I've invited you here because you're going to star in the new Jordan the Red saga!"

"I am?" The wizard sounded skeptical. "What's it called?"

"'The Wizard's Revenge: The Death of Jordan the Red.' Catchy, hey? And you're my man, right? A wizard out for revenge . . . It's got glamour all over it."

"I would get to kill Jordan?"

"Well, that's the idea, isn't it? Of course, he'll try and stop you, but that's where the excitement comes from. You've got a grudge against him, and he knows it—or maybe he doesn't know it yet. Maybe you're coming out of his past like an assassin's arrow. Yeah. Go with that." Glister sat back, turning on the gilded smile. "What do you say?"

"Hmm . . ."

Looking down, Cyral imagined the thoughts going through the wizard's head. Wizards' brains were vast, expansive places, capable of taking in the whole of the universe. Possibly this was the reason it took so long for anything to get from their ears to someplace where it could be processed. But on the whole, and, more significantly, on the ceiling, Cyral had the impression that this particular wizard was simply dense as a stack of bricks.

"Now, wait a moment," said the wizard. "Haven't other people tried to kill him before?"

"Quitters," said Glister dismissively. "No imagination. And, don't forget, Jordan's been out of practice."

Yes, thought Cyral, he's probably completely forgotten how to decapitate villains. Which end of this sword do I hold again? Where does the pointy bit go?

The wizard drummed his fingers against his staff. Glister's smile was getting to him; the gold tooth twinkled confidently. At last, he nodded. "Very well. I shall take the leading role in this saga of yours, in return for the opportunity to put an end to Jordan the Red. He will fall victim to the most cunning and intricate traps sorcery can devise, each one equal in humiliation and pain. I promise you, your audiences will cringe in horror at the merest description of what he will suffer."

He leaned over Glister's desk as he signed the contract. "You've got a good bard to do this, right? I don't want to be written as some poser with silly stars and moons all over his robe."

Without losing the gleam in his smile, Glister pointed a single finger at the ceiling. The wizard followed it.

". . . Oh."

Abruptly, Cyral could move freely again. He scarcely had time to savor his freedom before it brought him crashing to the floor. He dusted himself off without a word.

"I suppose he'll do," said the wizard. "You are most

fortunate, bard, to have the privilege of recording this historic event. Try not to get in the way."

"Don't worry about that," said Glister. "My boy Cyral here won't be following you. He'll be riding along with Jordan, so our audience can, er, feel the suspense building as Jordan walks into your trap."

"But then how will they hear about my plans? When will they get a sense of my burning desire for revenge, my motivations?"

"We could do that right now, if it's convenient," said Cyral. "I can take all your information now, rewrite it in the present tense, and then later, add a different backdrop and some narrative to make it sound as if I was there with you when it happened."

He dug into his portfolio for a spare piece of parchment. The wizard watched him with the bewilderment of one who had only ever been on the audience side of a saga before.

"'As if you were there'? Surely you don't mean . . . make things up," said the wizard.

"No, of course not," said Cyral. He reached toward Glister's desk. "May I?"

"It's all done through the wonders of technology," Glister explained, handing his golden goose-feather pen to Cyral.

The wizard grunted disapprovingly. "Very well. What do you need from me?"

"Well, to start with, sir, I could use your name."

There was a delicate silence, during which Cyral was afraid he was going to end up on the ceiling again. The wizard shifted uncomfortably in his chair, refusing to make eye contact.

"My name."

"Er . . . yes, sir."

"That's absolutely necessary, is it? I couldn't go by 'The Dark One' or some such?"

"I'd rather not," said Cyral. "Jordan the Red has already fought eight Dark Ones, two Dark Lords, and one entity simply known as The Dark. Three of them were wizards. Why? Is there some problem? It doesn't steal a part of your soul to know your name, or anything like that, does it?"

"No, no . . . nothing like that."

The wizard's ears were turning red. Until that moment, they had been quite overshadowed by the sheer angular size of his nose, but his ears were equally large and, in his embarrassment, gave him the look of a tomato split in half with an axe. Cyral mentally made a note of that image to save for later.

"Hey, why are we wasting time on this?" asked Glister. "We've got your name right here on the contract." He shuffled some papers. "Okay, here it is— Oh."

"Oh?"

Cyral leaned over, tilting his head for a better view.

"My name," said the wizard, remaining magnificently calm, "is Sardo Hopley, Junior."

"What, as in, 'Sardo Hopley's Famous Baked Goods'?"

"Yes."

"Mister Puffy Muffin and the Sugar-Crumb Goblins? You're that Hopley?"

Hopley showed his teeth in the most forced and unpleasant smile Cyral had ever seen. "Yes. Forever haunted by the legacy of my family's business. But I assure you, my grasp of cosmic powers is quite real! As will my vengeance be, when I have Jordan the Red in my clutches."

"Yes, I'm sure you'll rise to the occasion," said Cyral, who felt confident the pun would go over Hopley's pointy hat. It did.

"Don't worry about it," said Glister, hastily. "We'll

make it part of your angle. Secret identity, gimmick . . . something like that. Make a giant oven part of your master plan; we'll sell it to the tradesmen."

"I'm sure they'll eat it up," said Cyral. Hopley glowered at him.

"Mock not a wizard," Hopley intoned. "Your temporary necessity may save you from the wrath of my magic—but I can still give you a poke in the eye with my staff."

"Right, right, he gets the message. Cyral, kid, show a little respect to the guest artist here." Glister was on the other side of the desk so quickly he seemed to have teleported, putting a hand on the shoulder of each of the other men. "We're all friends, right? All working toward a common goal?"

"The death of Jordan the Red," said Hopley.

"Creating a saga for the ages," said Cyral.

Buying a solid gold desk, thought Glister. "Exactly," he said. "So let's be smart about this, and do it right. Sardo—can I call you that? Great—why don't you give Cyral here your vital details, and then you can go get your evil plan under way . . . What am I saying? I don't mean evil. I mean your rightful revenge! That's the way."

"What more do you need from me?" Hopley asked, folding his arms.

"We, er, could go over your grudge against Jordan the Red. A quick summary of it, perhaps?" Cyral raised his pen and offered what he hoped was a conciliatory smile.

"Yes. Yes, your audience should know the details. I should begin by telling you that soon after the family business came into my hands, I grew tired of running it—within minutes, in fact—and began exploring the arcane arts. Like many magically inclined young men, I was drawn to the darker side of wizardry . . ."

He went off on an account of sordid practices and illicit lessons with infernal tutors that, if told by someone else, might have evoked terror and fascination. Hopley mouthed his way through it as if he were pounding bread dough. Cyral listened patiently, taking notes and wondering if there would be anything worth saving from it all.

". . . Until, at last, I was inducted into the ranks of the A.T.C.B.S.O., where I was—"

"Hang on," said Cyral, risking another trip to the ceiling. "What is that? The A.T.B. . . . ?"

"A.T.C.B.S.O.!"

"Acronym That Cannot Be . . . something, something," provided Glister.

Cyral took a stab at it. "Spelled Out?"

Hopley sank into his chair, glowering. Outside the windows, small, dark thunderclouds began to form, rattling the glass. "I am beginning to feel as if I am not being taken seriously."

"Sorry," said Cyral. "Carry on."

"I was an up-and-coming Dark Wizard with the A.T.C.B.S.O. when I devised a scheme for turning children into swine. My superiors were immensely pleased with the notion. Everything was going along perfectly, until Jordan the Red ruined it all!"

Hopley raised his staff furiously, and the miniature thunderclouds crackled and spat tiny wintergreen sparks of lightning, which even Cyral had to admit were suitably dramatic.

"So he showed up and thwarted you," Cyral prompted. "How did you escape?"

"I didn't!" said Hopley. "Oh, no—Mr. Jordan the Couldn't Be Bothered never showed up. He didn't thwart me at all! So when the A.T.C.B.S.O. Grants Committee came by to see how my scheme was developing, I had to show them . . ."

There was an embarrassed silence. The thunderclouds slunk away behind the curtains. Glister closed his eyes and folded his hands in some sort of prayer over Hopley's contract.

Cyral coughed. "And you, er, couldn't actually . . ."

"Have you ever tried turning children into pigs?" snapped Hopley. "It's harder than it sounds. All I had was a warehouse full of the little brats getting fat on Traditional Recipe Gingerbread Scones. Jordan the Red was in town—I had been counting on him to break the whole thing up before the committee arrived! I lost my funding because of him!" Hopley gestured madly with his staff, but the storm had gone out of it.

"Will that be enough for you?" he asked wretchedly.

"Yes, I think that tells me everything I need to start writing the prologue," said Cyral. "And, er, your current plan?"

"It will be cunning and intricate. I shall inflict upon Jordan equal measures of pain and humiliation."

"You did say. But . . . any details?"

Hopley's eyes flicked toward Glister. "It . . . may involve a giant oven."

A manic enthusiasm took over Glister's face. He clapped his hands together as if giving CPR to a dying fairy, then started scribbling on the back of one of his cards. "I can see you boys are going to have your work cut out for you. Hopley, here's Jordan's last known location— village called Cheese, way over in the back of nowhere. He's got an apprentice, some kid called Eliott. Sound like bait to you? Of course, that's a brilliant idea—use the apprentice for bait. Wish I'd thought of it. Oven, giant mixing bowl, whatever else you can think of, run with it. Something that somebody can dangle over. Cyral, you got that? I want to hear about dangling."

Cyral nodded and made a note.

Hopley stared at the card with Jordan's location on it.

"Cheese," he murmured. "I seem to recall there being one of the old family mills near there . . ."

"That's great. Perfect. I can see you're already bursting with inspiration," said Glister. "Why don't you go gather yourself some henchmen and head over there. Take a couple days to get comfortable and set everything up. Don't worry about travel expenses; you can magic yourself there. Right? Of course you can."

"Um, I can't, Mr. Starmacher," Cyral pointed out.

"We'll take care of that in a minute, Cyral. Can't you see that our hero here is in a hurry to get on with his revenge?"

"I am? Oh. Indeed," said Hopley.

"Right. Have a good laugh over how perfectly everything is coming together, and go get him, magus! Remember, the sooner you set your nefarious scheme in motion, the better for your audience!"

Then Glister was shaking Hopley's hand and pushing Cyral out of the way to give the wizard plenty of room to teleport. His smile was everywhere, reassuring Hopley, encouraging Cyral, checking itself in the mirror, tidying away the contracts now that they were signed and no longer anything anyone else needed to worry about. Cyral could see the smile at work, even rationally realize what it was doing, and yet he was still powerless to resist its charm. Hopley stood no chance at all.

A flash and a thunderclap later, the wizard was gone. As soon as Hopley's pointy hat had spun out of sight, Glister collapsed back behind his desk, once again drawing Cyral into intimate conspiracy.

"He's perfect, isn't he? Nobody's going to be crying bitter tears when he gets killed off. I know, I know, it's not my place to tell you how to write but, Cyral, skewer him to the hilt. Go big—way over the top. And his ego? It'll have them rolling on the floor. The groundlings love laughing at someone who pretends to be—what's the word?—intellectual. Elite. If Jordan's going to come back with a vengeance, there's got to be some comedy, too."

"Are you sure about him?" said Cyral. "I'm . . . not sure I could make him seem like much of a threat."

"Of course I'm sure! Central Casting provided him and they never let me down. And who knows? Maybe Hopley'll hire himself a henchman with some real dramatic juice. Right now, the important thing is, we need to get you onto the scene . . ."

"Another wizard?"

Glister smacked his palms against his desk. "Don't be silly. Wizards charge money to teleport other people. You can't afford that, and I'm not going to let one of my writers get themselves into unnecessary debt! Go get yourself packed, and be back here in fifteen minutes—I'll have all your travel arrangements made by then."

"You will? Thank you, Mr. Starmacher!"

"You're on the hero circuit now, my boy. Turning everyday lives into adventures. You get taken care of! Trust me. Oh, and Cyral? Lose the mustache."

STILL BUZZING WITH the prospects of fame and fortune, or at least being paid enough to eat this week, Cyral raced back from his apartment, a room partitioned out of the cellar of an arrhythmic dance studio. Packing his bags to the stuttering drumbeat coming through the ceiling had taken him no time at all; everything he owned could fit inside a small closet, which was coincidentally the size of the only apartment in Palace Hills he could afford. The bottom shelf made a comfortable bed and kept him above the level of the gutter runoff, while the upper shelves provided enough room for his collection of scrolls, books, and crow-feather quill pens. He had one change of clothes, very plain, which he wore when he didn't want to look like a bard; this didn't happen often, because he was trying to be noticed.

And today, he had been!

Everybody knew Glister Starmacher kept the very best heroes in his stable, that he had launched the entire Jordan the Red series. Going to his office had been a long shot, but it had paid off! Forget the pompous, brainless wizard; forget the nagging feeling that Glister might not be as sincere as he seemed. Writing for Jordan the Red was the literary opportunity of a lifetime. Having shaved off his mustache, Cyral felt like he had become a new man, a man with a destiny. It was written in the stars that he'd be writing for the stars.

Barefaced and giddy, Cyral danced through the crowded streets. Everything sounded like music, even the shouts for him to get out of the way and watch where he was going. When he checked in again with Glister's secretary, he half expected her to start singing a pretty duet with him about how bright the future looked. She did not.

"He's waiting for you on the roof," was all she said.

Nevertheless, Cyral tipped his feathered hat to her. A lost opportunity, he thought. A waiting room full of bards would have made a perfect chorus, and been far more believable bursting into song than, say, a stagecoach full of traveling salesmen.

Four flights of stairs took most of the music out of Cyral's step. He found Glister looking out from the edge of the rooftop balcony, with a hand on the head of each of a pair of gargoyles. Palace Hills spread out before him like an overloaded banquet table, gleaming glass and polished copper roofs reflecting a pink sugar sunset. Spires rose like candelabras, each one competing to be the only tower in the city able to boast a view over all the rest. And

in the middle of it all sat the vast, circular bulk of the
Central Casting building.

Cyral had never seen it from above before. It was a
dwarf compared to the height of the towers around it, but
of such a diameter that if it had been hollowed out, the
wizards could have had chariot races within its walls. Its
flat roof supported a formal garden, full of statues of famous wizards, built around a central glass dome. Under
that dome, Cyral knew, was the heart of Central Casting:
the Wizards' Conclave, Where the Magic Happened. It
was in all their brochures. Nobody knew exactly what that
meant, but it sounded tremendously impressive.

"You're here—that's great! Some view, huh?" Glister
had noticed him at last. "Know what all that is? That's your
audience out there, a half million bums to put in seats. I bet
you can hear the applause already."

"I'll try not to disappoint you, Mr. Starmacher," said
Cyral, who was far more aware of the sound of the wind.

"Me? Oh, you don't have to worry about me—I've got
faith in you! It's them, out there, waiting in the dark for
the curtain to go up. They're the ones you've got to think
about. All those eager ears, waiting to hear the new adventures of Jordan the Red . . . waiting to hear the best damn
saga of their lives . . . waiting for you. Come over here and
take a good look down."

Cyral swallowed, hard. He had been afraid of this since
stepping onto the roof. "I can see fine from here, Mr. Starmacher. If it's quite all right with you . . ."

"Nah, I insist. What—you're not afraid of heights, are
you?"

"Not heights, exactly," said Cyral, edging toward the
railing. "More distances. Things a long way down getting
closer very quickly . . . I'm a bit afraid of that."

"Then I really hope you packed a blindfold." Glister lit
a thin cigar, and the moment he took his hands off the

gargoyles, one stretched its wings and scratched itself. A monkey face in a mane of granite gray fur turned toward Cyral and yawned toothily.

Cyral backed away. "Oh, no. No. Mr. Starmacher, I can't fly!"

"Of course you can! You want to get there fast, don't you? Can't be late to the scene." Glister waved his hand, dismissing Cyral's fears like so much smoke. "Now, just let the monkeys get a good grip on you—"

"What happens if they don't?!"

"Relax! They've never dropped anyone," said Glister, beaming with the confidence of a man not likely to be airborne anytime soon. "Not without making sure there was a haystack underneath. You'll be fine."

"I could hire a coach. I could pay for my own wizard."

"No, you couldn't." Glister shook his head with theatrical disappointment. "I didn't want to do it like this, but if you're not there when the action starts, you'll make the whole team look bad. Get him, boys."

There was a moment, right before four leathery hands seized him, when Cyral could have grabbed onto the railing, or bolted for the stairs, or, in fact, done anything other than stand frozen in front of the leaping gargoyle monkeys. Not that anything he could have done would have saved him, but it made him feel slightly better, as they carried him over Palace Hills like a sack of potatoes, thinking that he had had the option.

But not so much better that he didn't throw up twice before they dropped him onto an inn for the night.

SIX

ELIOTT KEPT HIS word and said nothing about his meeting with Glister Starmacher to anyone, though over the next two days this became harder and harder for him, as he could no longer look Kess or Jordan in the eye. Conversations became exercises in suppressing his anticipation. Finally, he retreated from them entirely and sank into an uncharacteristic silence, protecting his secret behind walls of noncommittal grunts and half answers. When Kess tried to keep him company, he lay in bed and pretended to be asleep, or muttered that he wasn't feeling well, while in his head, a thousand possible adventures thundered like wild horses through his imagination.

A star! The next big thing! *The Collected Adventures of Eliott, the Hero's Apprentice*!

Even Jordan noticed the change in Eliott's mood. One

evening, after an early retreat to his room, Eliott heard voices in the hall outside:

"No, he's not sick," said Kess, on the other side of the thin door. "He's only saying he is."

"Then what's the matter with him?" asked Jordan, and Eliott nearly forgot his ruse and leapt out of bed.

"Since when do you care?" said Kess, and then, before Jordan could answer, carried on, "I think maybe his hero let him down. What do you think? Could that do it?"

It's not him, Eliott wanted to shout. It's not anybody! But don't ask me what it is, because I'm not allowed to tell you!

"Did I ask to be his hero?" Jordan snapped. "I'm not responsible for anybody but me anymore."

"It wouldn't have killed you to hunt one troll with us."

"It might have! Look, I didn't come here for this . . ."

Their voices retreated down the hall, fading out of Eliott's hearing until they were only a distant murmur punctuated by the occasional Last Word. Eliott got out of bed and went over to the window, his stomach twisted into a knot. Kess and Jordan were arguing because of him. The adventure needed to hurry up and begin, so he could explain why it had been necessary for him to keep a secret from them.

Kess hammered at his door. "Eliott? I know you're faking. Open up."

Too exhausted to refuse, Eliott let her in.

They sat down on the bed together, Eliott with his knees curled up to his chin in determined silence.

"You missed Jordan," she said, pushing a strand of her hair back into place. "He still wouldn't give me his autograph." She drew her knees up to her chest in a parody of Eliott's position. "God, he can be irritating. And annoying. Do you think that means I'll be madly in love with him by the end of the saga?"

Eliott shot her a look. "Kess. You've been madly in love with him since I could crawl."

Kess grinned mischievously. "Longer. In a purely spiritual, conceptual way."

"You stole that painting I had of Jordan fighting the fire elemental because he had no shirt on."

"I had a good reason," she said, straight-faced. "The elemental didn't have a shirt either. If your parents had caught you with it, they'd have tossed it and we'd both have lost out."

Eliott laughed. "So, um, what did Jordan come here for?"

Kess uncurled. "There's a faire tomorrow. He said he'll take us. His way of saying good-bye."

"Are we really going to leave?"

"That's what I told him."

Then it'll happen soon, thought Eliott. It has to happen before we go. He slumped sideways, burying his face in the pillow to suppress an outburst of gleeful anticipation.

"Don't worry," said Kess. "The Braid'll do its magic. You'll get your adventure. You'll see."

"I know," said Eliott, with muffled certainty.

"It might be at the faire. You never know what sort of monsters could be attracted by boiled corn and folk music. You'll come, right?"

Eliott touched the Braid and thought about Glister's promises. He had complete faith in both, and yet . . . another tiny voice kept saying he could still mess everything up. Wishes could twist, and talent agents could change their minds, and it could all be his fault, if he told Jordan what was going to happen, if he let it slip to Kess. He had to keep his distance from them, for just a little bit longer; when the adventure began, it wouldn't matter if he was right there with Jordan, because the Braid had guaranteed they would all be together for it. He had to avoid the faire, for the greater good and the cause of thrilling heroics.

This, in his fizzing, imagination-soaked mind, passed for logic. He rolled onto his side and tried not to look at Kess.

"Nah. But you two go and have fun. Come get me when—if—anything starts to happen."

Kess stared at him. "So when are you going to tell me?" she asked.

Eliott's smile slid away like rain into a storm drain. "Tell you what?"

"What's making you mope like this. You know I'll get it out of you."

He shrugged. "It's nothing."

"Fine," she said. "Stay in bed tomorrow. Have fun there. But I'm going to go to the faire with Jordan and I'm going to dance and I'm not going to worry about you."

"Yeah, sure, okay."

With some hesitation, Kess got up and left him alone. When she had gone, Eliott reached under the mattress to his very secret hiding place and took out Glister Starmacher's black glass card. He turned it around and around in hands, looking at the etching of The Star. He could almost see his own face on it.

THEN IT WAS Friday, Kess and Eliott's last day in Cheese, and the day of the annual harvest faire. By noon, every house in the village was empty, and every man, woman, and child was up on the Dancing Green. When Eliott finally awoke, he found he had the Trout and Truncheon entirely to himself. Even the cooks and servers had been given the day off, he discovered, as he explored the kitchen in search of breakfast. He filled a mixing bowl with hot oatmeal and raided cupboards until he had added enough brown sugar, cream, and plums that he was satisfied it would no longer taste like oatmeal.

The empty common room still had hot embers in the fireplace, so he stoked them up and dragged a table over. As an afterthought, he went back upstairs and brought down three quilts to spread out over a bench. Breakfast and a comfortable place by the fire arranged, Eliott sprawled, immersing himself in daydreams, resolute in his decision to let Kess and Jordan go to the faire without him.

Out at the front of the inn, a bell clanged once for service. Eliott ignored it.

When the bell clanged again, he sat up and looked toward the front desk. After the third clang, he gave up and called out, "Yeah? Somebody there?"

"Ah, excellent. There is life in this rustic hollow." A figure strode into the common room, black robes swirling like a swiftly gathering storm, staff clicking on the floorboards.

Eliott forgot about his oatmeal and stared, taking in every detail of the stranger: The tall, black hat with the pointy tip bent down. The staff with a carved fist on the end. The robes. The white chef's apron worn over the robes. And the face—one look at the stranger's face and Eliott forgot everything else—a hard, lean face with prominent ears and the aquiline nose of an emperor. Between the square-cut, flour white beard and thin, sharp eyebrows, dark, studious eyes returned the scrutiny.

Eliott found his voice. "Hey, you're some kind of a wizard, right?"

The eyes showed no amusement. "I am indeed a wizard."

"Yeah, I knew it. The pointy hat and the staff kinda give it away. Cool. Who are you?"

"My name is Hopley. Does that mean anything to you?" asked the wizard, in a low, challenging growl.

Eliott considered it. He knew the names of a dozen wizards, good, evil, and comically mediocre, from his set of Central Casting trading cards, but Hopley had never been featured among them. Unfortunately, in Eliott's mind, this put Hopley in the minor magics league, along with hedge wizards, charlatans, and any sort of party magician. No matter how impressive the wizard looked, he was still nobody if Eliott hadn't heard of him.

Eliott shook his head and said, "No. Should it? I mean, you're not the famous Hopley the Magnificent or something, are you?"

"No. I am not famous as a wizard . . . yet. However, I should hope one does not have to be famous to receive service at this inn."

"Oh, I don't work here." Eliott swallowed a lump of oatmeal. "I'm not even from here. But if you want a room, go ahead and take one."

"I won't be staying that long." Hopley smiled coldly and leaned against his staff. "You may yet be able to help me, boy. I'm looking for someone . . ."

Eliott shrugged. "Everyone's at the faire. Up the road, you can't miss it."

"Ah. Would this 'everyone' include an older man, a warrior, perhaps going by the name of Jordan?"

"Yeah," said Eliott gloomily. "Jordan'll be there."

He slumped forward, his chin resting on his arms, thinking of the day he might have been spending at the faire with Jordan. There would be an archery competition, and weight lifting, and maybe even an all-comers wrestling melee. Eliott would have loved to see Jordan win all of those, which of course he would, and then still try to pretend he was—

Eliott bolted upright. "But he's not Jordan the Red!" he blurted. "He's another warrior called Jordan. Totally by coincidence. No relation."

"Yes? Luckily, it's not Jordan I'm searching for at the moment," said Hopley, and his wicked smirk said that he had seen through Eliott's clever attempt at misdirection. "Tell me, does this Jordan Not the Red have an apprentice?"

"He . . . Ooh. Wait, why?"

"Because I have a message for Jordan. One that I intend to use his apprentice to deliver." Hopley looked around the empty inn. "And that line was exactly why I should have insisted the bard stay with me. He had better be able to re-create it when I tell him about this. Stark, ominous simplicity—don't you agree?"

"It really gave me chills," said Eliott honestly. "Glister Starmacher sent you here, didn't he?"

"A well-informed boy," said Hopley. "'One that I intend . . .'" He rolled the rest of the line around in his mouth, committing it to memory.

Eliott looked over the wizard's black robes and sharp, haughty features once more, drawing conclusions. He could feel the bouncing thrill in his stomach of an adventure beginning, but it was mixed with the definite knowledge that this was his first encounter with the villain of the piece, and it was already too late for him to hide behind a tree or in an apple barrel. Now his only options were to throw his oatmeal at Hopley and run, or try to escape by cunning.

"Yeah . . . Jordan has an apprentice," he said carefully, with his hands on the edges of his bowl. "He's upstairs. I'll go get him for you . . ."

He rose and started for the stairs at a nonchalant pace, ready to become extremely chalant as soon as he was out of Hopley's sight.

"Wait a minute."

Eliott turned. The wizard's staff was pointed at him like a lance.

"I thought you said that everyone else was at the faire . . ."

"Oh. Right. Everyone's there except Jordan's apprentice."

"You're not."

"And me! Jordan's apprentice and me!"

"Eliott."

"Oh, hey, look! Oatmeal!"

He threw the bowl and ran. The wooden crash told him his throw had fallen short, but that wasn't the important part of the plan. The important part was to get away, and get away fast. Keep running. Find Jordan. Not get turned into a frog.

As he turned the corner, a tingling sensation burned across his shoulders, as if for a moment his back had gone all pins and needles. He lurched sideways, catching himself on the banister. If he could get to his room, he could get to the window, and if he could get out the window, he could get to Jordan.

Or he could rest for a moment right here. His thoughts were becoming fuzzy on the issue. If he put his head down, he could nap, just for a moment . . .

His eyes closed. He slumped forward, bounced quite gently off the stairs, and slid back down to the bottom.

Hopley stepped over him. "A sleeping spell. Entirely harmless on its own, though it does allow a great deal of harm to be dealt before you awaken. Luckily, I have no intention of harming you at the moment. Jordan is far more likely to come and find you if you are alive, after all."

With a wave of his staff, Hopley lifted Eliott from the floor like a marionette and floated him back into the common room.

"And this will make sure that Jordan comes looking for you promptly," said Hopley, taking an envelope from his sleeve. He placed it on the mantle over the fireplace and made a quick motion with his left hand. Large, glowing letters curled onto the front of the envelope, addressing it to Jordan the Red.

"You won't be able to ignore me this time," he muttered.

Then, on second thought, he moved the envelope to the center of the table and propped it up against a candlestick. He stroked his beard thoughtfully. He moved it back to the mantle.

"Now to the stronghold. Come along, boy."

With Eliott bobbing along after him, Hopley left the inn and boarded his waiting coach. He had done his best to turn the coach into a traveling symbol of his power, but underneath the black paint and iron spikes, it was still a bread wagon. He slid Eliott into the back and rapped at the driver's seat. The driver, who was short, rotund, and heavily hooded, snorted back.

"Home, pig," said Hopley.

A grunt and a whip-crack, and the coach trundled away from the village. Neither Hopley nor his driver noticed, as they crossed the last bridge out of the village, that they nearly ran down a young man in a feathered hat walking the other way with his eyes turned to the sky as if expecting winged monkeys to swoop down and carry him off—which was, in fact, the young man's chief worry at that moment, and the reason he was paying no attention to oncoming coaches.

"THEY WERE STARING."

"I can't help it. It's the ears. Anyway, you should thank me." Kess poked at Jordan's chest with a caramel apple. "Nobody was paying attention to you at all. You want that, right?"

"They know I brought you. There'll be gossip for months."

"Scandal." Kess rolled her mouth around the word, savoring it.

"No one around these parts would ever dance like that," said Jordan, but without much rancor. He had tasted too many samples of beer and cider and sugared pastries to be very annoyed with anything this afternoon, and he was forced to admit, Kess was good company when she wasn't arguing with him or fawning over his legend.

They strolled along the goat track from the Dancing Green back into the village, with the breeze behind them and warm sunlight washing over their shoulders. The faire was still going on, but Jordan had called for a tactical retreat. Kess's entry in the harvest ribbon dance had caused Mr. Gordium, the piper, to swallow his own whistle.

"It was modern," said Kess. "Or postmodern. I made it up last year, so whatever that makes it."

"You were moving like a crazed maenad."

"Thank you." She swatted away an overly curious fly. "You're sure this is quicker than going by the road? This caramel's starting to run."

"Quick enough. Not as dusty. We'll be there and back again before they've got the barbecue going."

"Good. If this doesn't convince him," said Kess, waving the caramel apple emphatically, "he'll definitely come for that."

They came up to the Trout and Truncheon from the back, through the kitchen garden. Usually, this guaranteed Jordan a chance to chat with one of the cooks, but with everyone at the faire, they entered through the pantry door without meeting anyone.

An odd, uneasy feeling prickled the back of Jordan's neck. The emptiness of the inn, the extra layer of silence and stillness, brought back the kind of apprehension he had known in his adventuring days. He had learned early on that saying, "It's too quiet," was invoking the god of surprise attacks, but this was the same sort of gut feeling you got right before you were tempted to say it. The feeling in your gut after you said it was generally sharper and more arrowlike.

This, however, was Cheese, and not some haunted castle. He put the feeling down to a touch of sunburn and ignored it.

"He's probably still up in his room," said Kess. "I'll go find him."

"Tell him, if he comes along, I'll let him in on the secret of the sauce," said Jordan, with a stiff smile.

"Thank you. I'll try that."

"You two've been good. Even him. Last couple of days, it hasn't bothered me, having the two of you around. You should both have some fun before you go."

"Sure you won't come tell him that yourself?"

Jordan shook his head. "I'm going to put a damp cloth on my neck and close my eyes for a minute. I'll be in the common room."

"All right. We'll be right back. Don't have any adventures without us!"

Jordan actually laughed, as much to his own surprise as hers. He was having a good day. "I won't," he called after her.

He found a clean towel and dipped it in the sink a couple of times, then slapped it across his neck, still dripping. The cool water felt like a plunge into the pond, and he was casually considering going for a swim after sundown as he wandered into the common room.

There was a letter on the mantle. It had his name on it.

His good day fell apart.

Jordan stared at it, waiting for it to make any sudden moves. The letter sat where it was, waiting for him in a similar manner. It was the tensest standoff Jordan had been in since he had caught up with Chemi Two-Blades in a cantina on the Ashgrit Frontier.

"Oh, hell with it," he muttered, which he vaguely recalled Chemi saying before they stabbed each other. He picked up the letter and broke the seal.

"'If you want to see,'" Jordan read out slowly, holding the letter at arm's length, "'your apprentice again, be at the hanging tree by the crossroads south of Cheese at sundown tomorrow. You will be met and brought to him. Come alone. Bring the bard. Sincerely, Your Nemesis. P.S. Alone means alone except for the bard, whom you may bring.'"

"What bard?" Jordan wondered out loud.

"Ah, I believe that would be . . . me."

The voice from the doorway had a poetic lilt and a breathless eagerness, as though its owner had been waiting for his cue to enter.

"You were lurking," said Jordan, without looking around. "No one's timing is that good."

"Well, yes, but not for very long," said Cyral. "I arrived and I asked myself, Where's the closest thing this village has to a tavern? That's where the adventure will start. That's where they always start, isn't it? Am I . . . Do I have the pleasure of meeting the legendary Jordan the Red?"

"No."

"Then could you tell me where to find him, please, so I can let him know you're reading his mail?"

Jordan turned over the envelope and glared at the traitorous glowing letters of his name. "You put this here?"

"Oh—no. But I, er, was waiting for you to read it," said Cyral guiltily. "Once I saw it there."

"All right, who are you and how much do I have to pay you to forget you met me? And what is this?" Jordan gave the letter an aggressive shake. As a threatening tool, it wasn't the best he had worked with, but it wasn't the worst, either. Cyral took a step back.

"If you're admitting to being Jordan the Red, then I'm your new bard. Cyral Gideon, sir, and may I say—"

"New bard?"

"Yes, Mr. Starmacher sent me to write your come-back—"

"Glister sent you? How the hell did he know where to send you?"

"Apparently, your apprentice—"

"I've never had an apprentice! I mean, Jordan hasn't. Damn. Go back to the part about the comeback."

"I'm sorry; I thought you'd be more excited. Yes, it's all arranged, though I don't know how much I should be telling you—"

"Everything. Talk."

Cyral took out his notebook. "Well, there's no firm title yet, but you'll be defeating an evil wizard in his strong-hold of doom, and saving the life of your apprentice."

"Fantastic. Bloody fantastic." Jordan rattled through a string of curses in five languages, only one of which Cyral understood, and that one only well enough to know that this part of the saga would never make it past the censors. "Look, I'm not interested, I'm not available, and I'm not playing along. Whatever Glister's set up for me, you go back there and tell him to call it off."

"I'm afraid I can't, sir. I haven't got a return flight, and as you've read, the scenario has already begun."

"Then this is going to be the dullest saga you've ever written." Jordan sat down decisively. "Call it 'Jordan the Red Does Nothing.'"

"Ah. Nothing. Certainly. Er . . . I hate to point out a possible flaw, but then, what happens to Eliott?"

"Eliott?"

Cyral double-checked his notes, suddenly afraid he had misremembered the name. "Yes, your—"

"—apprentice." Jordan looked back at the letter, then slumped forward in defeat, pressing one hand across his eyes. "He set this up, didn't he."

"Yes, I believe Mr. Starmacher spoke to him—"

Kess came into the room, still holding the caramel apple.

"Eliott isn't upstairs," she said, frowning. "Is he down here?"

"No," snapped Jordan. "If he was here, I'd kill him. Read this."

Kess took the letter. She read through it silently.

"Your appren . . . Eliott?!"

"Did you know about it? What he was setting up?"

"No."

"Lucky for you," said Jordan, but Kess was still staring at the letter.

"This isn't right," she continued distantly. "I should be with him. Him, and you, and me. Come on, we need to go after him. Now."

"What? Hell with that! Boy made his own bed; he can lie in it."

"He never makes his own bed!" She threw the letter down onto the table. "And he's being held prisoner by some sort of evil villain—"

"Wizard," said Cyral helpfully.

"—that's not a bed; that's a snake pit!"

"He made his own snake pit, then. Do you know what he's done? He talked to my agent. He brought a bard down on me. He's thrown me right back in with the wolves!" Jordan sank down into his chair, fuming. "They want another saga, and they won't stop until they've made me live one. I'm not doing it."

"But everything's arranged," said Cyral, who was beginning to form a mental picture of what Glister's reaction to all this would be. If Cyral was very lucky, he would merely never work in Palace Hills again.

"I'm retired."

"Eliott needs you," said Kess.

"I'm not going on another adventure!"

"Now, let's not make any hasty decisions," said Cyral, holding up his hands in an appeal to calm and rational thought. "By the terms of the letter, we don't have to do anything until sundown tomorrow. I'm sure that Eliott can survive—I mean, stay safe; sorry, bad word choice—I'm sure he'll be fine until then. After all, he is the apprentice to Jordan the Red—"

"He's not my apprentice!"

Kess grabbed Jordan by the shirt with both fists and hauled him to his feet. "I don't care if it's an adventure! You need to go out there and get him back! You're a hero—be a hero!"

"I used to be a hero," said Jordan. He pushed her hands away and straightened his shirt. "Ex. Former. I don't do it anymore. And I'm never going to be a puppet for these string-tuggers again."

He jerked his thumb at Cyral, and by proxy at Glister Starmacher and the entire industry of bards and talent agents.

"Then do it because it needs to be done. Because it's the right thing to do. Because Eliott needs help, and there is nobody else in this village who can go rescue him."

"Nobody? How do you know?"

"I've met them all. They're farmers and herders and—background characters! Nobody here knows what a wizard can do, let alone how to fight one."

An inspiration crawled over Jordan's face, insectlike, twitching a humorless smile up from his skin. He rubbed his jaw thoughtfully. "You do."

"I— What?"

"You know about wizards. Least as much as I knew back when I was starting out."

"I'm not a hero."

"Makes two of us, doesn't it? Hell, if you're not up for it, I bet our Little Boy Bard here knows enough about adventure stories; he could pull it off. How 'bout it? You hiding a pair of mighty thews under there?"

Cyral swatted him away. "You'd send us off to save your apprentice—?"

"Happily! And he's not my—"

"Fine," said Kess. "I'll do it. But you're coming with me."

There was no request in her voice, and no room for compromise. It was a voice that had sent a much younger Eliott to bed with no supper, and dissuaded the unwanted manly attention of barbarians with the same efficiency as a knee to the groin; it was the cold, iron tone that said the revels were ended. With an effort of will, Jordan kept his head from dropping and his hands from clasping obsequiously behind his back.

"How do you figure that?" he muttered.

"I'll need a guide," said Kess. "And I'll need your experience. And if you don't, I'll make your life an absolute hell."

She smiled. Jordan didn't.

"Because it's the right thing to do, huh?"

"You had your chance at the moral high ground," said Kess.

Jordan made a last attempt at walking away. He got as far as the back door. He closed his eyes and inhaled the oncoming evening, the mixed smells of hot earth and grain, the aromas of the faire wafting down from the Dancing Green. There would be the tug-of-war soon, and the raffle for the giant picnic basket, and then the fiddlers would start to play. His neighbors would be enjoying their simple lives, without magic or monsters; he tried to imagine how their lives would change, any one of them, if they had to face a vengeful wizard.

He shut the door.

"You're willing to do whatever I tell you?"

Kess nodded.

"Okay. You win. But he doesn't," said Jordan, pointing at Cyral. "I'll help you, but no heroics, no trying to make this a big adventure or any sort of story. We do this my way, not theirs."

"Whatever you say."

With startling speed, Kess reached over and snatched Cyral's notebook away from him. He opened his mouth to protest, only to be glared into silence. Jordan nodded with satisfaction.

"Good. Now," said Jordan, making himself comfortable in a big chair by the fire, "what's the plan, boss?"

"Oh. The plan." Kess looked around for inspiration, and settled on the letter. "We go to the rendezvous—"

"Nope," said Jordan. "That's still playing their game. You want to beat Glister and his toy villains, cut straight to the heart of the thing. You, bard—you've met this wizard? Where's he working from?"

"How would I know? I was literally dropped off by flying monkeys not an hour before I got here. I haven't spoken to anyone but the two of you since then—when I have been permitted to speak, that is!"

"You're allowed to talk now," said Jordan. "So shut up and tell me everything you know about the wizard."

Cyral arched one eyebrow. "And you'll let me finish a sentence?"

"Yes!"

"Very well. But I'm afraid I don't know anything about where he might be. I think he may have said he remembered the name of this village, but I'd need you to give me back my notes to be certain."

Jordan folded his arms. "Make one move to start writing anything down . . ."

"I won't! You have my word. But if you want my help, I'll need my notebook."

"Kess. Give it back to him."

Cyral took the notebook from her hands with the care of a musician picking up his instrument. He flipped through the pages, frantically deciphering his own shorthand from the meeting with Glister.

"Yes, here we are— Glister suggested some sort of trap that your apprentice could be dangled over, and then Hopley said—"

"Wait, Hopley? The wizard is a Hopley?" Jordan frowned. "As in, Hopley's Famous Baked Goods, with the stupid sugar-goblins?"

Cyral winced, but managed a smile. "One and the same, I'm afraid."

"The Puffy Muffin Man is the big bad villain Glister's throwing at me?" For a moment, Jordan's cold rage was shoved aside by indignant disbelief. "If that's the best he's got, he really has gone downhill without me."

Cyral felt he should defend his antagonist. "He's really quite powerful. And menacing. I'm sure you'll find him one of the worst enemies you've faced."

"Yeah, he sounds like the worst. Right. At least now I know where we're going," said Jordan. "Other side of the Wild Forest, there's an old mill. Place used to be a Hopley's Bakery outlet. If he's half as stupid as he sounds, that's where we'll find our Bread Wizard. We'll cut through the forest and get there while he's still trying to figure out which henchman he's sending to meet us."

"Good plan. You lead," said Kess, opening the back door of the inn for him.

"Now? No. Not happening."

"You'll take me through that forest—"

"We're not prepared. We've got no food, no gear, no idea what Hopley might be planning for us, and we'll be in the middle of the forest when it gets dark. Tomorrow, Kess. We'll leave at dawn."

"Yes," said Cyral, standing up. "We will. At dawn!"

Kess and Jordan stared at him.

"I am coming with you," he clarified. "Whether you intend to allow me to record the adventure or not."

This did nothing to abate their stares.

"Look—I know about wizards and things, too, just like you said. And I've met Hopley before, which is more than either of you have done. I could be useful."

"I wouldn't put money on it," said Jordan.

"You can come," said Kess.

"He can?" said Jordan. "Why?"

"Because he wants to be useful and that's more than you do." She crossed her arms. "There's a story about the biggest fool in the world trying to win the hand of a princess. He manages it because, when he sets out, he accepts the company of everyone he meets along the way."

"Oh, I know that one," said Cyral. "The man with the straw, and the man with one leg tied behind his back . . . It happened in Bulgaria, I believe?"

"I've never done anything like this," Kess continued, all her attention focused on Jordan. "I'll need all the help I can get."

Jordan pushed himself stiffly out of his chair. "Biggest fool in the world's our inspiration. Oh, yeah, this is going to go great. Start gathering supplies. I'll meet you here in the morning."

SEVEN

DAWN CAME WITHOUT metaphor. Cyral stared blearily out the back door of the inn, trying to think of one, but after spending the better part of the night planning and packing with Kess, and the worst part trying to steal a few hours of sleep on the floor, he had already exhausted his mental resources in the act of being awake, dressed, and ready to set out in the predawn hours. His neck and back were lobbying for a few more hours' sleep in a real bed, but Cyral was determined to seem eager and diligent in his duty—which was, he reminded himself, to Glister Starmacher, not to Jordan the Red. One way or another, he was going to return to Palace Hills with the story of an adventure.

"Looking for something?"

Cyral turned, and found Kess beside him, pale and silent as the morning mist herself.

"Nothing," he said hastily. "I was thinking of opening lines I might have used, if I was writing this saga. Which, yes, I know, I'm not allowed to do."

"It's too bad you're not." Their eyes met, and Cyral felt as clear as water, with all his plans and thoughts exposed. But all she said was, "Jordan's here."

They found Jordan in the common room, finishing a large breakfast. He glanced up as they came in, daring them to say something enthusiastic about the day ahead. When no one did, he pushed his plate away and, with a grim expression, picked up his knapsack. Every move he made was stiff and forced, with reluctance or arthritis or both.

"Here's how it is," said Jordan. "Until we find Hopley, I lead; you follow. After that, you're on your own. And nobody tries anything heroic."

"If you need to do something heroic to save Eliott," said Kess, "you will."

"I'm guiding and giving advice. That's it." Jordan flexed his fingers. "Think of me as the old mentor who sends you on your way."

"Definitely not," said Cyral. "The old mentor is always killed off midway through, to allow the young heroes their chance to rise to greatness."

"Good thing this isn't going to be a saga, then," said Jordan.

He took his wolfskin cloak off the back of his chair, and, from underneath it, in a cracked leather scabbard, an old, cruciform sword with a plain, round pommel.

Cyral drew a breath. "Surely that's not the Sword of Empire, the legendary blade gifted to you by the lost heir of Charlemagne himself!"

"No. It's not," said Jordan, buckling it to his hip.

"Oh. What happened to that one?"

"Beats me. Doesn't matter right now, does it?"

"You had it in the 'Skarbolg Saga,'" Kess supplied. "But then you didn't use it against the skeletons of D'loom."

"Yes, I always wondered about that," said Cyral. "After all, it was a holy weapon."

"It was a piece of shit, all right?" Jordan glared at them each in turn. "The metal was lousy, the balance was awful, and it went blunt if you looked at it funny. It was a cere-monial sword made for looking pretty. Now can we go?"

Without waiting for an answer, he strode out.

". . . Not the most auspicious start," Cyral muttered, but he refused to let it shake him. He set out into the damp, fresh morning, following Jordan but walking in the footsteps of the bards of legend. In his head, an over-ture soared.

At first, they cut across the village fields, traveling northward by the most direct route to the forest. Then, when they had left the tamed outskirts of Cheese behind them, their path began to twist and turn, taking them through moorlands and lowlands where vast stretches of heather made the green hills blush purple. They walked in single file, and Cyral came last, trying his best to commit to memory every image, color, and sound of the journey. He was still afraid that, if he risked stopping to take notes now, he would be accused of slowing them down, or worse, of writing something about Jordan.

After a while, they found the road Jordan had been searching for, if it could be called that. At best, it was two wheel ruts running toward the forest, now and again deep-ening into small pools of stagnant water, but most often lost under years of unchecked growth. Behind them, it began to curve back toward the village, but dwindled away to nothing long before it reached even the outermost of the cultivated fields. Ahead, it plunged into a stand of whispering poplar trees at the edge of the forest. With a last glance back, Jordan followed it.

Within the forest, the road was clearer, shored up and leveled with beams from the same massive trees that had been felled to build it. On either side of the road, a wide swath of the forest had been reduced to young poplars and alders, but here and there, a massive oak or cedar, too stubborn to be cut down, still showed the forest's age.

"This used to be a lumber road," said Jordan, "but they stopped cutting about eight or nine years ago. It was called the King's Lane."

"Why?" asked Cyral.

"Who knows. Maybe someone called King built it. There's never been a real king anywhere near Cheese."

The King's Lane took them deep into the forest. Jordan continued to guide them, but as the road ran straight and obvious, his directions became little more than the occasional, "Yeah, keep on going this way." His steady, trudging pace never changed, and as the morning wore on, Cyral and Kess got farther and farther ahead, until they found themselves obliged to pause and wait or lose sight of him.

During these starts and stops, Cyral weighed his options. There had been sagas written about heroes without their knowledge or permission, but they rarely ended well, as the Candid Crusader experiments had proved. But even if this adventure wasn't likely to sidetrack into a drunken rampage through the Holy Land, the whole notion of trying to work in secret felt wrong to Cyral.

Which meant he would have to take a chance.

The next time Jordan was a safe distance behind, Cyral caught up with Kess. "Could we talk?"

She considered this. "Talk," she said, not as a command but as a general invocation to some unseen muse of conversation. Cyral cleared his throat.

"I wanted to say," he began, as he had practiced in his head, "that I am honestly sorry for all this. For my part in it. I thought that you—that is, Jordan and all of you—that you were willing participants, that you wanted to be involved. I've had to look at a lot of things differently. It's changed my perspective—though not on everything."

"What does that mean?"

Cyral glanced back over his shoulder. "I'm still going to write this saga."

This didn't appear to surprise her. "Jordan won't like that," she said, with barely concealed amusement.

"I know. But I'm not going to write about him. I thought, instead, perhaps I could put the focus on . . . you."

She didn't laugh, which ruled out several of the scenarios Cyral had imagined, but she also didn't leap at the opportunity, which ruled out most of the rest. As no horrible monster crashed out of the bushes to interrupt them, Cyral found himself at a loss for what to say next.

"If you were willing," he tried.

Kess shrugged. "Right place, right time?"

"That's not the only reason." Cyral took off his hat and held it sincerely over his heart. "You've got all the qualities an audience would want to hear about—I mean, you're young, beautiful, full of spirit and determination. And you are in charge, after all, so it only makes sense that this should be your story."

"I still don't know what I'm doing."

"We'll play up your innocence."

This time she laughed, and quickly covered her mouth with the back of her hand. "Please don't."

"Or however you'd like it," said Cyral. "This would be your story."

"My own story . . ." She let the words melt on her tongue. "Okay. Write whatever you want. You have my permission."

Cyral smiled and took out his notebook. He dipped his pen into the vial of ink sheathed on his belt. "Could I ask you something, then?"

"Me first. Why didn't you give up?"

An inch from the page, Cyral's pen hesitated and froze, the ink building to a drop at its tip.

The drop fell.

"Oh . . . well, I suppose it's my job." He stuck his pen into his hat band and dabbed at the blot with his sleeve. When he looked up, Kess was still watching him with an unsatisfied frown.

"Just a job?" she said.

Cyral opened his mouth, tempted to answer without reserve, to tell her about his wild ambition of becoming a bard of great renown, and hopefully of great reverb, too; about his humiliation in front of the Ugly Crowd; and about the deep-down certainty that had driven him to this career in the first place, that stories needed to be told, and that he needed to tell them.

Instead, he faked a cough in the name of professionalism. "Isn't that enough?"

Kess looked away, as if he was suddenly less interesting than a pair of squirrels chasing each other through the undergrowth. "What was your question?"

Cyral tried to remember. "It was about you and Jordan's apprentice—"

"Eliott."

"Yes. I wanted to ask . . . I gather the two of you are . . . close?"

Kess tightened her lips. "That's not a question. But, yes, we're close. But not dot-dot-dot close. Don't call him my lover or anything stupid like that."

"No? As you say. How would you describe it, then?"

"I could say it in Elvish . . . He imagines worlds for me.

He trades my old dreams for new ones. He makes me laugh, and I bug the shit out of him. Have you got a word for that?"

". . . I don't believe so, no," said Cyral.

"I don't worry about him. I'm not worried. Eliott will be all right. He gets away with everything," said Kess, as if this was a source of personal pride. "And he's got Elvish magic to protect him. He'll be all right."

She quickened her pace, pulling ahead, but Cyral read the tightness in her shoulders and her voice. He could feel the unspoken words rising, like the tide creeping up a shallow beach. ". . . But?"

"But I should be with him. If I'm not there, if something happens . . ."

Kess let out a breath. Slowed. And then, to Cyral's astonishment, she leaned against him and wrapped her arm around his. "Tell me a story," she said. "One with a happy ending."

"I'm not sure I can think of—"

Her grip tightened.

"Well, I suppose . . . Yes. Once upon a time," he began, reaching into the first story that came to mind, "there lived a species of migratory horned toads—"

But before he could go further, Jordan caught up with them.

"Something's coming," said Jordan, without breaking stride.

Cyral stopped, his curiosity getting the better of him, and in the distance he heard it: a faint and metallic noise, as if someone were having difficulty carrying buckets of nails along the road.

"Move," snapped Jordan.

"We should see what it is. This could be somebody we need to meet," said Kess.

"Fat chance," said Jordan. "We don't want to meet anything out here."

But it soon became clear that whatever was behind them was making better speed than they were. The noise grew slowly, relentlessly, louder, broken now and again by harsh voices speaking in an unfamiliar language.

"I can slip back and look," said Kess. "I won't be seen."

"You know that? For a fact? Because you've done this before? No. No splitting up. That's how your enemies get ahold of the body parts to send warnings to your friends."

"Oh, charming," said Cyral, but he took advantage of the distraction to write a short description of the moment: *Kess looks back as thrilling and unknown danger approaches.*

"Anyway," continued Jordan, "you don't need to. Up ahead. I think there's— Perfect."

The road bent back on itself here to avoid a deep hollow, so that for a stretch of a hundred yards, they could look back through the trees and see the source of the pursuing noise. As it appeared, Cyral abandoned his previous reservations and wrote as rapidly as he could. A large number of short, spindly creatures, spread out in double file, was approaching at a steady march. They carried weapons and wore armor covered in spikes, all rusty and blackened, so that the overall appearance of the troop made Cyral think of toxic, crawling things normally found beneath rocks. One in the lead was singing—if the word could be tortured sufficiently to stretch that far—and beating out a rhythm with a length of chain.

"Goblins!" said Kess.

"Yes, I can see," said Jordan. "Thank you for stating the obvious." He pointed to the forest on their left. "Trees."

"Trees?"

"Oh, for— You and you," he explained, in helpful tones for the dense of thinking, "follow me off the road into the trees. Now!"

"Ah, we're going to ambush them," said Cyral, holding on to his hat as he stumbled through the undergrowth into the protective shadows of a broad cedar.

"No," said Jordan, "we're staying out of their way until they're past." He dragged Cyral close to him. "Did you set this up? You and Glister?"

"What? No. As far as I know, Hopley is the only antagonist arranged for you. These must be something incidental."

"No one's ever seen a monster in this forest. No one. You drag me here and there's suddenly goblins? This reeks of Starmacher grease."

"Unless the plot changed—"

Kess made an urgent gesture. "Jordan. They've stopped."

"Oh, hell."

Back on the road, a harsh voice snapped a command, and the centipede formation broke apart. Small clusters of goblins moved to the edges of the road, poking their weapons into the undergrowth.

"We'll have to fight," said Kess. "Here."

She drew a pair of carving knives from her knapsack and handed one to Cyral.

Jordan grabbed her wrist. "Where did you get those?"

"The kitchen at the inn. They don't have runes on them, but they'll do."

"Stealing cutlery." Jordan shook his head. "Do either of you even know how to fight with a knife?"

"I learn fast," said Kess.

"And I've read books," said Cyral. "There were knife fights described. Mentioned, at least."

"One of us is going to end up missing fingers," said Jordan. "Look, there's at least forty goblins out there. That's almost . . . fifteen to one. And you two barely count as ones. You know what they call people who go up against those sorts of numbers?"

"Heroes?"

". . . Yeah, exactly right. Stupid, dead heroes. Now, come on, before they see us. Most important rule of adventuring: know when to run."

Keeping low, Jordan struck out into the trees, and Kess and Cyral followed him.

"I can't believe he's running away," said Kess, looking over her shoulder. Behind them, the goblins were slowly beating paths into the bushes.

"You have to admit," said Cyral, "it did sound rather bad when he worked out the odds."

"But he's Jordan the Red. He's fought armies."

"I haven't! Have you? Don't worry; I'll write that you made a strategic withdrawal. Showing wisdom and cunning." Cyral risked a smile. "Discretion being the better part of valor?"

But Kess remained unconvinced.

Soon, they were completely out of sight of the old lumber road, and the goblins were only a distant rattle of metal and an occasional harsh shout, far behind, but Jordan still pressed on into the depths of the forest. Cyral tried to call to mind everything he had learned from his research for *Druid Today*, but the forest seemed to have a dearth of horned toads migrating through it at the moment. He vaguely recalled something about moss growing on the sides of trees.

"Jordan? Aren't we . . . I mean, I thought we'd be staying within sight of the road?"

Jordan glanced back. He was well ahead of Cyral now,

stepping over fallen branches and treacherous roots as if they were puddles in the street. "Nope."

"Are you sure that's the best thing to do? We won't get lost out here?"

"I know which way we're going. We're only getting lost enough that none of Glister's pets can find us."

"Honestly, I don't think he sent those goblins. But, look, what about plain, ordinary dangers? What about bears?"

"Don't worry about bears."

Cyral considered this. "Do you mean, if any bears try to eat us, you'll step in and save us?"

"Nope."

"No, of course not. That would be pandering to your legend. I can only imagine you lying on the ground having your intestines gnawed, stoically refusing to do anything lest I write it down. Ow!"

"Watch out for the branch," said Jordan cheerfully.

Cyral rubbed at his watering eye. He was coming to the conclusion that forests were better left to scenery painters. One large, dappled canvas sheet and a couple of potted shrubs would have signified everything quite adequately.

"It's okay," said Kess. "We won't meet any bears. Trust me."

"Elvish wood-sense?"

"No. Common sense. The way we've been crashing around, we must have scared away all the animals by now." She smiled. "Too bad. I'd like to see him fight a bear. I know he would, if we really got attacked."

"Fat chance," Jordan called back.

"You wait and see," Kess continued. "When something happens, he'll come through."

After a while, Jordan slowed down enough that Kess and Cyral could catch up with him. The sound of the goblins had faded away, so Jordan allowed them a brief rest under the shade of an enormous cedar and the chance to share some food and water before they pushed onward. The forest grew denser and darker around them as the trees pushed the sun away. Hills and gullies shepherded their path, often in broad curves that turned them this way and that, to the point that Cyral feared they were walking in circles. He discreetly took a loaf of bread out of his knapsack and began tearing off crumbs and dropping them on the trail behind him.

A rustling in the bushes made him look back. A bristly tailed squirrel stared up at him hopefully, its mouth already full of crumbs.

Ah, right, Cyral thought gloomily, I knew there was part of that story I was forgetting.

He put the rest of the loaf away and caught up with Jordan and Kess.

"Look, can we be reasonable?" said Cyral. "Those goblins must have given up by now—if they were even looking for us. Shouldn't we head back and find the road again?"

Jordan shook his head. "They might be gone, or we might walk right back into them. No. For now, farther away from the road we stay, the better. Anyway, another half mile of bushwhacking'll be good for you both. We'll keep going this way," he said, and led them over a rise.

And stopped. Here, in the heart of the forest, the heavy canopy of ancient fir and cedar had been torn open and left for stunted, withered saplings, nettles, and thornbushes to patch. Thickets of crab apple, gray and scaly beneath their golden leaves, marked out the path of a winding stream and spilled berries the color of royal blood down into the water. Everywhere, the tendrils of wild blackberries crept and curled around anything that reached for the sunlight, and their overripe berries were dark as royal sins. If there had been birds gorging themselves on the fruit, if a small, fleeting animal had shaken the leaves, if a single insect had droned over the stagnant stream, it would have been a pleasant glade. Instead, it was as silent as a poisoned well.

In the middle of the place, the thornbushes had grown into a massive wall, so high and tangled that at least one dead apple tree had been engulfed, its gnarled branches reaching out like a hand sinking into the ocean.

"What is this place?" asked Kess.

"Beats me," said Jordan. "But I don't like it. And I get the feeling—"

"—that it doesn't like us," Kess finished. Jordan glared at her.

"You had no idea it was here? Really?" Cyral eased forward to the edge of the thornbushes. "It looks like something came along and simply ripped up all the trees. Have there ever been giants in these parts?"

"What? No. Completely giantless. Where do you think you're going?"

"Into the heart of all this. It looks like there's something through there. It could be a pile of boulders or it could be a house . . . Either way, I want a better look. Kess? Would you care to come exploring with me?" Cyral struggled out of his knapsack and hung his broad, feathered hat on a suitable spike of a branch. If he ducked down, there was just barely enough space for him to squeeze through the gap in the hedge.

"Yeah, there's a bad idea," said Jordan. "We're giving this place a wide clearance."

"First we run away from goblins; now we run away from plants?" Cyral threw up his hands. "Kess, tell me we're not going to pass this up. Think of—"

"Eliott," Jordan cut in.

"Yes, think of the story you'll be able to tell Eliott after you rescue him. Imagine if there is an ancient treasure horde in there—you could find an enchanted ring to give him as a present."

Kess hesitated. "He's waiting for us . . ."

"He'll be perfectly safe until we get there. Hopley's following the rules of plot—there's always time for at least one adventurous detour along the way. Please? A quick look." Cyral moved closer to Kess, murmuring so that only she could hear, "It would give me something to write about."

He could see the temptation creeping like a shiver up Kess's long ears. She gave in. "All right," she said. "Let's see what's in there."

Jordan grabbed her by the shoulder. "Are you crazy? You can feel the wrong of this place; why would you want to get any closer?"

"To see why it feels wrong," said Kess, with a grin. She slipped away from him and into the tangle of thorns.

"Fine," Jordan called after her. "But I'm staying out here." He folded his arms and leaned against a tree, in a very bad impression of a man relaxing at his ease. "Scream if anything horrible happens to you."

"And you'll come running?"

"What'd give you that idea?"

Kess laughed at him and disappeared into the bushes. Cyral, with guilty self-satisfaction, added a polite bow and followed after her.

JORDAN WAITED. HE could feel the sledgehammer of inevitability coming for him, ready to drive it into his head one more time that heroes couldn't retire. He had stayed out of the forest for twenty years, and for twenty years, it had been nothing but a forest: branches, leaves, birds, fluffy woodland creatures happily trying to eat one another. Now he had been drawn in, and suddenly there were goblins and creepy, mysterious glades waiting for him. He wondered if Glister Starmacher had tapped into ancient Atlantean mystic powers, and was secretly running the universe.

Which meant, it was only a matter of time . . .

"Here! Jordan, I think you should come and see this!" Jordan was almost relieved to hear Cyral's shout.

Take the hit now, he thought, or catch it coming back the other way.

"Fine," he said, in case any of Glister's secret Atlantean spies were listening. "Let's get this over with."

"WHAT DO YOU think it is?" asked Cyral, shielding his eyes against the sun as he looked up at the thing they had found.

It had been a tower, before long centuries of collapse pulled it to the ground. From the amount of rubble strewn around, it must have once risen high above the tallest trees in a much younger forest. Now all that remained was a two-story stump in a clearing the thornbushes had yet to overrun, and the broken crown of the tower perched precariously on top, barely hanging on. The fractured, conical roof, its blue clay tiles bleached to gray and overgrown with weeds, pointed crookedly toward the sky. All that was keeping the tower from collapsing completely to the earth were the vines coiled around and through the fallen stonework.

"What does it look like?" said Jordan. "It's a ruin. Let's leave before it falls down on us."

"But what's it doing here in the middle of the forest? Aren't you the least bit curious?"

"No."

Cyral shook his head. "I don't understand you. There's a story here; I can feel it. This may have been the watchtower of a long-forgotten kingdom, or the hiding place of a dread and terrible sorceress. If these stones could talk, they could tell us a history that no living man has heard, and you want to leave it unexplored."

"Yes. Exactly," said Jordan. "You've seen it; let's move on. Shouldn't keep the wizard waiting."

"We've been making excellent time. I think we've earned the chance to look around—a moment longer, please. I need to find out what happened here."

"Nothing happened here. Nothing heroic or historical or interesting. If it had, you would have heard of it. Everybody would have. The tower was built, and then it fell down. End of story. Now, let's go."

"Jordan," said Kess quietly. "I think you're wrong."

She knelt among the brambles and held up a thin, silvery strand of something. Weeds and thorns had grown up around it and entangled it, but when she lifted it, there was an obvious trail of it winding down from the narrow window of the tower. "It's hair."

"Oh, hell."

Jordan backed away, gripping his sword. Kess let the twisted strands of hair sink back into the weeds.

"Clearly, I'm missing something," said Cyral. "Why are we suddenly afraid of hair?"

"Not the hair," said Jordan. "This place—it's a setting. Think of your childhood stories."

"Oh . . . !"

"And in the heart of the forest, the wicked witch locked the princess away from the world," said Kess, in a lullaby voice. "In a tower with no doors, guarded by thornbushes, there to await the rescue of her handsome prince."

"Let down your long hair," said Cyral.

"Right. Except no prince ever comes for this one," said Jordan, still watching the silent hedges apprehensively. "The princess dies waiting for a hero who never comes. The tower falls down, the story never gets told, and somewhere, someone's agent writes the whole thing off for a tax break. Come on, we need to get away from here."

Cyral stared up at the crown of the tower. It looked remarkably intact, and the window was by design the perfect size for climbing in through. "Shouldn't we at least try to find out who she was?"

Jordan stepped in front of him. "No. Listen to me, I used to live in these stories. See all the thorns? They were here to guard the place. They've festered and wormed their way into the heart of the forest. Ever seen a heart full of worms? Now, out the way we came, and fast."

"But we've come this far!" He turned to Kess for support. "Could you leave and never know what's in there? 'Then came she to the ruined tower, and looked upon it, and turned around and went away again'?"

"Sounds good to me," said Jordan.

"No," said Kess. "No, I want to see this, too."

Cyral smiled at her. "My hero," he said, with genuine enthusiasm. "Now, how do we get up there?"

"We climb," said Kess. She crouched down and slid her fingers into the weeds again, picking out the fine strands of hair. "That's what it's here for. After you."

"Pair of idiots," said Jordan, as he retreated to the gap in the hedge. "You're on your own. I'll wait for you outside."

"Whatever would we do without him," said Cyral, under his breath. He checked that his notebook was secure in his belt, stepped carefully to where Kess was waiting, and began to climb.

The rubble was easier to ascend than he had expected, and more painful. The cascade of hair was unbelievably sturdy, and the vines ensnaring it held it firmly in place; at the same time, every vine nipped and stung him with tiny spines, even when he avoided the larger thorns. Every stone had a jagged edge, and even the moss between the stones prickled his bare hands. He passed a bird's nest crouched among the weeds, and, farther up, a bird's skeleton impaled by long thorns.

He was halfway to the window when the vines began to shake.

His breath caught in his throat. He froze, imagining the creeping vines suddenly coming alive, like snakes, skewering him with thorny fangs. Jordan would be so smug, he thought.

"Something wrong?"

He risked a glance back. It was only Kess coming up behind him.

"No, I'm fine. A moment of . . . I'm fine." He swallowed heavily and continued upward. He was almost at the outcropping of the tower's fallen crown, where the uppermost room, still intact, jutted out from the heap of broken masonry. The weeds and thorns grew sparser here, as the hair narrowed into a single, thicker skein, hanging from an almost vertical wall. Cyral reached up and took hold.

The hair went limp in his grasp.

A hollow sound bounced out of the tower, through the window—toc, toc, toc—and pale silken hair unspooled past Cyral's face. He clung to the stone, scrambling for a grip on anything solid, as an ancient skull, still wearing a tarnished coronet, tumbled past him. He screamed. It struck the stones and shattered, and suddenly everything was moving—the hair, the thornbushes, the loose stones beneath Cyral's flailing feet. He caught the edge of the window-sill and hung, dangling by one hand. As he swung around, he saw the whole of the glade writhing and lashing out. Then he twisted again, and all he could see was the tower wall, festooned with wisps of hair like cobwebs. He grabbed out with his other hand, caught the windowsill, and dug his fingers in until his knuckles went white. His arms started to shake.

Something caught his ankle.

"Climb down," Kess shouted, pulling at him. "There's still a gap!"

"I can't!"

"Just let go. It's not far to fall!"

"I really can't!" He tried to turn his head, but his whole body was turning to stone, everything except his pounding heart. "Kess, I can't move! Please . . . help . . ."

"Then . . . then stay really still. I'll climb over you and pull you in. We'll wait this out. Okay? Can you hang on?"

Cyral felt his jaw hardening, his tongue becoming a petrified block between his teeth. He managed to nod.

In a series of agonizing movements, Kess hauled herself up over Cyral's back. For one awful moment, her whole weight was on Cyral's shoulders, nearly wrenching them from their sockets; then she was over him, scrambling through the window into the tower.

"Okay, now I'm going to grab your wrists and—"

There was a muffled thump, and then silence.

"Kess?"

Something inside the tower walked across the broken floor on slippered feet, softly swishing as it moved. It came over to the window. Cyral could feel it looking down at him, but he didn't dare to look back. If he didn't see it, it might not be a thing without a head . . .

He felt cold, thin hands take hold of his arms, lift him up and leave him sprawling across the windowsill, gasping for breath. He kept his eyes pressed shut. The occupant of the tower leaned over and brushed against his cheek; the touch felt like silk, dry and whispering. He heard a soft voice speaking in an unfamiliar language, and the voice was like the touch. *"Aeoling,"* it murmured. *"Carmin aeoling."*

A kiss touched his lips. Numbness crept through him, from his lips to the rest of his body, like the shock of a bee sting before the pain hits. He slid backward off the windowsill.

Then the pain hit.

Cyral tumbled down, snagging his clothes and skin on brambles and broken masonry all the way to the ground, but as he fell, he felt a strange resistance slowing him down. When at last he lay unmoving at the foot of the tower, once he was sure that nothing was going to kill him, he risked opening his eyes.

He was webbed from head to toe in fine, blond hair. He pulled at it and it fell away, pooling around his feet.

He looked up. "Kess . . . ?"

The tower remained silent. The glade, however, did not. All around him, peeling from the rubble, twisting beneath his feet, vines rustled. Dry leaves crackled. The ensnarled trunk of the dead apple tree groaned and bent as its moorings strained toward their prey. Cyral looked around desperately for the gap in the hedge, but the landscape had changed. There was no way out. Kess was gone and Jordan was gone and he was trapped.

And if he died, no one would ever hear about it. No one would tell their story. He would die a failure as a bard.

He looked back into the churning, serrated mouth of the thornbushes. There were still open patches between the thrashing vines. Someone quick enough, desperate enough, might just be able to get through . . .

"Kess . . . if you can hear me . . . I'm going to try to find

Jordan. Stay there until we get back. Stay . . . Just stay alive, please."

And with his arms wrapped around his head and a fervent hope that he was indeed desperate enough, Cyral threw himself into the jaws of the hedge.

EIGHT

A LIGHT SLAP brought Eliott awake.

"Send one of the servants," he mumbled. "I don't need a lesson today."

"Oh, I believe you do," said an unfamiliar voice. "And I have a very valuable lesson prepared for you."

Eliott frowned, confused. He kept his eyes closed, but started paying more attention with his ears. He could hear a repetitive wooden clunk, and something mechanical, and several people moving around. Behind all the other sounds, he could hear a steady rush of moving water, but he tried to ignore it and the pressure on his bladder it invoked.

"Come," said the voice, rich and well mannered. "You've slept for more than a day already. It's time you make yourself useful."

"Where am I?"

A memory, ill defined as a dream, hung in front of him, but something was keeping him from seizing hold of it.

"Open your eyes and see."

Reluctantly, he did.

The wizard, Hopley, smiled down at him; a horrible sight to wake up to. He could see every hair in the wizard's hatchetlike nose. Every patch of bad skin beneath the glue holding Hopley's beard to his chin loomed large. Eliott grimaced and twisted to find something else to look at.

He was tied to a chair inside some sort of big wooden barn. The chair was on a catwalk, extending out from the second floor. Below him, a complex machine of cogs and wheels and spikes thumped and rumbled in a menacing way.

"Now," said Hopley. "First of all, tell me what you think. I'm sure you and Jordan have seen plenty of torture chambers, but I believe I have constructed something . . . unique."

"It's . . . Yeah. I've never been in one like it," said Eliott honestly. "You were going for rustic, right? This is, like, your evil lair in the country?"

He took another look around. There were rats in the rafters, tiny gray faces watching him curiously. He played with the idea of charming them down to eat through his ropes.

"Kinda dusty," he added.

"Sometimes one must make do with what is available," said Hopley. "This is an old family mill, abandoned in response to shifting market demands. Honestly, hire an ogre as a financial planner and suddenly you find yourself having to make changes everywhere. I told—"

He stopped himself with a small cough.

". . . In any event, when I first arrived, the building was in an impossible state. The mill wheel machinery was broken, the place was infested with goblins, and a swineherd had set up lodgings with his entire herd of pigs in the bakery. Consider it a testament to the power of my arts that I was able to make this much of a restoration. I may yet have to resort to enchantments to get the smell out of the bakery."

"What happened to the swineherd?" said Eliott. "Have you got him tied up somewhere, too?"

"No. I killed him."

Eliott's eyes went wide. "Just for being on your property?"

"Hardly," said Hopley, with a good imitation of regret. "The intention was not to kill him. The intention was to transfigure him into a beast of monstrous ferocity, to serve as a guard. Unfortunately, the magic involved proved too complex for his body to withstand."

Eliott shuddered. "Harsh," he said, with feeling; partially revulsion, partially macabre fascination with the image in his mind.

Hopley stalked away to a window, hands clasped behind his back. "Fortunately, his herd of swine were more adaptable. Perhaps I should have attempted to turn pigs into children all those years ago. What would the A.T.C.B.S.O. Grants Committee have thought of that, I wonder."

"My dad's always complaining about committees," said Eliott conversationally, as he tested his bonds. "How they make everything take ten times as long as it needs to. He says tradesmen shouldn't be allowed to interfere with the business of nobility. Er, no offense meant."

"No offense caused," said Hopley. "I have elevated myself far beyond the ranks of a mere tradesman. I am a wizard, and soon, I will be a celebrity. The Man Who Killed Jordan the Red."

Eliott kept a carefully straight face. "Yeah? And how are you going to do that?"

"You will sit there until Jordan arrives. Then I will hoist you over the edge and leave you hanging from that rope, where you will dangle as bait. Jordan will come to rescue you. When he walks out onto this narrow bridge, I will knock you both off the bridge, into . . . the Machine." Hopley snapped his fingers, causing an ominous roll of thunder. "Where you will both die," he added for clarity.

"Got it," said Eliott. "Walk, knock, die . . . Effective, simple. Really simple. Like, way simpler than anything Baron Clockwork ever tried."

"Are you implying that my trap should be more complex? I would remind you"—Eliott's world filled up with Hopley's glaring nose again—"that you are the one currently held in the middle of it, one snap away from your own spiky doom."

Another echo of thunder rattled the shingles, made slightly less ominous by the involuntary twitch of Hopley's fingers as he realized that he had caused it. He carried on quickly. "Do you have no fear of death, boy?"

Eliott thought about this. "Nah, not really. Not right now. You've got to keep me alive if I'm going to lure Jordan here, and when he gets here—I'll get to be rescued by Jordan the Red! How cool is that?"

"And then . . ."

"Oh, right. Then the death thing." Eliott shrugged as best he could; the ropes were too tight for easy expression. Deep down, he knew he probably should be scared, but Hopley and the Big Barn of Doom simply held no terror for him, not after a childhood growing up with stories of the Necromanticore and the Three-Headed Beast of Skulp, not after a lifetime of Elvish practical jokes. Instead, he felt the thrill of finally being part of something—he was getting to live the story!

"I'll be scared when Jordan gets here, okay? I'll make it look good for you," he said sympathetically.

"That's all I ask for."

"You promise you won't put me to sleep again or anything? I want to watch your big showdown."

"You may watch. So long as you give me no cause to expend unnecessary magic on you." Hopley smiled. "I have, however, instructed my guards to be merciless if they need to subdue you."

"Yeah, that's fine. That's fair."

Hopley smiled coldly. "I may yet permit you a measure of recognition in the saga."

"That'd be great," said Eliott. "So have you rehearsed what you're going to say?"

"For what?"

"For the big entrance scene!"

Hopley looked at him blankly. ". . . Should I have something prepared? I was intending to extemporize."

"Oh, man! It's a good thing you kidnapped me. You've got to have the big speeches planned out." Eliott sat up straighter in his bonds. He decided it didn't really count as collaboration to improve the villain's dialogue. "Let's start with some taunts . . . How about, 'If you have any courage in your heart, try and save him!'"

Hopley tested the sound of this.

"Go on . . ."

BARBED VINES LASHED at Cyral, catching and tearing at his clothes, his hair, anything they could reach. Thorns stung his skin and sprang back bloodied. He could see nothing but leaves and brambles all around him, but wherever he felt a space, he pushed his body into it. When the vines tangled his feet, he scuttled ahead on hands and knees. Stopping was unthinkable.

And then something crashed into the bushes ahead of him, and he cried out involuntarily. The hedge broke apart, and strong hands grabbed him and yanked him forward. He felt sunlight on his back, and blessed open space above him.

"Jordan? Is that—"

Jordan shoved him toward the trees. "Move!"

In a daze, Cyral stumbled on, away from the grasping, choking vines now stretching toward him from behind. "Kess—she's still in there! What do we do?"

"Keep running," said Jordan, keeping pace beside him. "Run."

Oh, good, Cyral thought maniacally. I know how to do that. I'm getting quite good at that.

He plunged ahead, into the cool, green, and above all nonmurderous bushes. Then, out of the corner of his eye, he caught a glimpse of bright plumage flashing and flapping on the edge of the surging brambles.

"My hat! That's my hat!"

He skidded, pivoted, and flung out his arm—then, looking back into the churning, writhing maw of the living hedge, decided that if he had to choose between being the sort of man who always went back for his hat and the sort who still had two hands, he would much rather be able to clap. He turned again and ran to catch up with Jordan.

When they were beyond the reach of the thorns, they slowed down. Cyral collapsed against a tree and sat there until his heart stopped racing and the tremble had gone from his limbs. Jordan gave him a length of bandage to clean the blood from his cuts and scratches, followed by a long drink from Jordan's waterskin, which did not in fact contain water. After he had finished gasping and coughing, Cyral told the story of the tower.

". . . And I left her there," he finished hoarsely. "I shouldn't have. I know. We need to go back."

To his surprise, Jordan didn't argue. "You got a plan?"

Cyral wiped the sweat and dirt from his forehead. "No," he admitted. "I don't know what to do. What would you have done?"

"Not gone in there in the first place."

"Yes, but if you had to. If it was your quest, to get through a wall of thorns to save a maiden trapped in a tower, what would you have done?"

"If it wasn't in the middle of a forest, burn the damn thing down. Towers aren't too flammable. Place like this?" Jordan squeezed out the last of the home brew. "Dunno. Probably track down some old artifact like the witch's bones that'd let me pass through safely. There was always some piece of junk like that lying around."

"You . . . wouldn't throw yourself through and hope for the best?"

A thin smile cracked the corner of Jordan's mouth. "What kind of a fool'd do that?"

"Right. Yes. Well, do you think we'll find some sort of artifact of safe passage around here anywhere?"

"No." Jordan stood up, grunting and stretching. "But, can't hurt to look. Gives the glade time to fall asleep again. I'm thinking that's going to be your best chance— sneaking back in."

"Our best chance, you mean."

"Let's go find an artifact."

Cyral scrambled after him. "Jordan—"

"We're looking for a dead witch, maybe. Keep your nose peeled for the smell of gingerbread."

"Jordan, wait! You're not seriously saying you're going to make me do this on my own!"

"Old mentor, remember? Advice only. Doing things is up to you."

"But I can't do this on my own. I can't! I don't know how to rescue someone from angry plants. I'm just the bard. I sing; I write; I do poetry! You need to—"

Jordan turned on him, sudden and angry as an avalanche. "What? What do I need to do? You want me to put on a show for you? Give you something to write about? Hell with that."

"Oh, I'm sorry—did you not want to be written about? You should have said something earlier." Cyral raised his hands in mock surrender. He was pushing his luck, he could feel it, but he had spent too much of the day running away from things. "In fact, you have made that perfectly clear. I'm not writing anything about Jordan the Red."

"Yeah? Then what's in here?"

Jordan grabbed for the notebook, but Cyral was quicker, and held it out of reach. "These are my notes for 'The Adventures of Kess.'"

"'The Adventures of'— Does she know about that?"

"I have her full permission. Believe it or not, some people are still interested in being heroes!"

"And getting trapped in towers?"

Cyral winced. "I never meant for her to get in trouble."

"Yeah, but what sort of story would it be if she didn't?" said Jordan nastily. "You shoved her into the trap, so you're the one who gets her out of it. I'm going to make sure of that."

They walked on in silence, a heavy, pressing silence that reminded Cyral of Kess failing to answer him from the tower. He tried to distract himself with memories of other stories, but with no success. Everything brought him back to the fact that he had lost his heroine, and it was all his fault.

"I wish I'd never left Palace Hills," he said, as a relief from hearing himself think. "I've never liked forests. Shouldn't there be birds singing or something? It's so quiet here. Too quiet."

Jordan stumbled to a halt. His shoulders tensed and he

hunched over as if he had been struck by a stomach cramp.
"Oh, you did not just say that. Dammit."

"What? What did I . . . Oh."

The bushes around them shook and parted as the goblin army emerged from the shadows, blocking their path with long, jagged spears. Cyral turned to run, anticipating the usual plan, only to find more goblins closing in from behind. A spear jabbed toward his sternum, forcing him back.

"Well, well," said a goblin, with a malicious sneer. "What have we got here?"

COLD HANDS LIFTED Kess off the dusty floor and set her down on a stack of ancient mattresses. She could see and feel it happening, but only dimly, through a dark curtain. She let her eyes fall shut again, and sank back into dreams, which were much more interesting.

She was still in the tower, but in her dream the room was a round gallery full of paintings, lit by bright sunlight but without windows or doors. Each painting, as she looked closely at it, held a story in miniature. Peasants chased geese out of the way of advancing armies. Knights rode out to subdue dragons, while maidens chained to rocks cheered them on. A princess with long, flowing hair leaned wistfully out the window of a high and lonely tower.

Kess leaned closer. Behind the princess, inside the tower, a painting hung on her wall, too, showing a room full of tiny squares of color, too small to see in detail, and barely visible within that room, a female figure with long ears . . .

She pulled herself back, out of surprise, then quickly looked again to see if the figure had moved. She felt a twinge of disappointment when she found it had not; but her dreams had always behaved by their own rules, not to meet her expectations, so she let it pass.

Her gaze drifted back to the watercolor face of the princess, over whose shoulder she appeared in the painting within the painting. Sad eyes, she thought. The artist had captured something within the flecks of gray and blue that spoke of discontent and hope denied and stories that had no ending, but carried on until no one cared to hear any more and the storyteller's voice withered away.

"Do you like them? I taught myself to paint."

Until that moment, Kess knew she had been alone, but when she heard the voice, she suddenly wondered how she could have failed to see the girl sitting on the huge canopy bed in the center of the room. For that matter, it was hard to believe she had overlooked the bed. So, the dream was changing. Kess smiled.

"They're good," she said. "You've got me in this one."

"I've got everybody. Everything. I had a lot of time to do them all." The girl picked at a bit of lint on the lap of her dress. When she leaned forward, her hair spilled down to her waist. "You should see who else you can recognize. Do you want to play that game?"

"How old are you?" asked Kess, sitting down beside her.

"Twelve."

"And you painted all these? That must have taken a long time."

The girl nodded. "Oh, yes. Hundreds and hundreds of years. I was going to start painting the walls next."

"But now you're not? How come?"

"Because now you're here," said the girl, as if this was the most obvious thing in the universe. "Why did you come?"

Kess shrugged and brushed her fingers down the girl's long, blond hair. "I was curious."

"But nobody comes here. Not ever. Were you running

away from somebody? Did somebody tell you I was out here? My stepmother said no one would find me until my prince came along, and then we'd leave together and we'd all be famous. She made a contract with a traveling bard. I was supposed to learn to sing so my prince would hear me, but I can't sing, so that's why I started painting instead. Are you waiting for a prince?"

Kess sat up sharply. "He's waiting for me!"

The girl laughed. "That's not how it goes, silly. You wait for him, and he rescues you. Then you both live happily ever—"

"Ever after is too long. What am I doing here? I need to go. How do I leave?"

"Do you really have to? You could stay. Look, there's lots of pictures you haven't seen yet. Let me show you."

"I really have to," said Kess. "Please, tell me how."

"No!" The girl threw herself off the bed, her long hair streaming out behind her like the string behind a kite. She grabbed a painting off the wall and threw it to the floor, shattering the frame. "I don't want to be alone! You can't go! I'm sick of this!"

Kess reached for her, but the girl's hair was flying everywhere now, filling the room, tangling Kess's hands, wrapping around her face, choking and blinding her. "I have to go. I have to wake up."

The girl's small fists beat against her chest. "You can't! You can't! Don't leave me!"

The hair wrapped tighter, becoming a cocoon. Kess hugged the girl close to herself and closed her eyes, and waited for the dream to change.

JORDAN GROANED AND slowly raised his hands as the goblins closed in. Inevitability, he thought again bitterly. "There a problem here?"

The leader of the goblins pushed back the visor of his rusty, spiked helmet. "Someone's been sneaking through our forest. Using our roads. Not paying their tolls. Looks like we've found them, haven't we, boys?"

"We're just travelers," said Cyral. "Bona fide travelers, just passing through. We don't want any trouble."

The goblin spat on Cyral's boots. "Then you should've stayed out of our forest."

Cyral backed into Jordan. "Please tell me I'm finally going to get to see you fight."

Jordan snorted. "Me? I'm just a helpless old man."

Cyral's eyes went wide. "Don't tell me you're expecting me to do something, because the pen is definitely not mightier than lots of spears—"

"No. Now, shut up. This isn't the time for heroes— They're not attacking."

Cyral nodded rapidly. "Yes, and I like that very much."

"If this was one of your stories, they would be."

"Oh, please don't give them any encouragement."

That was the problem with sagas, Jordan considered. Nobody ever wrote about the times when the goblins didn't attack on sight. Everyone walking away alive made for dull entertainment. "Leave this to me. And learn something."

And then, to a look of utter incomprehension from Cyral, Jordan unbuckled his sword and set it on the ground. He pinched his nose and made a snorting, gargling noise that sounded as if an irate duck were trying to escape from his sinuses. Funny, how it all came back . . .

The leader of the goblins squinted at him suspiciously, then made a similar noise in reply.

Cyral stared. "You speak Goblin? Why—?"

Jordan shrugged. If the bard was so inexperienced that he had to ask, then there was no way that he, Jordan, would be able to satisfactorily explain the dynamic between hero

and monster that developed in the middle of nowhere, between fights and chases, when the only lights were their
campfires and yours, and there was no one else to listen or
talk to. Yes, there was an obligation, usually contractual,
to end up in mortal combat, but there was also a kinship.
The monsters Central Casting summoned and sent out
were playing their part, too, for their five dollars a day.

"Just something I picked up," he said. "Not important.
What's important right now is that they're not going to kill
us yet, so I'm going to keep talking to them. You got a
handkerchief? One you aren't going to want back?"

Around them, the goblins began to step back, their
faces trading expressions of cruel amusement for doubt.
The ones farther back, sensing the stabbing and slaughter-
ing had been at the least postponed, shifted their spears to
a more relaxed position. One lit a cigarette. Jordan cracked
his knuckles, squatted down, and began to negotiate.

KESS ROLLED OFF the pile of mattresses and hit the
cracked wooden floor in a sprinter's crouch. Her mind
told her she was still webbed with hair, that there was no
way she could move, but her body said otherwise, so she
ran. The thing without a head slid in front of her, but she
knocked it down without hesitation. It was empty now,
nothing but bones in a dress pretending to be alive. There
was the window, and there were the uneven bricks on the
other side that she could grip and hold and swing down to
the lower stump of the tower where there was solid rubble
for her to stand on while she caught her breath.

Then she opened her eyes.

The glade rustled softly around her, barely moving but
still alert and aware of her. Branches and vines shifted,
curling ever so slightly toward her when they thought

she was looking the other way. It might have been the wind.

Cautiously, Kess lowered herself down from the ruin. She felt a pang of fear clutch her, but it was fear belonging to someone else, someone who had never been allowed past the guardian hedge. The hedge felt it, too; the fear, and the wisp of another presence wrapped close around her chest.

"Hold on to me," she whispered. "It won't hurt you. It can't. Stay with me to the other side. Just to the other side; then you can go wherever you can imagine."

Half-dreaming, half-awake, Kess walked into the hedge.

JORDAN CLEARED HIS throat with finality. Cyral, who had lost the edge of his panic to the tedium of listening to the negotiations, looked up. "Yes? What was that?"

"Phlegm," said Jordan. "Starts sticking after a bit. Good news is, they've agreed to let us go. In fact, they're going to escort us out."

Cyral waited. He knew a setup for bad news when he heard it.

"Thing is, 'escort'?" Jordan rubbed the back of his neck awkwardly. "In Goblin, that's the same way they say 'throw.' As in, getting thrown out of a pub for bad behavior."

The leader of the goblins, who spoke both languages, grinned and nodded in agreement.

"But what about Kess? We can't abandon her," said Cyral. "They need to give us time to get her out. Tell them that!"

"Look, we're not in a good place to argue terms," said Jordan. "Squib here only looks happy because he's getting what he wanted—us gone, fast, and a promise not to tell anyone they're here. Funny story—seems they were living in this old mill on the other side of the forest until a few days ago when an evil wizard moved in and kicked them out."

"Funny. Yes— Ow!" Cyral pulled his foot out from under Jordan's boot and glared. He hadn't been about to say anything incriminating.

"Now they're hiding in this forest, living in caves and constantly watching out for the wizard," Jordan continued unapologetically, "in case he decides to enslave them and start some sort of minion breeding program. And this bunch hasn't got any women anyway, so they're already not very happy."

"I'm very sorry for them, but we can't leave without Kess."

Cyral knelt down to face the goblin leader at eye level. "We can't go yet. There's still someone else in the forest, a woman, and we have to find her. It's very important. We'll leave as soon as she's with us; you have my word on that."

The goblin growled. The finger bones and teeth adorning his helmet rattled violently as he shook his head. "And our word is 'no,'" he snapped, in a crude mimic of Cyral's own voice and dialect. "No delays, no tricks. We're getting you and him out of our forest right now."

"At least throw her out, too!" The words tumbled out of his mouth before he had time to consider them. "You don't want her in your forest, either. You should go find her and throw her out—we left her in a ruined tower, in the middle of a glade not far from here. You might have to hack a path in—"

Jordan grabbed Cyral by the collar and hauled him to his feet. "You're going to get yourself killed."

Cyral shook him off. "Please," he continued. "She might be hurt. Her name is Kess. She's an elf."

The goblin laughed. "Elf? An elf can stay. Have an elf in your forest, that's good luck; ain't it, boys?"

Around him, the other goblins who were still paying

attention threw their laughter in with their leader's. There was a sharp, vicious edge to the chorus that made Cyral uncomfortable and reminded him that a rabbit's foot was lucky, too, but not for the rabbit. He glanced at Jordan, but found no reassurance there.

"She's lucky for us, too," he tried, but this only fueled the goblins' amusement. "Fine! Fine—I'll pay you to find her and escort her to the end of the forest with us, alive and in one piece. I'll pay you."

The laughter died a sudden and violent death. For the first time, every goblin was paying close attention to their captives. Every beady, coal black eye crawled scrutinously over Cyral, as if gauging his exact worth and plotting how it could best be extracted. The suspicion crept into his head that he might possibly be doing something very foolish.

"What price?" the goblin leader demanded.

"Er . . ." Cyral took stock of what he had left to offer. Apart from the clothes he was wearing, which were torn and dirty from crawling through the hedge, all he had was his notebook and the pouch of inks and quills that went with it. "I could . . . write you into a saga. You could be very famous goblins."

The leader of the goblins made a rude noise.

"He says, 'Getting into sagas is a death sentence,'" Jordan translated. "He's not wrong."

"You're a bard, are you?" said the goblin, fingering the tattered and ink-stained silk sleeves of Cyral's jacket. "You got any songs?"

"Yes, a few."

The goblin slapped his hands together, and with a cunning gleam in his eye, said, "Done. Paid. We'll take your best song for finding your elf. All rights?"

Cyral nodded. He heard Jordan make a low, warning noise, but too late. "All right. Agreed—but no tricks. You find her and bring her out today, and we all leave the forest at the same spot, unharmed."

"Yes, yes. Sing."

Cyral straightened up and cleared his throat, and tried to imagine himself back in Palace Hills, at one of the grand concert halls where he had never in fact been able to perform. He thought through his repertoire, discarding the various Jordan the Red ballads out of courtesy and self-preservation, and finally settled on a song of his own creation about traveling through the rain. It had a sad melody, but hopeful words, and he had always been pleased with it. He began to sing.

When he had finished, the goblins murmured among themselves and nodded. None of them threw spears at him. Under the circumstances, it was better than applause.

"Now," he said, crossing his arms firmly. "I've sung for you. Will you go find her?"

"Your elf?" The leader of the goblins smirked. "Done. Found. There she is."

He pointed his spear past Cyral, to where Kess stood leaning against a tree. She looked drained, as if something had left her, but she wore a tired smile, which brightened when Cyral ran over to her.

"That sounded great," she said, and hugged him. "I followed it right to you."

"They wanted my best," said Cyral. "The price of getting you back."

Kess frowned. "Oh. I'm sorry."

Jordan ambled over, rebuckling his sword to his belt. He sized Kess up. Then, without explanation or ceremony, he handed her his cloak. She wrapped it around herself gratefully, pulling her arms close across her chest, and shivered.

"You're in one piece," said Jordan. "You've got luck. Did you get a good taste of real adventure?"

Kess didn't answer.

The goblin leader gave Cyral a whack across the shin with the shaft of his spear. "Yes—yes. She gets cloak; you get elf; we get song. Now, out, all of you, out," he ordered. "On this way, and get out."

Poking and prodding, the goblins herded them to the far side of the forest at a rapid march. To Cyral's irritation, every goblin had picked up his song and was marching along singing or humming or whistling it, each in his own key and to his own rhythm, beating the poor melody into a bruised discord.

"Everything worked out well, then," he said, with forced cheer. "Not so bad, in the end, even if the goblins didn't do much for us. And now one of my songs will be slightly more well-known."

Jordan shot him a sideways glance. "You know what you did, right?"

"I sang my way out of trouble." Cyral smiled. "I know it wasn't anything heroic or even all that brave, but I did something. And I feel good about it."

"Try singing that song again."

Cyral opened his mouth. Nothing came out. He blinked several times. "I, er . . ."

"Yeah," said Jordan. "And you'll never be able to again. You gave it to them. All rights, unreserved."

"But, I didn't . . . How did they . . ."

The goblins stamped to a halt. The trees were thinning out, old growth giving way to new, with flashes of open sky beyond.

"Here," said their leader. "You go out from here, and we don't catch you back in our forest again, on pain."

"You took my song!"

The goblin whistled a few notes up into Cyral's face. "Yeah. Good deal."

Then he and his troop plunged back into the deepening shadows, and a few moments later, they were lost from sight completely. Only a distant and now almost-unrecognizable tune hanging on the breeze lingered after them.

Kess touched Cyral's arm. "Goblins are thieves. They'll take anything they can trick away from you. Money. Blood. The color of your eyes. The taste of your next meal. Then they have it, and you don't. Goblin magic. You didn't know?"

"No! I've never personally met a goblin before—I mean, I'd heard, but I thought those were just stories."

"Just?" She drew back abruptly, the sympathy fading from her face. "It's going to be dusk soon. We've got to go."

"Wait; hold up." Cyral took his notebook out of his belt and hurried after her. "You never said how you escaped the tower."

"I walked away. The hedge let me go," she lied, without making any effort to hide the lie.

"But it can't have been that easy." Cyral poked his pen into one of the holes torn in his sleeve. "You must have made a daring escape, beating through the thornbushes, darting nimbly between . . . No? Surely . . ."

His imagination broke against a wall of silence. Rather than stop to pick up the pieces, he tried a different approach. "What was in the tower?"

Kess shook her head. "Nothing. There was nothing." She exhaled slowly, as if letting the adventures of the last few hours drain out of her. "Listen, I've changed my mind."

"About what?"

"You. About you, writing about me. I don't want to be your hero."

"But you'd be fabulous! I think, if you gave it a chance, you'd see— Here, let me show you how I'd write you.

'Approaching the tower . . .'" He fumbled to find his notes. "Please, I've got to write about this."

Kess put her hand on the notebook. "I don't care." Then, seeing his expression, her voice softened, and she continued. "I mean, I don't care if you keep writing, or if you don't. Go on, write about what happens. Tell me the story afterward. But this isn't my story. Don't make me responsible for it. I want Eliott back. That's it. I'm not going to do all the other things you'd want your hero to do. So." She pushed the notebook gently back against his chest. "Good luck."

She walked away, leaving Cyral staring after her. Each step seemed to put countless miles between them.

"But I need you," he called after her. "I can't tell a story without a hero!"

He smacked the notebook with all its useless, pointless scribbles against his thigh. It hurt more than he expected. "How am I supposed to write this saga now?"

"Beats me," said Jordan, "but you're running short on time to figure it out. Another half mile, we'll be at Hopley's mill."

NINE

THE MILL LOOMED. It had no right to, being only three stories tall and wider than it was high, and yet it did, a crooked and wooden-shingled monstrosity impaling the sun-burnt sky with its chimney, daring brave heroes to come closer. The big wooden wheel creaked and groaned like a torture device, endlessly clawing at the torrent of water rushing down on it from the broad, deep mill pond, inevitably forced to surrender what it captured into the stream beyond. Everywhere, there were signs of the disrepair the old mill had fallen into—broken fences, missing shingles, weeds grown tall around the foundation—but there was evidence that someone had returned to the place, too. Young trees had been felled and left lying in the yard, and the sign hanging over the big front doors of the mill had been repainted, turning HOPLEY MILL & BAKED GOODS into HOPLEY'S STRONGHOLD. The effect was slightly di-

minished by the cutout of a smiling, dancing Puffy Muffin
Man still visible under the black paint.

The other telltale clue that the mill had been reoccu-
pied was a dozen or so guards in ill-fitting armor lurching
around between the mill and the detached bakery.

"What are those creatures?" asked Cyral. "They can't
be human."

Kess leaned out from behind the crumbled retaining
wall at the head of the mill pond, where they had taken
shelter. She could feel the aura of magic around the mill,
the faint shimmer of its touch where Hopley had cast
spells, the glow of it on the guards. She knew that glow;
she remembered it from her grandmother's lessons. She
looked through it.

"Pigs," she said, fighting a feeling of revulsion. "They're
pigs. He's tried to make them look like people, but he isn't
very good at it."

"That's good news," said Jordan. "Bad news is, we've
still got to get past them." He eased his back against the
wall and made himself comfortable. "Got a plan?"

The window above the waterwheel, thought Kess. The
wall was high, and scaling it would be risking a plunge into
the churn of the pond and the machinery, but there were no
guards watching that side of the mill. If she was quick and
nimble, she could do it.

Or she could fall and drown.

"What would you have done?" she asked instead.
"You're the guide."

"Killed 'em all and let the bards sort it out," said Jordan grimly. "We're not using that plan."

"Then I guess we find another way in. Maybe a
window?"

Jordan pushed a sigh past his teeth, a little sound that
carried a full load of disappointment and resignation. "Or
a back door," he suggested. "See how there's no one watch-

ing the wheel? I'd bet money there's a way to get at the mechanism down there, and if you can get to that, you can get inside."

"Are you sure?" asked Cyral, risking another glance around the wall. "I mean, if there was a back way in, wouldn't it be likely to have guards around it, too?"

"Back doors are never guarded. Or never by more than one goon, and he's never hard to take down. For some reason, villains always expect you to go in the front."

"You usually did," said Kess.

"I still checked the back doors first." Jordan folded his arms. "Are you going in there, or are you going to sit around here all night?"

"We are going in," said Kess. She eased to the edge of the wall again, at once annoyed and impressed with Jordan. He had looked once at the mill and seen it all, so he could sit back now with everything worked out, while she still had to guess at the details and the odds. "There's nothing more to hide behind from here to the waterwheel. How do we get to it?"

"We could swim," suggested Cyral. "With hollow reeds in our mouths to breathe through."

"Fine. Which one of you brought the hollow reeds? And they'd better be at least two feet long, because the only thing growing around this pond is duck grass, and we'll need to swim deep not to get noticed."

Cyral looked at his boots. "I was only trying to help."

"It was a good thought," said Kess. "Maybe if it was darker."

"You can still help," said Jordan. "In fact, you're going to be the key."

"I am?" said Cyral, in the dubious tones of someone who has just been volunteered to assist with a magic trick.

"Yeah. You're going to make a diversion. Go knock on the door of that bakery and buy some bread."

"What? No. No!"

"You'll give Kess—and me, yes, I know—you'll give us time to get over to the wheel. Look, you and your flashy suit, you're a walking distraction already. Put it to use."

"I am not going off on my own and missing all the action," said Cyral firmly. "Not now. This is the heart of the saga, the climactic moment where the villain is confronted. I'm staying with the two of you, to observe and record."

"That's what you want to do, huh?"

"That's what I mean to do."

Jordan put a friendly hand on Cyral's shoulder. "Then it's time you learned something. Open your book and take this down. Being a hero is about doing things you don't want to do, for people who don't want to do it themselves. Also, violence is involved."

Jordan patted his sword, still resting in its sheath. It didn't gleam, or sing, or do any of the things usually associated with the swords of heroes. It just hung from Jordan's hip looking like a sharp, heavy piece of barely secured metal.

"One of us is going to have to do something he doesn't want to do," said Jordan, through a grin with no friendliness in it at all.

". . . I'll go create a distraction at the front," said Cyral. "Perhaps I could tell the guards a story about a Big Bad Wolf."

"Tell a story, sing a song, whatever. Just don't get yourself killed," said Jordan. "What's the most important rule?"

"Know when to run," replied Cyral wearily. "Yes, all right. I'm going."

Jordan caught him by the sleeve. "Back that way. Come at them from the forest, not from where we're hiding now."

Then Cyral was gone, and Kess and Jordan were left alone together, crouching behind the wall with nothing to do but wait. Kess touched her fingers to the earth, feeling the grit of the dry soil, focusing her mind. She ran through the names of the top ten best Jordan the Red sagas, and the tactics he had used in each one; it was a game she had played with Eliott, attempting to teach him concentration. Name ten villains, while she tapped his forehead. She could feel him tapping on her skull now.

The heart of the story, she thought, again and again. This is where everything gets decided. Win or fail.

Jordan gave her a nudge and held out a small leather pouch. "Peanut?"

Before she could answer, they heard a voice across the other side of the pond and the yard. "Excuse me! Is anyone there? Yes, I'd . . . er . . . like to buy some bread!"

A puzzled grunting and squealing followed, but Kess had no time to pay attention to it. Jordan was already on his feet, moving with remarkable speed and quiet along the grassy edge of the pond, down to the sluice gates feeding the waterwheel, and disappearing into the shadow of the mill. It wasn't that he moved silently, Kess noticed, as she followed along behind; it was simply a steady, practiced pace that blended the rustling of the duck grass into the sound of the breeze and the water rushing through the wheel. It was as close as she had ever seen to a human moving like an elf.

Then he reached the millstream where it emerged below the waterwheel and, trying to ford it, lost his footing and slipped heavily on the submerged stones. Drenched to his waist, he staggered out, splashing and swearing under the roar of the wheel. Kess took a chance and cleared the stream at a running leap.

"Show-off," Jordan muttered, rubbing his bruises. He checked his sword and his knapsack and, finding both secure, waved Kess over to the moss-covered wall of the mill. "Okay. Door."

"It's here."

"Then open it carefully and get in there," Jordan growled, watching above and below for undistracted guards.

Kess pressed against the damp, slimy wood. "It's locked. I can't . . . *Casaba!*"

Jordan stared at her.

"It's an Elvish opening spell," she said defensively. "He's a wizard. I thought it might be a magic lock."

"There a keyhole?" asked Jordan, rummaging through his knapsack. "Aha."

"Yes. Do you have— Is that a picklock?"

Jordan cupped his hands around the keyhole. There was a sharp metallic scratch and a click. "Yeah. Heroing isn't exactly steady work . . . You pick up a thing or two if you want to eat regularly."

"You learned that in Skulp?"

"Huh?"

"From the Thieves' Guild in Skulp? When you were—"

"Gods, give it a rest! Get in there, get Eliott out, and talk ancient history when we're a few miles away from here."

Kess hesitated. "You're coming in with me."

"No. I'm making sure this door stays clear." He tapped the threshold of the door with his boot. "That's the line I'm not crossing. Your turn to be the hero."

He took a step back, into the shadows and the spray coming off the wheel, and rested his hand on his sword. "But no actual heroism. Keep your head down and stay away from Hopley."

"If I'm not back soon—"

"Don't."

"All right."

Kess drew the Trout and Truncheon's second-best carving knife, took a breath, and, with a litany of the names of Jordan the Red's ten best horses running through her head, crossed the line.

The basement of the mill was so near to completely black that Kess had to pause for her eyes to adjust. Everything creaked and thumped with the motion of the mechanism, axles, and cogs turning some fiendish device overhead. The smell of mildew and rotten grain and rats—especially of rats—somehow managed to surpass every impression of fetid stenches Kess had ever imagined from the stories of slaughterhouses and sewers where Jordan the Red had battled zombies and hell-spawned monsters of pure bile. She pulled Jordan's borrowed cloak around to cover her mouth and nose, amazed that ancient, mangy wolf hair could smell better than the mill, and ventured farther in. Dimly, she could now make out pillars and beams and, at the far end of the basement, a flight of stairs.

There was a hatch at the top of the stairs. Kess listened at it for a moment, but the only sound from the other side was the ceaseless grinding and scraping of the mill's inner workings. She put her shoulder against the hatch and pushed. With a shower of grain husks and dust, the hatch rose, lifting a precautionary inch, and then an elf's width, as Kess pulled herself through. She looked around.

She saw the Machine.

A metal bowl had been built around the old millstones, pieced together with bands of iron three inches wide and spaced just far enough apart to poke a spear through, or for a grasping hand to reach out. Inside the bowl, two curved and serrated blades swept the circumference with deadly purpose, their rotations controlled by a complex series of gears and levers labeled with speeds from DICE to PUREE. The Machine was large enough to trap two or three people; more if the blades spun fast enough. Of course, at that point, the word "people" would no longer be applicable.

Kess stared in horror, her purpose momentarily forgotten as her imagination raced ahead to see the Machine in action. A trough on one side kept drawing her attention, making her think of limbs and bones and blood.

A noise from the loft above broke her horrible fixation. For the first time, she noticed the catwalk overhead, and the figure tied to a chair directly above the Machine.

It was Eliott.

Kess bit back her first impulse to call out to him, to rush up to the second floor and out onto the catwalk at once. Eliott was motionless, and something above her was still making a noise, shuffling and stumbling. Kess retreated behind a heap of discarded metal and lumber, and watched as one of Hopley's guards edged out onto the catwalk toward Eliott. It looked human, in a monstrous and distorted fashion, but some part of it was still a pig, and knew that a pig's place was on solid ground; it crossed the catwalk at such an awkward gait that Kess thought it might fall before it reached the middle of the span, and found herself feeling sorry for it if it did.

But the pig kept its balance and made it out to Eliott, where it pressed a bowl to his lips, trying to force him to drink. Eliott's head rose and smacked the bowl away, followed by a sound Kess knew well. The bowl and a glob of spit tumbled from the catwalk and landed defiantly in the Machine.

The guard snorted and hit Eliott across the face.

Kess felt her heart stop. The chair rocked and the catwalk swayed, but both steadied, and Eliott remained safe.

The guard backed away and, soon after, came unsteadily down the stairs. It passed by Kess's hiding place without seeing her and went out of sight behind the workings of the Machine. Kess took a chance and darted out, slipping through the shadows between the dusty rays of the sunset, up the stairs, and onto the second floor with barely a creak of the floorboards to give away her movement.

There were two rooms built onto the second floor, but their doors were shut, so she ignored them. The important thing, the only thing, was reaching Eliott on the catwalk. The orange blaze of the sunset through the window behind him gave him a wreath of light, like a martyr in stained glass. Kess crept out to him, forcing herself to breathe normally.

"Eliott? Eliott, are you okay? Come on, say something . . ."

His head lifted again. His cheek was bruised and his hair looked like he had had his head stuffed in a sack, but when he met her eyes, he grinned. "Hey, Kess. Did you see the thing Hopley's going to dangle me over? Cool, huh?"

"You little shit," said Kess, and hugged him. "Let's get you out of here."

She crouched down and began sawing at the ropes around Eliott's feet and wrists with her carving knife.

"Wait, Kess! Jordan—where's Jordan?"

"Outside."

"Then don't free me yet! He's got to come in here and rescue me and defeat Hopley!" Eliott squirmed in his bonds, causing Kess to almost slice his thumb.

"Quit moving. Hold still. Jordan's waiting for us."

"But Hopley's promised that there will be a big showdown scene, and I've got to be here for that. I've earned it, Kess! I let his guards beat me up, you know."

"You let—" Kess cut through the second rope, leaving only the one around Eliott's chest. "Eliott, this isn't a story—getting hurt will actually hurt!"

Eliott rolled his eyes in the most infuriating way possible. "Nah. If I really get in trouble, I can just wish my way out of it, remember?"

He twisted his arm around and tapped the two remaining threads of the Braid, pinned to his jacket and half-hidden under the restraining coils of rope. Kess grabbed his arm.

"Has— Do you have any idea how dangerous— Does Hopley know you have that?" she sputtered. "Has he seen it?"

"No! I wouldn't say anything to someone who's obviously the bad guy. It's totally safe."

"Eliott, you don't go showing off a Braid! It's way too powerful. And a wizard doesn't need to be told about it—if he sees it, he'll know what it is!"

"Yeah, seriously, don't worry. I don't think Hopley's that good of a wizard."

A roll of thunder rattled the roof. Kess suddenly noticed that the light burning through the big window had gone dim. Black storm clouds were rolling in from a clear sky. She tightened her grip on the carving knife and spun around.

A fist of invisible force lifted her off her feet and flung her across to the platform at the far end of the catwalk. She had time to scream before she hit the wall, but not the ability; her mouth and body felt frozen. In her mind, she swore at herself and her own stupidity. She knew how stories worked—never talk out loud about the all-powerful artifact while inside the villain's lair. The villain was always listening.

"Good enough of a wizard, it would seem," said Hopley.

IN THE SHADOW of the waterwheel, Jordan glanced up as the sky went dark. He frowned. A few hundred yards away, the sky was still clear, but around the mill, a stormy nimbus was gathering, and he knew the reason why.

Dramatic effect.

"Bugger," he muttered.

WITH A SMUG, self-amused chuckle, Hopley walked out
onto the catwalk, followed by two of his guards.

"So. An Elvish Wishing Braid. How generous of you
to provide me with such a toy. You're quite right: I did
fail to recognize it, but I would have been looking for
three pieces of thread, not two." He reached down and
tugged the Braid off Eliott's jacket and held it up to the
light. "How I wish I'd had this before I went to all the
trouble of building this trap for Jordan."

Kess winced, or tried to. Even her eyes were paralyzed.

"But then, why should I waste a wish on Jordan? I'll
save this for after he's dead. Revenge against the
A.T.C.B.S.O. Grants Committee, perhaps, or— Aargh!"

Hopley staggered. Eliott had kicked him hard in the
shins.

"Brat," Hopley snarled, making a cutting gesture with
his free hand. Eliott rocked back in his chair and froze,
while Kess abruptly found that she could move once more.
She edged toward the side of the platform, hoping for a
way down.

"Don't think I've forgotten about you, either," said
Hopley, raising his staff toward Kess. His eyes flicked between her and Eliott. "However, I will deal with you with
more mundane force. Get her."

Kess barely had time to think, He can only hold one of
us at a time!—before Hopley's guards came at her with
cudgels, rushing across the catwalk with more fear of the
wizard's power than of falling. Their grotesque, snarling
faces no longer evoked any sympathy at all. The first
guard lunged at her and she spun away, but a second was
there, shoving past and grabbing at her. They corralled

her, trying to back her into the corner. The floorboards bounced and protested under the guards' heavy feet, making Kess dance for balance as she dodged around the confined platform. Twice the guards collided with her, and twice she broke away.

No way down, she thought desperately. Down is not an option. Up!

There was a ladder against the wall, rising to an upper loft that was nothing more than planks laid across the joists. She saw the ladder, and then she was climbing it, pulling herself up onto the dusty beams, while Hopley shouted at her, at his guards, promising pain to all of them.

And then a hand closed on her ankle. She kicked out wildly and held on. Her leg turned in an unexpected way. For a moment, the guard clung to her, dangling over the empty air; then it fell, gracelessly, crashing off the edge of the platform and down into a heap of splintering wood far below.

Kess dragged herself up into the loft and pulled her legs out of reach. Her struggle with the guard had partially pulled the ladder away from its mooring already, but she gave it an extra nail-popping twist for safety. Finding another way down could wait. Right now, she needed to have a serious discussion with her leg about some agony it was feeling. She huddled back against the musty sacks of old flour that filled the loft and tried to massage out the pain.

"Stay up there if you wish," Hopley called up at her. "There or here, I have you trapped, and that is what matters. Jordan the Red will have no choice but to come and attempt to rescue the three of you shortly."

Painfully, Kess wriggled to the edge of the loft. Another pair of Hopley's pig guards had arrived, dragging Cyral in between them. He looked slightly stunned, as if he had had the wind knocked out of him, but otherwise unhurt.

"Ah, Cyral. You will forgive me if I count you among Jordan's allies," said Hopley, walking over to grace the bard with his presence, "but since you appear to have taken his side in things, I am forced to treat you accordingly. Don't let it be said, however, that I have no respect for journalistic neutrality."

He gestured at the guards, who thrust Cyral's notebook and quill into the bard's hands.

"I hope you can appreciate what I have accomplished here in so short a time," said Hopley, walking out along the catwalk. "I have a strength of guards created by my arts, and this fortress—"

Kess managed a derisive laugh. It was the least she could do, she felt.

"—built up from the ruins of my ancestry," Hopley continued, ignoring her. "I have the bait." He put his hands on Eliott's shoulders. "And soon, I will have Jordan the Red as well."

"You weren't expecting him yet," said Cyral. "We took a shortcut. You aren't ready."

Hopley glared at him, then gave a nod to one of the guards, who jabbed Cyral viciously in the ribs.

"I knew Jordan would arrive in his own time. He never arrives when he is expected! So I have been ready from the moment I brought his apprentice back here. Do you not see the Machine? I call it the Giant's Mixing Bowl, because it will grind bones to make bread."

He walked out onto the platform at the far end of the catwalk and leaned against his staff.

"I hate waiting," he added unhappily.

"You have my sympathy," said Cyral. "While we wait, would you care to tell me the details of your plan for Jordan's, er, final demise?"

Hopley looked back scornfully. "Do you really expect me to?"

"It is traditional . . ."

"Only for the villain."

"Ah," said Cyral. "Of course."

Hopley drummed his fingers against the window frame. "He's out there. I know it."

"He could be a while," Kess called down. "If you wanted to go get a cup of tea or anything. Maybe a muffin?"

"Do not vex me, elf. If you—"

"Vex? Seriously? Nobody says 'vex,' Hopley. I can try not to make you angry," she offered, carefully shifting a bricklike sack of flour from the stack to the edge of the loft. Every movement made her leg twinge. "I could even try not to piss you off. But I wouldn't try very hard."

A satisfyingly predictable bolt of force punched up between the planks and hit the sack of flour with a frustrated puff of dust.

"I told you," said Kess. "Eliott? Can you move again?"

"Yeah," Eliott called back weakly. "Good one."

"Enough," said Hopley. "Do nothing, elf, and I may let Cyral write a verse about how you daringly tried to escape. But I have no time for further games."

He pushed open the window and leaned out into the gathering dusk. He licked his lips.

"Jordan! I have your friends here at my mercy! Come in and try to save them, if you have any courage left in your heart! Or leave them, and hear their screams as the Giant's Mixing Bowl grinds them into a slurry flour, and my magic bakes their dust into loaves of revenge!"

He glanced back at Cyral.

"Did you get all of that? I chose the wording very specifically."

Cyral, who looked slightly green, nodded weakly and scratched something down in his notebook.

Hopley turned back to the window. "Jordan! I know you're out there!"

"Wrong," said Jordan, coming up the stairs at the opposite end of the mill with a sack of flour on his shoulders. Without breaking stride, he swung the sack around and lobbed it lightly at Cyral. It knocked the bard off his feet and exploded in a cloud of dust. As the guards choked and coughed, Jordan grabbed them by their helmets and brought their heads together with a dull clunk. He stepped over them.

"And these aren't exactly my friends, either," he added casually. "Well, the elf's all right, but it doesn't look like you've caught her. The kid and the bard . . ." He shrugged. "Anything you bake out of them is going to be pretty dense."

Hopley found his voice again. "You dare— Guards! Grab him!"

"Don't make me draw my sword," Jordan snapped, and the onrushing guards faltered. "This is our big scene, isn't that right, Hopley? Hero and villain. Pick a side; I don't care. You throw guards at me, and I wade through their corpses to have the final showdown with you. And you know what happens then?"

He kept walking. The guards got out of his way.

"You die, Hopley. Stupid villains get killed off."

There was nothing menacing in Jordan's voice, no more anger than his usual simmering desire to give the world a good smack to make it behave itself and stop annoying him, and yet Hopley backed away as if Jordan had him at spearpoint. Unfortunately, the wizard already had his back to the wall, and Jordan was still advancing across the catwalk, passing by Eliott without a pause. Hopley looked out the window at the waterwheel and the churning pond below. He made a decision. He retreated.

Into bravado.

"Fool! Do you really think you can defeat me? Strike at me if you can, but I will return to plague you again and again until I have my revenge! I will face you in a hundred sequels to this brief saga!"

"Eliott," said Jordan, without turning his head. "How many villains have come back for another try?"

"Ooh . . ." Eliott's chair bounced and rocked as every Jordan the Red story went rushing through his head like water through the wheel. "Three, not counting organizations like the Thieves' Guild of Skulp! Baron Clockwork, General Sarod—who came back as a fiery floating head—and the Witch Queen of Hellsbrogdt!"

Jordan sighed. "Helga. What a girl. Fifteen below freezing, and she wouldn't wear more than chain-mail lingerie . . ."

"But they came back!" Hopley shouted. "And so will I—"

Jordan poked him in the chest with one finger. "Son, those three were far out of your league. You're a gimmick. A one-shot. Walk away now, while I'm giving you the chance. Believe me, I've faced a thousand more terrible things than you, Mr. Bread-Maker Wizard, and every time, the story ended the same way."

He broke eye contact long enough to glare at Cyral, who was taking notes. When he looked back, Hopley was trembling.

"Walk away, Hopley," said Jordan, with a voice of weary kindness. "Don't let some slimy talent agent kill you for the sake of a story."

"I'll . . . I'll be immortalized," Hopley whimpered.

"Yeah, for the way you died!" Jordan threw up his hands. "Cyral, you want to tell him how you and Glister've set up this saga to end? Because I'm about ready to kill him just to get out of here—"

"No, Jordan. For the way *you* died," said Hopley suddenly, and his face lit up with the crazed satisfaction of the perfect comeback line. He held up the Braid. "By my hand. I wish . . . I wish all of those terrible things you fought and killed before were here now, for you to face again."

And he snapped the silver thread.

TEN

HOPLEY GLANCED DOWN at the broken thread and the white thread that remained in his hand, and a look of confusion crept over his face. "Er . . ."

"Fine. You've had your last words," said Jordan. "Now, we're leaving, and you're letting us go. Happy ending—"

There was a knock at the front door of the mill, a quick, sharp blow as if the one knocking knew about doors but had forgotten how to open them. It came again, with greater force, and was echoed by the sound of breaking glass somewhere around the back of the building. Something landed on the roof with a leathery slap. A light rain of dust drifted down from the disturbed rafters. Hopley straightened up.

"So, a slightly delayed reaction," he said calmly. "That will be your ending now. And it will be a happy one—for me, anyway."

Kess crawled to the edge of the loft. "Jordan! Get the other thread! Get it away from him!"

Without comprehending, Jordan moved, but Hopley moved faster. The wizard's hand snapped around in a complicated gesture, still holding the last thread of the Braid, and one of his guards lurched into Jordan's way, propelled bodily by Hopley's magics and looking terrified about it.

"No!" shouted Hopley. "You won't take this from me!"

The things outside the door struck again, and this time, there was a splintering crash. Somewhere outside, someone shouted in a cruel, foreign tongue. One of the pigs squealed in pain.

"The thread!" Kess tried again, but at the same moment, Cyral yelled from the other end of the catwalk, drowning her out. A thing with three heads and the body of an eel was trying to climb the stairs.

"That's a hydratch," said Eliott helpfully, as Jordan rushed past him. "From the 'Rotwood Saga.'"

"Oh, God," said Cyral.

"Do you remember how it burrowed into its victims'—"

"Yes!"

Jordan grabbed a barrel and flung it at the creature, knocking it back down the stairs. It collided with something at the bottom that growled and bit back.

"Block the stairs. Anything you can find," he ordered, hauling Cyral toward him. Confusion later, his face said. Act now. Cyral grabbed an old sack and heaved it after the barrel.

"Make whatever preparations you wish," said Hopley, standing back smugly, as though everything were unfolding exactly as he had planned from the beginning. "Make peace with your gods, if you like. There will be no escape for any of you. Especially not for you, Jordan the Red— there's no cliff for you to hang on to here!"

"They won't spare you, Hopley," Kess called back. "Do you know what you've done? Break the other thread!"

"I think not. These are Jordan's old enemies I've brought back—we have a common goal."

"Um, are you sure about that?" asked Eliott, looking down. "Because I don't think you want to have anything in common with those . . ."

The door had broken, and the mob outside was pushing in. They looked mostly human, until the light through the windows showed off exposed bone and missing flesh, scars from previously fatal wounds and faces distorted by death itself. They neither lurched nor shuffled, as Eliott would have expected, but moved with cold, predatory purpose.

"Wish them away!" Kess yelled. "Hopley. Do it!"

"Not yet."

The walking dead were still on the ground floor; some were taking a keen interest in the Giant's Mixing Bowl, pulling and prying at the metal spikes and blades, but it was only a matter of time before they discovered the stairs. Kess looked at the carving knife by her hand, then back to Hopley. The unpleasant thought shot through her head: if the white thread breaks, he'll come back to life. So it wouldn't really be like killing him.

But she would remember . . .

She had never killed before.

She couldn't do it now.

With a grunt of frustration and fury, she pushed at the nearest stack of old flour, bombarding the dead. Zombie henchmen and minions of a dozen defeated armies staggered and fell as forty-pound sacks struck them from two floors above. Clouds of flour dust blossomed like fog on a haunted moor.

"I think you're slowing them down," said Eliott encouragingly. "Did you see the ones wearing the uni-

forms from Brok? Those must have been the Traitorous Men."

His chair thumped on the catwalk as he tried to turn for
a better view.

"Hey, Kess? This is great just watching, but can you
cut me free? I want to help Jordan defend the stairs."

"I'm coming. Hang on."

Kess pushed one more volley of flour sacks down
onto the dead, then scrambled along to the far end of the
loft, above where Jordan and Cyral stood guard. They
had choked the stairs with every loose scrap of wood or
piece of debris available to them; sacks and barrels and
the doors to the upper rooms. On the top of the barricade,
the two guards Jordan had knocked unconscious lay like
ballast, holding the rest down. Kess swung herself down
from the rafters and handed the carving knife over to
Cyral.

"Get Eliott."

The bard nodded and went. Kess turned to Jordan.
"This won't hold, will it?"

Jordan shook his head. His sword was still sheathed,
but he had found a long gaff to prod anything that tried to
come through the barricade. "Slow 'em down at best."

"Then you need to listen to me. Listen—Hopley has a
thread, a white thread. Break it and everything goes away.
Break it, or kill him. Jordan, you need to—"

"Wait. You hear that?"

"No, but the thread—"

Then Kess heard it, too: a broad, sweeping pulse of
beating air, broken by unnerving silence. The things gnawing at the roof had stopped. The shouts outside the mill
had died away. Only the walking dead on the floor below
were still making any sound at all.

"I know what that is . . ." said Jordan.

The beat stopped. A weight crunched against the end

wall of the mill, and the whole building shuddered. For an instant, a vast, leathery limb pressed up against the window behind Hopley, blacking out the sky. Everyone turned and stared.

The roof and the wall split apart. Beyond the gaping hole of broken boards and shingles, a massive black body clung to the side of the mill. A head made of claws and horns rose from a serpentine neck, high and higher against the twilight sky. Outstretched wings wrapped around the corners of the building, hooding the creature's prey from other predators, as if it could have any opponents to threaten it.

"Dragon," said Jordan.

"Yes, thanks," said Kess, finding her own voice, "for pointing out the obvious. What do we do?"

"Be ready. Just . . . be ready."

The dragon scratched and tore at what remained of the wall and roof at that end of the mill, opening a breach wide enough for its horned head and sinuous neck to reach inside. It swung its head like a snake, jerking from side to side as it peered through the broken shadows and clouds of flour dust filling the mill.

It's looking for us, thought Cyral. It knows we're in here.

The last of Hopley's pig guards, panicked and disoriented, tried to run, but it was already too close to the dragon. The massive, swaying head smacked it off the catwalk without consideration. The pig fell, screaming, down to the mill floor. Now only Hopley stood in the way of the dragon.

The wizard smiled.

"Halt! I command you!" he shouted, raising his arms magnificently. "By my arts, you are reborn and summoned here for vengeance! It is only fitting that you join me, and together we will defeat Jordan the Red once and for all!"

The dragon looked down at Hopley as if he had tried to stop it with a particularly complex algebra problem, and then did what all dragons do when faced with math instructors or other human-sized annoyances. Its great jaws opened. There was a snap and a gulp and Hopley was gone.

The dragon's head rose and tilted back, carelessly smashing away more of the roof on the way up. Its throat undulated as it swallowed the slight bulge that had been a wizard. In Cyral's horrified imagination, he saw the shape of a kicking foot distend the dragon's skin.

"Okay," said Eliott. "That was cool."

"Run!" said Jordan. "Go!"

He grabbed Eliott, who happened to be nearest, and ran at the gaping hole in the wall beneath the dragon's bulk. Cyral faltered, mesmerized by the silhouette of the monstrous head still pointed toward the sky. Its cheeks had begun to glow, red as a second sunset but far less likely to please sailors, unless they wanted their ships burned to the waterline.

"Ah," said Cyral, finding himself alone on the second floor of a dry, wooden building about to be lit on fire. "Aha."

Then Kess darted back out of the clouds of dust, caught his hand, and dragged him. He had a brief awareness of the dragon's talons passing within spitting distance of his face, then a gut-wrenching scramble over broken beams and shingles onto what remained of the roof, a leap. A terrified thought went through his head as he plunged through empty air that there was no possible way he could jump far enough to land deep enough in the pond, and then a cold pain struck him, all over.

The dragon opened its jaws and belched fire into the old mill, lighting up the interior of the building for a brief, clear view of the horde of zombies and assorted other monsters still inside. The particles of flour dust hanging in the air glowed, beautifully incandescent in their final moments.

And then, in accordance with the twin powers of chemistry and dramatics, the mill exploded.

FIVE FIGURES ROSE out of the millpond and sloshed toward the shore, resolving into Jordan, Cyral, Kess, Eliott, and a tentacled monstrosity of a forgotten age. Jordan kicked the creature squarely in its eye, and it sank back into the churning water with a cephalopodian yelp.

"Jordan—Jordan, I'm sorry. I'm so sorry. Wait for us." Kess waded out of the pond after him and toward the forest. "You need to know. Hopley, he—"

"He made a wish," said Jordan, his voice like cold iron. "I heard. And it's come true. When we're safe, you'll tell me the rest of the story. Not now."

He slid into the concealment of the forest, not waiting or caring to see if any of the others followed him. Though some indigo light still lingered after the sunset, the moon had risen, fat and smug with the promise of werewolves. Between the moon and the glow of the burning mill, the night was uncannily bright, and the shadows were crisp and stark. Jordan stumbled through them, cursing his lost night vision. His eyes felt as tired as the rest of his body.

Every terrible thing you fought and killed before, he heard again. All of them, out there, in the dark, searching for him. In the distance, he could hear drums and shouts and the sounds of predatory chaos; he forced his ears to ignore them and focus on the range of immediate danger. Every unnatural twig crack, every rustle of anything larger than a squirrel—but don't count out squirrels, he reminded himself. Remember the man-eating squirrels of Rotwood, looking so cute and harmless?

Rotwood.

At the same moment he thought the name, he heard a laugh like a dead branch creaking, a laugh that read his mind. He turned to run and collided with Cyral.

"Jordan? What is it?"

"Out! Out of the forest!" he shouted, as the trees around them began to sway.

"Why, Jordan . . . how old you've gotten. Too old to play? Too old to dance with the little sister of the oak?" The voice chittered from tree to tree, chasing them as they fled. Branches whipped across Jordan's path. Roots clawed at his feet. "You burned me. You hurt me. I made such sad songs for you."

"Little sister— Is that—wow, is that Viscaea? You called her Venomberry," said Eliott, managing to crash through branches and pull up useless trivia at the same time. "She can take over the souls of trees, right?"

"Yes!" said Jordan, over delighted wooden laughter.

"Can I watch you fight her?"

"No!"

A tall pine bent down across their path, limbs and needles shooting out of the dark. Jordan threw himself to the ground as the lance tip of a branch stabbed past him. On every side, the forest closed in and blocked his escape. Through the thrashing leaves, he could see moonlight on open fields—so close. That would be Venomberry's idea of a game.

Then, through the trees behind him, he heard a familiar tune being pounded into noise by crude voices.

He could hate himself in the morning, he decided. If he lived that long.

"Hey! Over here," he shouted. "Squib—guess who's back in your forest!"

An angry yell shot back out of the darkness. "Deal breakers!"

Jordan scrambled to his feet, raised his hands, and waved at the looming pine. "Venomberry! Look, you've got goblins. See the goblins? Nasty, sharp axes. Remember the last time you were chopped down?"

The possessed tree creaked upward, distracted by this new threat. The first ranks of goblins crashed out of the undergrowth, spears and axes held high, only to be thrown back by avenging branches. Squib howled and flung himself bodily into the fight, ignoring Jordan for now. Shrugging off lashing blows that rang against his bone-decorated armor, he sank his spear deep into the trunk of the pine and held on like a deranged ornament as Venomberry tried to dislodge him. Jordan caught Eliott by the arm, ducked, and ran.

"Will that really work?" asked Cyral, struggling to keep pace. "Pitting them against each other?"

Jordan grunted. Words wasted breath, but if he had had any to spare, he would have explained that it was working for now, and now was all that mattered.

Guilt later, he reminded himself, as the war shouts and axe blows of the goblins gave way to screams and the cracking of great branches falling on rusty helms. Deep down, past all the ambushes and attacks and thefts, he liked goblins. You knew where you stood with them, even if they were gnawing on your knees while you stood there. And now he'd set them up to fight an entire forest so he could escape. Because he was the hero.

He glanced back. At the top of the wildly pitching pine, silhouetted against the moon, a ball of enraged goblins still held on, pruning for their lives as other trees tried to swat them down. Venomberry had forgotten her other prey completely.

That's one enemy escaped, thought Jordan, but too many others still out there. He pushed himself to keep running, out into the open fields far beyond the reach of the trees, until a shallow hollow opened up in front of him, surrounded by tall weeds. He sank down into it, pulling the others down after him. "Too old for this . . ." he said, breathing heavily as he tried to keep his muscles from seizing up.

"Are you all right?" asked Kess.

"Out of practice at running for my life." He arched his back, vertebrae returning loudly to their accustomed places. "Amazing how it all comes back. Catching my breath. Tell me the damn story."

Kess huddled away from him, one arm draped over Eliott. "This is my fault. I gave Eliott a Wishing Braid, and Hopley took it from him. It wasn't supposed to happen like this."

"You . . . gave him . . ."

"I gave Eliott—"

"—a wish."

"But it can be broken. If you'd listened to me—"

Jordan cut her off with a look. "So what about you, kid? You made a wish, too, right? That was it—how you found me. You wished yourself here to meet me."

"And to go on an adventure," said Eliott. "And so far, it's been awesome—did you see that dragon?"

Jordan slumped. "Couldn't you have wished me dead and got it over with? Couldn't Hopley?"

"I'm sorry," Kess said again.

"How 'bout you, Cyral? You make any wishes lately?"

"I wanted to write for you," Cyral answered flatly. He held up a limp, soggy block of paper that had been his notebook. "A little fame would have been nice."

"So what's next?" asked Eliott, poking his head up above the edge of the hollow.

"We keep running," said Jordan. "We run and we hide and we live through tonight. That's all we worry about right now. Tomorrow we figure out how to undo your wish."

"I tried to tell you," said Kess. "There's a third thread, a white thread. Break it and it sets everything right. All the monsters go away."

"Yeah? Where's this magic thread?"

". . . Hopley had it."

"Great. That's just great. See, even when you kill the bad guys, they manage to screw you over. There, you can write that down."

"So the thread is gone," said Cyral, ignoring the last remark. "Being inside the dragon makes it rather hard to get at—and I'm certainly not volunteering to go in after it . . . Speaking of the dragon, is it too much to hope that it died in the explosion?"

"Nah, I saw it fly off," said Eliott. "But I think we managed to stun it!"

"We? We didn't do anything to it," said Jordan.

"Okay, you. You blew up a mill on it and you stunned it—and I know you could have taken it if you hadn't been distracted."

A shadow swept over them on leathery wings, high above. Cyral cowered.

"Back to the subject of running away," said Cyral, when the flying thing had passed. "Where do we go? Back to Cheese?"

Jordan shook his head. "They might follow. We go south, try to get to the hills. Cover as much ground as we can."

"We could take that coach," said Eliott, standing up before anyone could stop him. "Look, over there!"

Jordan looked. On the far side of the fields, rattling and bouncing along the narrow road, a black coach drawn by two gray horses was approaching at speed, its lamps rocking wildly.

"Go—we've got to stop it."

He rose and ran, against the hot protest of his legs and

lungs, despite a confident pessimism that they had seen
the coach too late, that it would have driven past before
they could hail it down; but while he was still a distance
away, the driver hauled back on the reins and brought
the coach and horses to a sudden halt. A figure in a short,
ragged cloak strolled around in front of the horses and
bowed to the driver.

"Hey! Someone else is taking our coach," said Eliott,
in what he probably thought was a quiet voice. "We saw
it first! Are we going to fight them for it?"

There was a flicker of steel and a short, sharp squeal,
and the driver slid sideways onto the road. The highwayman crouched over the body, going through his pockets.

Jordan froze, signaling Eliott to do the same. "Stay
very still. Get down. Slowly."

"What's going on?" asked Cyral, catching up. Jordan
grabbed him by the shirt and pulled him to the ground,
clapping a hand over his mouth.

The highwayman stood up. He unhooked the coach
lamp from above the driver's seat and shone it out across
the fields. Jordan squinted, trying to get a glimpse of the
highwayman's face without looking directly at the light.
The shape, the cloak, the movements all pricked at something in the back of Jordan's memory.

"Do you—" began Cyral, pulling free.

The light swung onto them, and stayed there.

"—think he's seen us," Cyral finished lamely.

"Safe to say I have," the highwayman called back. "Jordan! I hoped I'd be the one to find you! See, I've got a little
wager going with a bunch of the others out here . . ."

He raised a horn to his lips and blew three long notes.

I know that voice, thought Jordan. Damn, damn, damn.

He got to his feet and walked toward the coach cautiously, expecting to find a knife in his gut at any moment.
"That you, Two-Blades? I figured you'd be dead by now."

"Oh, I died years ago, but it looks like I get to come back in the same shape you left me after the last time we squared off. Should have finished the job, Jordan. Maybe I'd've come back brainless and corpsey as one of them." Chemi Two-Blades smirked and nodded to his left, where a small army of the walking dead were advancing under a tattered banner. "Guess this is my lucky day."

"No need to do this," said Jordan. "You let us take that coach, Two-Blades, and get out of the way. You know I can beat you down if you don't."

"Like old times. But here's the thing . . . you've gotten old. I'm back in my prime. Still liking the odds?"

"Jordan," said Cyral urgently. "Behind us."

More dark figures were arriving, answering the horn blast. Living men and dead edged closer, wary of one another but temporarily on the same side. Among their ranks, beasts and monsters beyond count or description shoved and snapped to get at Jordan, but their allies held them back. The horde fanned out into a ragged circle, blocking every escape.

Chemi Two-Blades grinned. "How 'bout now?"

"Kill him!" someone shouted, and a scarred warrior in blue war paint surged forward, raising an axe taller than he was.

One of Chemi's knives met the warrior's heart before he had taken two strides toward Jordan.

"Mine!" Two-Blades shouted back. "My kill!" He looked at Jordan. "Did I mention? What I win is you. The right to make the kill. And the rest of them get to watch. I've been waiting a long time for this."

"That's what you said last time," said Jordan grimly. He glanced around at the horde, now standing as an audience for the blood sport. Some had climbed onto the coach for a better view. There was no escape left.

Jordan drew his sword.

"Aw, yeah," said Eliott, bouncing with excitement. "This is gonna be good."

Chemi Two-Blades bowed artfully, without taking his eyes off Jordan. Dying once had made him less of a fool. When he rose, he had a long dagger in either hand.

"Gentlemen. Ladies. And all the rest of you," he called out. "Give us some room. A man needs space in the grand arena."

The horde shuffled back grudgingly, throwing taunts and oaths at both fighters. Kess drew Cyral and Eliott out of the way; they huddled together in the narrow margin between the duel and the ring of enemies.

"What do we do," asked Cyral quietly, "if he loses?"

Kess looked at him oddly. "He's not going to lose."

"Yeah," said Eliott. "He can't lose. He's the hero. The hero always wins."

"Yes, all right, but—"

Steel rang against steel. Chemi Two-Blades had made a swift, testing lunge, striking his daggers off Jordan's sword. It was almost painful to watch how slowly, stiffly, Jordan reacted.

"—but what if he doesn't?" said Cyral pointlessly. Kess and Eliott had their full attention fixed on the duel, with none spared for wild and unlikely speculation. Because of course the hero always won. The hero was luckier, more clever, or simply the better swordsman; everyone knew that. He might be bloodied once or twice, take a fall—

Jordan missed his footing and staggered back clumsily, scarcely bringing his sword up in time to turn aside another quick stab. Chemi's dagger nicked his arm below the shoulder.

But that was only for dramatic tension. Heroes never died before an audience. They died when no one was watching, off page, to be revealed later, pierced by many swords or arrows, lying amid the bodies of their enemies. That was how it went.

But as Cyral watched Jordan stagger and drag his sword around to meet Chemi's swifter, darting strikes, the bard recalled that Jordan no longer wanted to be a hero. He certainly wasn't fighting like one. Chemi Two-Blades was fast and slippery, and Jordan's blade never came close to touching him the few times it rose in a counterattack. Every move seemed to enflame Chemi's spirit further, while Jordan faltered and slowed. Another cut, unguarded, stung Jordan's thigh.

"Just wait," said Eliott. "Anytime now."

Anytime now, thought Cyral, we'll all be dead. He felt completely useless in the face of it; he had no way even to write an account of Jordan's final battle.

The gathered horde could feel the end approaching, too. Their jeers grew louder and wilder, and those with weapons rattled them against the sky. Kess and Eliott still seemed to be holding out hope, but even Kess was biting her lip.

Then Jordan tripped over the coach lamp. He sprawled heavily onto the grass, his injured leg twisting back beneath the other. When he raised his left hand, it was a gesture of defeat.

Chemi Two-Blades crowed.

"Oh, you've gotten old!" he said, to general laughter. "Poor old man—should have been done in long ago!"

"I'm not dead yet." Jordan grunted, struggling to prop himself up on one elbow. "Give me a moment . . ."

"You hear that? He's still not dead!" said Chemi, playing to his crowd. He spread his arms wide, looking like a vulture in his ragged cloak. His raised blades gleamed with tracings of silver. He turned to the horde, raising a frenzied roar. "I'll take care of that!"

For one brief moment, he turned his back on Jordan. A moment was all it took.

"Oh, wow!" said Eliott.

"What? What?" said Cyral, whose eyes had been on Chemi Two-Blades. He looked back at Jordan at the same time Chemi did, just in time to see the still-burning coach lamp go flying off the end of Jordan's boot. It hit Chemi squarely in the mouth. Fire and glass exploded.

That should have been coupled with a quip, thought Cyral, and made a mental note to add one when he wrote the scene. It was hardly heroic to say nothing.

Jordan was still moving. His sword followed the arc of the lamp, deceptively slowly. There was no style to the strike, no grace, just straight, deadly precision. When it was done, Chemi hung suspended from the point of Jordan's outthrust sword, deadweight on the blade. At the other end of the thrust, Jordan crouched in counterbalance, almost as motionless. Only his chest moved, fighting its own rapid battle for breath. In the cold moonlight, with a cold sheen of sweat on him, Jordan looked like a glass statue.

Chemi Two-Blades slid to the ground, grinning out the back of his throat. The horde, no longer an audience or an army, howled and snarled, but still they hesitated, holding their distance out of fear or awe. It wouldn't last. It couldn't. But while it did, Jordan risked kneeling and wiped his blade on the grass.

"That was amazing," said Cyral, hurrying over to him. "I wish I could write it down."

"You touch that notebook and I'll put you with him!" Jordan snarled. "Get away from me!"

Cyral opened his mouth, but found nothing to say. He could feel the sodden pages of his notebook pressing under his belt like a cramp in his side, paining his breath.

He backed off, as much as he was able within the circle of enemies.

But as he retreated, a troll, hairy and stinking of the sulfur of the Mountains of Fire, broke through the press of the horde. Its broad, flaring nose sniffed it toward Jordan the Red and old vengeance—but in its way, the troll discovered another warm body. Peeling back its lips, it roared at Cyral and swung a clublike arm that knocked him off his feet. He hit the ground yelling what he wished had been something manly and defiant, but wasn't. He scrambled to his feet, ready to run, only to be struck and sent sprawling again. The troll bounded after him, temporarily distracted by more interesting prey. When Cyral regained his footing for the second time, the troll was on him, looming over him with fists upraised.

Not like this, he thought, bringing up his hands to block the blow. I haven't got any famous last words. I've never had any famous first words! I've never had—

A cold breeze whipped over Cyral's head. With a soft moan, the troll fell backward, pawing at its face. Between jaw and eye socket, it had sprouted three inches of arrow shaft, white as driftwood and fletched with goose feathers; then a shadow passed across the moon, and when Cyral looked back, the arrow was gone. He backed away, fearing that the troll might realize it had been killed by a phantom shot and get up again, but the brute lay where it had fallen.

"Did you see—" he began.

He was cut off by a wild whoop and a flurry of gusting winds—each one a ghostly white arrow, he realized, seeing them sleet past. The arrows fell amid the horde that had followed after the troll to attack Jordan; among the untamed monsters and unorganized men that had begun fighting with one another instead; among the ranks of those holding back to see where they could best profit. An arrow landed in the grass at Cyral's feet, sticking there like a warning until it melted into mist. Everywhere the arrows fell, men and monsters died.

Again, a taunting whoop echoed over the battlefield, coming from everywhere and nowhere at once. The sky shimmered, and Cyral was struck by the sudden smell of horses. A noise of hooves stampeded overhead.

And then, at last, he saw them. A score of skeletal horses, trailing steam, their bones white as frost. A score of riders, pale ghosts with stars shining through their flying coats and scarves, bows in hand. They circled the battlefield, notching arrows and letting fly with wild abandon into the field of targets below them. Leading the charge, their ghostly captain cheered them on with words that had no meaning and wild gestures that made no sense. When he spread his arms wide, Cyral would have sworn that he was laughing.

The horde saw the riders, too, and those that were still living broke and scattered. Arrows returned at the riders glanced futilely off bones or passed through the ghosts with all the effect of shooting clouds. Within minutes, the riders had only Jordan and his companions and the animate dead within the circle of their charge.

"There he is!" their captain called. "Take the living!"

Four skeletal horses followed their captain, swooping down to earth. They snatched up Kess and Eliott and dragged each onto a horse that rose high and fast into the sky. Cyral tried to run, only to be blocked by a pack of ghouls, their rotting bodies pecked with many goose-feathered arrows but not halted. He heard hooves behind him, then felt hands lifting him away from the ravenous dead as if he were no more than a ghost himself; as he was placed into a saddle that felt like old ivory, he looked down, half expecting to see his body left behind. Instead, he saw Jordan the Red, ringed by fallen and unliving enemies, standing before the captain of the ghost riders.

The captain reached out. Cyral's last sight, before the terrible height pinched his eyes shut, was the ghost grasping Jordan by the wrist and hauling him up onto a skeletal horse.

ELEVEN

THE GHOST RIDERS landed in a broad silver patch of moonlight, on the sheared-off top of a mountain surrounded by a vastness of cloud. They were a tremendous height up, with nothing above them but the stars and the cold lash of the wind. One by one, the horses touched hooves to the bare stone, bones clicking as they found their footing and bent their necks to feed on phantom grass. One by one, their riders vaulted from their saddles, slapping intangible hands against fleshless flanks, stroking vertebrae and murmuring soft praise into the empty sockets of the horses' skulls. A torch flared among the rocks and set a heap of dry brushwood ablaze with a warm, living flame.

Eliott dropped from his horse and ran at once to the edge of the mountaintop. No one tried to stop him, so he leaned out and looked down. The clouds were a long way below. Out in the black night, other mountaintops hung like islands, but none rose higher than this one. For a moment, he felt certain that, if he was this far up, he must have been transformed into a bird. If he wanted to, he could leap out and fly.

"Wow . . ." he murmured. "Where are we?"

Kess came over and stood by him, slipping her hand wordlessly into his. Her fingers were colder than the night. Behind her came the rider who had led the charge, a tall, slender specter in coats that whipped and flared around its ghostly frame independent of the wind. It had no face, but between its hat and mask burned two red stars that could have been eyes. In its hand, it carried a coiled whip, and it gestured with this at the desolate mountain around them.

"This here is Shortfall," it said amiably. "And you all're gonna stay here for a while."

It touched a glove to the brim of its hat, said a respectful "ma'am" to Kess, turned, and walked away again. The rest of the riders didn't seem to be paying much attention to their captives; the mountain itself could keep anyone from escaping.

"I think we're in trouble," said Kess.

"We'll be okay," said Eliott. "We're here with Jordan."

But even Eliott couldn't help noticing that Jordan was still standing where he had dismounted, staring blankly toward the fire as if his mind had left his body back on the ground miles behind and below. His sword, notched and smeared darkly with blood, hung limp from his hand. He didn't look like a hero at all. Of course, it had to be part of some elaborate trick to escape the mountain, but even seeing Jordan pretend to look so hollow and lost made Eliott uneasy.

"This is just the part where things look hopeless," said Eliott. "Before something happens to steel his nerves. Like in the 'Wendigo Saga' where he came back to the farm, and his cousin and her family were dead? And he spent three days—"

Jordan turned toward them. With the bonfire at his back, his expression was shadowed and unreadable.

"Skip ahead to the part where he pulls himself together," said Kess.

"Which time?"

"Any time."

"Sure . . . I could do the comeback scene from 'Last of the Merovians.'" Eliott glanced at the ghost riders, and dropped his voice. "You want a diversion, while you and Jordan figure out how to make our escape?"

"Eliott, look at him. He's not going to do anything heroic right now. He needs to hear something with some hope."

"He does? No, he doesn't. You really think so?"

Kess nodded.

"Well . . . okay," said Eliott. "I'll do it, then."

Against the wind, Eliott walked into Jordan's hollow stare, trying to find the right words. The thrill of being the one who would inspire Jordan the Red with hope wrestled with the strangeness of thinking that Jordan the Red could even need inspiration.

"Hey, Jordan . . . can I talk to you?"

Jordan said nothing. Eliott took it as permission.

"You've been in worse situations than this, right? And gotten through them and managed to save the day. I mean, you killed that wendigo tribe. Or—remember when you climbed out of the snake pit at Antigran and stopped the Doomsday Blade? Or when you were being chased by the cannibal cave dwellers, and you got cut off by the river flooding, and had to push over those giant columns to make a bridge? You didn't give up. Right? You never give up."

Jordan stared at him, or through him.

"Or, what about the . . . um . . . the Sky Prison on Mount Canine? I know you were only there for, like, a week, but that must have felt pretty bad. Sort of like here! And you escaped from that, easy."

Jordan's lips moved. "What about the guards?" he asked, winching up the words from somewhere far below.

"Oh, you killed them," said Eliott brightly. "With an avalanche."

"I killed them," Jordan repeated, with such weariness that even Eliott's unending enthusiasm wilted. "Of course I killed them. But they're out there. Right now. Dead and walking around. Guards with faces I never saw. And every wendigo, every pirate, every demon. General Sarod. All of them."

"Yeah, but you beat them. You killed them all before— you can do it again."

"Do it again?!" Jordan's face twisted into something ugly and barely controlled. "How many?"

"Huh?"

"How many people have I killed? In all your gods-damned precious sagas. How many?"

"I . . ∴. I don't know," said Eliott, though he tried to come up with a number. It wasn't easy, even to guess. Too many times, the sagas skimmed over exact body counts, relying instead on phrases like, "and he slew all within the evil place." The avalanche on Mount Canine had destroyed an entire bunkhouse before the end of the prologue, but the guards inside had died vague and numberless, unimportant to the plot.

"I do. I counted 'em. Every last one of them. After the temple city of Zebek burned. It took a week. And then I was done. Sent Glister the total and said I was out." Jordan's voice rose. A few of the ghost riders looked around, their horses picking up on Jordan's mood and stamping their hooves in agitation. "So I know something about me that you don't. I know that number. Want to find out?"

He lurched forward. "Here's your chance. You and your wish. I should chuck you off this mountain right now."

Startled, Eliott backed up; then, after the reflex had passed, he checked behind him to make sure he hadn't gone over the edge. He glared back at Jordan. "I didn't wish them back! It was Hopley!"

"You gave him the damn Braid. You wanted your adventure. You told Glister Starmacher where he could find me— Where the hell do you get off, playing around with my life! Never again! I said never again!"

Jordan's sword carved circles in the air beside him, but he still seemed unaware of it, as if his arm had grown a steel extension and developed a slashing tic. His knuckles were white, clenched around a tension that ran the length of his arm and up into the shadowed crags of his face.

"You're a hero," Eliott protested. "Killing monsters and bad guys is what you do! Come on, don't be mad at me. We'll deal with this. I'll help you!"

"I don't want your help!"

Eliott nodded. He recognized this one. "I know, it's something you've got to do for yourself. But we're here for you—"

"Get away from me!"

Jordan raised his sword. Eliott's eyes went wide—real fear struck him for the first time as he understood, too late, the fury of Jordan the Red. The blade swept down—

The lash of a ghostly whip snared Jordan's arm.

"Hey, now," said the captain of the riders. "You two've gone far enough. Ease off. No fighting up here. There's no room for it on Shortfall."

Jordan twisted, and his sword was in his other hand, and the whip was a severed shimmer of mist, blowing away. He drew his arm back and crooked it across his chest, grimacing as the motion stretched the wound Chemi Two-Blades had inflicted. He stared from Eliott to the ghost, pale and panting as if he had just awakened from a nightmare. He seemed suddenly, terribly old, beyond Eliott's power to help or understand.

It was the hardest thing he had ever done, but Eliott walked forward. He held out his hand, palm down, fingers curled under, as if he were approaching an injured dog in the kennels back home; even in pain, the dogs knew him and knew that he would comfort them. He reached out.

"Hey. It's okay," said Eliott. "Jordan? It's okay. You don't have to do anything. I bet you could sit down, y'know, for a little while. You want to?"

Jordan sank to the ground. "No. No fighting. I'm done. I'll sit here until I'm bones."

"Not that long, you won't," said the ghost. "You can stay until the danger's died down out there, but we can't keep guests that long."

"Guests," said Jordan, and at the same time Eliott said, "We're not prisoners?"

"What, you don't know a rescue when you see it? No wonder you ain't said a thank-you." The red stars between the rider's hat and mask sparked with amusement. Behind him, the other riders drifted closer.

"All right," said Jordan. "Who are you?"

"You don't recall? Think back, oh, thirty-six years."

Grudgingly, Jordan glanced at Eliott. "What ghosts was I fighting back then?"

"I don't know," said Eliott, to his own surprise. "Unless there's a saga I haven't heard, they can't have been a really significant fight. Maybe . . . Did you kill a bunch of horsemen when no one was looking?"

Jordan ignored the question. He frowned at the ghost. "I don't remember you."

"Suppose that ain't surprising," admitted the ghost. "You only met us the once, and we had a bit more flesh on our bones back then. We were hired marauders for the Count of Coldstone Castle—cheap outlaws, you know? I think we tried to ambush you on the road to Port of Sanguea. Guess how well that turned out."

"Buckets of blood?" said Jordan.

"Mostly ours," said the ghost, nodding. "We never had time for no formal introductions. Vaughn Garrick."

"Charles Crib."

"Skilling Hayes."

On and on around the mountain, the voices of the ghost riders rose momentarily above the wind, long enough to give their names. It was like a guided tour of a graveyard, every man reading off his own tombstone. When the last had spoken, Jordan turned from face to invisible face.

"Why?" he said, eventually. "Why did you bring me up here? You want me to know your names; is that it?"

"Nah," said Vaughn, the captain of the riders. "We got yanked out of the sky, saw you down there, saw you were in trouble, and decided you could use some cavalry. Figured we owed you one."

"Owed? What'd you owe me for?" asked Jordan suspiciously. "Didn't I kill you?"

"Right in one," said Vaughn. "Best thing that could've happened to us. Turned out our eternal reward for our lives of crime is getting to ride the skies forever. We were a bunch of starvin', petty thugs—now we get to go anywhere, see everywhere—best damn views in the world up here. Comets trailing fire over Valhalla, sea snakes glittering in the Aegean. Right before we got pulled back to that field where we found you, we were racing the Northern Lights. Most beautiful thing you ever saw."

This got a drifting chorus of agreement and amens from the other riders.

"We're never hungry or cold no more," said one. "We don't want for nothing up here."

"Freedom," said Vaughn. "Which was all we ever really wanted. Saving your hide was the least we could do."

"You're not planning on giving us the same freedom, are you?" said Jordan.

"Nah. Couldn't say for sure where you'd end up. Might be there's some kind of a hell waiting for you."

"I don't doubt it."

Jordan looked out at the ocean of clouds. The wind sleeting across his face and through his hair seemed to carry something away with it, eroding some hard edge from his expression. He returned his sword to its old, cracked scabbard. Then he looked back at Vaughn and the other riders.

"Thanks," he said. "For getting us out of there."

"Not a problem. Anything you need while you're up here—can't offer much, but what we got's yours."

"Right now? I need sleep."

"There's caves," said Vaughn. "Over that way, out of the wind. Take a brand out of the fire; they ain't lit."

"Again . . . thanks."

With a hand pressed against an ache in the small of his back, Jordan headed slowly into the caves. Eliott hesitated, mouth open, torn between letting Jordan rest and needing to talk to him about everything that had happened. Nothing made sense. But as Eliott tried to decide if he should speak, the opportunity slipped away. Jordan went into the cave.

And came stumbling back out at speed.

"It's full of skeletons in there!"

"Oh. Right," said Vaughn. "Yeah. Right. Those'd be ours."

"Yours!"

The ghost managed to look amused and abashed at the

same time, a complex feat for something without a face. "What can I say? We used to be pretty attached to them, so we brought 'em up here, made 'em comfortable."

"You set them up playing poker," said Jordan.

"Some of the boys do still have a sense of humor. Who's winning?"

"Ain't you, Vaughn," said another rider. "You got stuck with aces and eights."

Deceased laughter rippled through the wind.

Jordan scowled. "Look, is there someplace I can lie down with nothing dead around?"

"Deeper in. Behind the bearskin, if that don't count."

"Okay," said Jordan, with finality. "Good night."

Eliott gathered his courage. "Jordan, could I—"

"No."

And that was that. Jordan slouched in to the back of the caves to sleep, and the ghost riders drifted away to watch the stars or tend their horses. Eliott stood around aimlessly for a bit, then wandered over to the fire. Even with the hood pulled up and his arms folded tightly, the wind drove a chill straight through his wool-lined jacket to his bones. He sat down beside Cyral, whom he remembered Hopley saying was Jordan's bard.

"Hey," he ventured.

Cyral glanced up. On the bare stone in front of him, he had carefully laid out a semicircle of damp squares of parchment, held down with smaller rocks. "Hello."

"I'm Eliott."

"Yes, I know," said Cyral. "You're the Device."

Eliott thought about this, and what he knew about heraldic devices, and if this was some sort of obscure, bardic-slang way of recognizing that he was born to nobility. He summed up his thoughts. "Huh?"

"You're the reason Jordan the Red came out of retirement," Cyral clarified gloomily. "The Device by which he was set into motion. I'm sorry; I don't seem to be able to do much right now besides compositional analysis. Cyral Gideon, at your service."

"What're you doing?"

"Drying my notes. They're not much, but I'd rather come out of this with more than nothing." He sniffed and wiped his nose. "More than a head cold, at any rate."

"You should write about that fight. How Jordan kicked the lantern and stabbed that guy—it'd be awesome. I'd hear that again and again."

"I don't think Jordan would be very happy if I wrote anything specific about his . . . exploits. I may be able to use some of the imagery for my next saga, though. Assuming, of course, that I'm given the opportunity to write for anyone else, after this fiasco is over with."

"What do you mean? You're writing the new adventures of Jordan the Red," said Eliott patiently. He almost said "the new adventures of Jordan the Red and his Apprentice," but a twinge of modesty stopped him.

"Jordan the Red? Really? Have you seen him around somewhere?"

Eliott had been kidnapped, chased, threatened, and ignored; he was in no mood for patronizing stupidity. "He's the old guy with the sword—the one who saved your life back at the mill. Remember?"

"And he begrudged every minute of it! That isn't Jordan the Red. Not Jordan the Red, star of 'The Ice Demons of Brok' and 'The Jungle of Jeopardy.' Haven't you heard him? He'd rather run away than fight. He'd rather hide than be a hero."

"He fought when he needed to!"

"For all the wrong reasons," said Cyral, and sighed. "It's useless. I'm useless. I may as well go back to Palace Hills and look for a freelancer."

He gave Eliott a thoughtful look.

"I don't suppose you'd have any interest in becoming an adventurer hero yourself, would you? There'll be plenty of work, dealing with all of Jordan the Red's revived antagonists."

"Oh . . ."

Temptation curled around Eliott and gave him a squeeze. He imagined himself, woven onto a tapestry, spearing monsters and rescuing distressed—and scantily clad—damsels from evil sorcerers. He thought about going back to his parents to tell them that they could forget about grooming him for court; he was off to the wilderness to be a warrior hero, who needed no grooming at all, and in fact wore stubble and dirt as marks of station. It sounded too good to be true.

And it was. The tapestry unraveled as he spotted the flaw in Cyral's offer.

"There wouldn't be a lot to do. Jordan's going to take care of all his old enemies again."

Cyral sniffed. "You honestly think so? What's he done that could possibly have given you that impression?"

"Well, he defeated Doctor Novay, and the Shadow Army of Mount—"

"Recently!"

"He killed that Two-Blades guy."

"Yes, and then he just stood there. He didn't kill the troll. Our ghostly friends had to do that. He didn't fight his way to freedom. He didn't save us!"

"No, but he would have!"

"He was going to attack you! You can't have missed that!"

"He's hurt," said Eliott sharply. "He wasn't himself then."

"No. He's not himself. He's not anybody. And he's certainly not Jordan the Red. Whoever he is, I'm done with him."

"Could you two stop?" said Kess, stepping between them. "You'll wake him."

"Yeah," said Eliott, in a quieter voice. "He needs his sleep."

"In case he decides to do anything heroic tomorrow?"

Kess put her hand gently against Cyral's arm, and a flicker of jealousy lit in Eliott's stomach. "Leave it," she said. "Just give him a break."

"Very well," said Cyral stiffly.

They settled into a sullen and shivering silence as the bonfire burned down, feeding it sparingly from the stack of wood the ghosts had provided. When it had dwindled to the size of a small campfire, they huddled under furs the ghosts brought out for them. Vaughn came and sat with them for a while, humming a tuneless, mournful song when it was clear that no one was going to speak. Cyral fell asleep soon after, snoring in harmony with the ghost's song. Kess lay down with her head on his chest and began quietly counting stars, which was nearly sleep for her.

Eliott had spent more than a day asleep as Hopley's prisoner, and now he felt relentlessly awake, a complete stranger to the idea of closing his eyes and willingly missing whatever happened next. He was as jealous of the adventures Kess and Cyral had had without him as he was of the way they lay together now; if anything did happen during the night, there was no way he was going to let it happen without him.

Anything.

Anything at all.

The night rolled on, bitterly free of dragon attacks or monsters falling from the stars. Eliott wrapped his arms around his knees, feeling like he had come too late to the party, when there was nothing left to eat except the dip, and all the pretty girls had gone home. He watched a

storm boil around a distant mountaintop; he watched the
ghosts ride out to play in the thunder without him. He
watched Kess, still counting, with her eyes closed.

"Bored," he muttered.

Vaughn stopped his tuneless hum and glanced at Eliott
from under the brim of his hat. "You need somethin' to be
happening? What for?"

Eliott shrugged. He just did.

"You'll have a long life ahead of you, full of doings,"
said Vaughn. "Enjoy the time you can waste not doing a
thing. Can you whittle?"

"You mean carving?"

"Yeah, if you want to make it sound like you're making
something. Whittling's turning a stick into less of a stick.
Good way to pass time."

"I've seen Jordan do it. With a turnip."

"Yeah, he'd be chippin' away time at his age. Young
men and old men ain't so different . . . Both need ways to
occupy themselves while they wait."

Eliott mulled over this bit of folk wisdom dubiously.
"Wait for what?"

"Life. Death. That sort of thing."

"Could I be . . . maybe waiting for something more
solid?" said Eliott. He glanced at Kess again; he couldn't
stop himself.

Before Vaughn could answer, there was a clatter of
hooves on the stone beside him as a skeletal horse touched
down. It had been ridden hard; there were still wisps of
cloud trailing off its flanks, and it snorted steam through
the bones of its skull. Its rider leaned forward, without
dismounting.

"Vaughn. You'd better come quick."

Eliott sprang to his feet. "Take me with you, too."

"You don't know where I'm going," said Vaughn.

"Neither do you! It might be somewhere where you'll need another set of eyes, or extra hands or—it's something happening, okay? Please?"

The ghost shrugged. "Mount up, then."

Where they were going turned out to be a spur of rock farther down the mountain, submerged deep in the sea of cloud. Stunted shrubs rustled wetly as Vaughn's horse and their guide's horse landed. A third rider hailed them as they set down. "Over here," he beckoned.

As they followed in that direction, Eliott realized there was a fourth horse with them in the dark, one without a rider. Its skull and neck were charred black. It nuzzled him as he passed by, and he felt soot rub off onto his hand.

They discovered the missing rider stretched out on the rock, arms spread wide, gloves grasping at the dirt. As Vaughn rushed to kneel at the fallen rider's side, one of the others said, "It's Skilling Hayes. He was like this when we found him."

Eliott stared. It was easy to see how the riders had found him; Hayes glowed like a hot coal in the dark, burning from the inside.

"Can he speak?" said Vaughn. "Can you speak, man?"

"He was calling for you before. Said he needed to tell you a thing he'd seen."

Hayes opened his eyes. There was a fire in them, too, burning like a furnace. When he rolled his gaze toward Vaughn, Eliott had to squint against the brightness.

"Vaughn," he groaned. "Damn, it hurts . . . I'd forgotten how much it hurts to hurt!"

"What happened to you?"

"I got seen. I know; I got clumsy, but I had to get real close . . . had to be sure."

"To who? Who did this to you?"

"Some holy woman. High priestess. Vengeful Virgin or

somethin'. She shot me with some sort of light. It was like starin' into the sun. Left me blind. But . . . listen . . . Vaughn, don't worry 'bout her. She ain't important . . . She—"

A shaking fit overtook him. His horse stomped and reared, pushing to get closer to him, but the other riders held it back. When the fit had passed, Vaughn said, "Go on. Who's important, if the one that hurt you ain't?"

"I saw the Count," said Hayes, weakly. "The Count of Coldstone Castle. He was at a big meeting . . . with all generals and high priests and . . . crazy-lookin' wizard types. They'd got all manner of allies gathered around. Some of them's human, but a lot of them ain't . . . I was tryin' to get close enough to see them all, get you a good count, when someone shouts, and then they're all pointin' up at me. They called me down, and when I wouldn't come, they started firin' arrows up at me. Arrows. I was laughin', Vaughn. I was laughin' an' just thinkin' I could get close enough to put an arrow of my own into the bastard's shriveled heart . . ."

He let out a groan of agony, and a hot vapor rose off him that made the air shimmer.

"And then this woman at the Count's side steps up, and she raises this golden wand . . . and I felt hot. Haven't felt heat like that in so long. Like starin' at the sun. I'm done, Vaughn. I know I'm done. Settle up for me?"

"We'll settle," said Vaughn. "And we'll see you again."

"You'll kill him. You'll kill the Count."

"We'll kill him," said Eliott impulsively. "I promise."

"Whatever you want, Hayes," Vaughn agreed.

"Man, I'm dying for a drink . . . a cup of cool water?"

Hayes gave a final gasp, and his body arched and shook. The fire in him erupted, all at once; for one brief moment, he shone like a beacon on the dark mountainside. Then the fire went out, and he was gone.

"Fetch a white linen sheet," said Vaughn. "Wherever you can steal it from, and the boy here can give Hayes's bones a proper stitching up. Rest him well, on the other side."

They rode out, and when they returned to Shortfall, they brought the mortal remains of Skilling Hayes away from the poker game of eternity in the caves. Another rider brought Eliott a linen shroud to wrap around the bones, and a needle and twine to sew it shut. Vaughn watched him carefully, directing each stitch. After that was done, the riders set Eliott to work piling a cairn of stones over the shroud—work Vaughn said should be performed by the hands of the living. By the time Hayes was finally covered to the satisfaction of the other riders, Eliott no longer felt the chill of the wind; he was hot and sore from his hands to his spine. He stumbled back to the remains of the bonfire.

"Hey, Kess," he muttered, nudging her. "Kess, you awake?"

"One million and six—no. I'm dreaming."

Eliott paused. "What about?"

"Being a star. Falling. Burning up. I think it's going to be a nightmare."

"O . . . kay. Cool. Listen, can you wake up? I learned something . . ."

He crawled close and told her the story of his adventure. By the end, Kess was sitting up, wide-awake and listening intently. Her half-conceived nightmare had left shadows of worry on her face, but she nodded enthusiastically when Eliott said, "This'll get Jordan back into action. I'll tell him first thing in the morning."

"And he'll stop them," said Kess. "And then we'll be safe, and have time to find another way to break the wish. He'll save the day."

Eliott frowned. "Yeah, of course he will. Kess, are you okay?"

"Just a bad dream," she said, with a sudden, brittle cheerfulness. "And tomorrow, Jordan saves the day. Like he always does. Everything's good."

She lay back down and closed her eyes again. Eliott, who had always trusted her in everything, settled down beside her and tried not to start doubting her now.

It was a long time before he eventually dozed off.

THE NEW DAY finally came, unaware of the saving that awaited it. Jordan emerged from the caves, fever-flushed and with fresh strips of bandages around the wounds on his arm and thigh. The night had not been kind to him. When he pushed his hands through his hair, he looked like a thistle going to seed, as gray and badly preserved as the bearskin hanging off his arm.

Eliott approached him cautiously. "Hey, Jordan . . ."

"Breakfast?" said Jordan.

"Huh? No. Look, I—"

"Bugger. You can always tell how the day's going to go by the breakfast it starts off with. What?"

"I found something out last night," said Eliott, forcing himself to ignore a sudden pang of hunger. "You're not going to like hearing it, but you were right."

Jordan folded his arms. "Yeah," he said warily, "I hate hearing that I'm right."

"No, I mean, it's what you said about everyone being out there—all your old enemies, like General Sarod and the Count of Coldstone Castle and everyone."

"Kid, if you want to give me a bad wake-up, why don't you hit me with a bucket of ice and get it over with."

"Wait; listen—they really are out there, and they're getting organized. One of the riders saw them, a whole bunch of them together, last night." Eliott ran to the edge of the mountaintop and pointed down. "Don't you see? Those guys took a hero to beat them when they were alone. It's going to take an experienced, expert hero to beat them now! It's going to take somebody like you."

He sidled back to Jordan, grinning. "And, you know, there is nobody like you. Except for you. So we're going to fight them, right?"

Jordan gathered the bearskin around his shoulders and stared out at endless clouds shielding him from everything below. He might have been the father of all gods, looking out at the beginning of creation, preparing to carve the formless pink marble of the clouds into a world.

"No," said Jordan finally.

TWELVE

THE STORY ENDED. The saga was over. Cyral threw up his hands and put the crisp, dry pages of his notebook away. Now there was nothing left to do except stand around the fire arguing about it. It was as good a way as any to spend a morning at the top of the world.

"But you've got to," said Eliott. "I made a promise to a dying ghost—okay, he was already dead, but you know what I mean—I promised we'd kill the Count!"

"Don't make promises for me," said Jordan. "I—"

"Okay, this is our fault," said Kess, the negotiator. "Hopley getting the wish was my fault. But all those villains need to be stopped. They could be marching on Cheese right now. We can't fight them without you, Jordan. We need a hero."

"Talk to Glister; he'll set you up with a dozen. I'm not—"

"You wouldn't need to fight all of them—give me a sword," said Eliott, to a general look of horror. "I could take out a couple of them. I've practiced."

"I wouldn't trust you to take out my compost," said Jordan. "If you go down there to fight all my old enemies, you'll get killed, and with my luck, you'd come back to haunt me—not that I've got anything against ghosts in general."

"Thank you," said Vaughn's disembodied voice.

"I know how to use a sword," said Eliott. "I had to take fencing lessons last year." He slid into a defiant, sidelong pose, one arm held above his head.

"You're not fighting them. And neither am I."

"But you can't just give up!"

"I'm not giving up!"

Jordan raised his hands for a truce, long enough for him to say what he needed to. "I'm not playing the game, either—not the way you or Glister Starmacher or any pub audience wants me to." He shot an undeserved glare at Cyral. "I'm cutting straight to the finish. I'm breaking the white thread."

It was a well-delivered line. Cyral had rarely heard thread-breaking given such dramatic foreboding, other than in extremely exclusive fashion boutiques. He regretted having to spoil it.

"You do remember," he said hesitantly, "that it was eaten by a dragon?"

Jordan grimaced. "Yes. I know. So, I'll probably have to end up killing it, cutting it open, and crawling through its intestines to find the damn thing."

Which was, in Cyral's professional opinion, likely the least dramatic battle cry of a dragon slayer ever.

"Of course, if I'm lucky, the dragon'll have already passed it through, and I'll get to save the world by shoveling crap," said Jordan, forcing Cyral to amend his previous assessment. "But I doubt it. Dragons digest slower than sharks, and I bet that stringy little piece of magic is pretty tough."

Kess nodded. "It can't be destroyed like that. It won't even get dirty." She glanced at Eliott before adding, "You've got a good plan."

"Yeah," agreed Eliott, "one dragon's worth a whole army of no-name guys."

"Glad you approve," said Jordan. "But so we're clear, I'm still retired. This isn't becoming a habit. It's getting done and getting forgotten. And if it's getting done, then it's best it gets done quickly."

He shook his head as if there was still a chance he could dislodge the idea.

"It's the start of a plan, anyway. Vaughn, I need to ask for your help. You don't owe me anything anymore, but I could really use you. I've got no idea where that dragon went, and likely not enough time left to find it on my own. Could you track it down?"

The ghost nodded. "I lost a man yesterday, on account of all this craziness. You might say I'd like to see that answered for. If killing this dragon'll help do that, then sure, you'll get help from me and mine." He whistled to the rest of the riders, then looked back at Jordan and said, "We've both got enemies out there now. If you get a chance, I hope you'll oblige me by killing the sumbitch Count of Coldstone Castle. Again."

"This'll deal with him, too," said Jordan.

The ghost riders left their horses and gathered around their leader. They were almost invisible in the light of day; a shimmer in the air when they moved, a faint haze when they stood still, and a fleeting scent of saddle soap and old leather.

"What's the plan, chief?" asked one.

"Ridin' out," said Vaughn. "As a favor for our guests.

Out in all directions. You're lookin' for that dragon that flew off yesterday, the big one. Find where it's gone and come straight back. Be back before dark, whether you find it or no."

There was a chorus of agreement from the ghosts, a hollow sighing on the wind that did no justice to the speed with which they returned to their horses and charged off the mountaintop into the sky. Perhaps two-thirds of them went, while those who remained, including Vaughn, took stations around the edge of Shortfall to watch for their return. They wheeled about once, like a flock of skeletal starlings, then scattered in all directions.

Jordan watched them fly until they were lost in the clouds, then walked up to Vaughn. "Thank you. Again."

"You just do what you need to do," said the ghost, the faint stars of his eyes trained on the horizon.

That settled, Jordan returned to the fire and shoved another stick into the glowing coals. He sat down heavily and let his arms hang over his knees, a man with nothing better to do than keep warm.

"So how are we going to kill the dragon?" said Eliott. "Set up some sort of trap? Challenge it to single combat? Do you think we could catch it sleeping and collapse its lair on top of it, because I've always wanted to see how you do that."

"We?" said Jordan coldly. "You think you're coming with me?"

"Well, yeah! We're in this together—you and me and Kess. And Cyral, I guess, 'cause somebody should tell the story afterward. I know I'm sort of responsible for things, so I've got a—an obligation to help you." Eliott grinned. "Plus, if you're going to kill a dragon, I know a hundred ways to do it. I've heard all the sagas of the great dragon slayers."

"You don't get it, do you. You really don't."

"Get what?"

"Everything you've done . . ." Jordan pinched the bridge of his nose. "Okay. I'll explain this to you. Once. So pay attention."

He took Eliott aside, far enough away from the fire that it was clear no one else was invited, but not quite far enough not to be overheard. Cyral, who had been writing about the ghosts' departure, briefly resisted temptation, then put aside his notebook and listened.

"I need to hear something from you," Jordan was saying. "You want to mess around, take away my comfortable life, call up my enemies, make me risk my neck again, fine. Not the worst that's been done to me, and being young and stupid ain't the worst reason for doing it, either. Anyway, it's done, so there's no stopping you. But if you think you can do all that and be my friend . . . no. You're not fighting at my side. You want to even stay around me, you've got to say it. Here. Now."

There was a pause, a moment split by the sharp edge of the wind, before Eliott answered. When he did, he spoke with such defensive disdain that Cyral cringed. "Please?"

Jordan stared. The wrinkles around his face compressed into tight, angry strata. "I could leave you here."

"What?"

"Nothing saying I have to take you with me. Been an adventure so far, hasn't it, so you got what you wished for. I'll go deal with the dragon, and you can ask the ghosts for a ride home. See if you can make a good impression on them."

"But . . . I've got to be there when you fight the dragon," said Eliott, with conviction. "I can't miss that!"

"Yeah, I'd hate for you not to get everything you wanted," said Jordan bluntly. "That'd be as bad as growing up."

"I do not get everything I want!"

"You're a spoiled child with delusions of hardship because the rest of us aren't being entertaining enough. I've known a hundred like you."

"And I'm not a child! Everyone treats me like that because I want to have adventures and kill dragons—"

"—because you can't think about anyone but yourself. You only need to do one thing right now, and you can't even do that. Go home, kid."

"Okay—I'm sorry! Okay? Is that what you want to hear?"

"For what? Getting left behind?"

"No! I'm sorry I met you!" Eliott's voice cracked, carrying out over the clouds to the far mountaintops. Even the wind and the fire had gone quiet. When he spoke again, it was scarcely more than a mumble. "I should have left you alone."

Jordan remained impassive. "Yes. You should have."

"I'm sorry I didn't. I really am."

They stood, still squared off against each other, like pieces in an abandoned chess game, neither sure if the game was over or who had won. Finally, Eliott looked down at his boots and said, "You know, you're still my hero."

"I'm not—"

"I mean, I still want to be like you. Or how you were. Or are. Or, I don't know, like anybody that's not me."

Cyral, who had given up all pretense of not listening, watched Jordan's face. There was no softening of the older man's eyes, no sudden forgiving smile, but a grim sympathy tightened in his cheeks as he said, "Why? Who're you?"

Eliott pulled at the torn, filthy lace cuffs of his jacket. "Whoever my parents make me. Lord Nodding Agreement the Twenty-seventh. One more nobody at court, feeling all proud and self-important because I clapped at the right time for the right person. It's what they do—it's all they do. Dress nice, talk soft, never do anything to stand out."

He met Jordan's eyes. "You won't really leave me here, will you?"

Jordan put a hand on his shoulder. "You let me have my life, and I'll let you have yours. Don't try to make me do anything, and you can come with me."

Eliott brightened. "So, are we—"

"No. But you can stay around."

They returned to the fire, where Cyral was suddenly very busy with his notebook again, and neither of them said another word about it.

THE DAY STRETCHED out, long and thin. Through the rest of the morning and into the afternoon, they waited for Vaughn's scouts to return. They fed the fire with what remained of the wood supply, and ate a little, and took turns napping inside the cave. Eliott suggested they play cards, but in the end, nobody wanted to disturb the skeletons.

"Or we could tell stories," Eliott tried again, the next time they were all sitting around the fire.

"No stories," said Jordan.

Eliott gave out a deep sigh, in case anyone had failed to notice that he was bored, but let the idea drop. He leaned back onto his elbows, tapping his boots together without rhythm. Twitches of expressions chased one another across his face, hinting at something else brewing in his mind. Cyral waited for it to boil over.

"What dragon was it?" asked Eliott, sitting up sharply.

"Huh?"

"The dragon that ate Hopley. Which one was it?"

"I don't know. I didn't have time for introductions."

"Well, it's got to be one of the dragons you killed before, right? And there weren't that many of them, really—maybe a couple dozen—so I bet we could figure out which one it was, and then we'd know the best way to kill it again, like, if it had a special vulnerable spot under one loose scale or something. It makes sense to me."

". . . That's not a bad idea," said Jordan grudgingly.

"You killed two dozen dragons?" said Vaughn. "Seriously?"

"Yeah. Toward the end, before I retired, 'The Adventures of Saint George' got real popular again, and his big claim to fame was killing some foreign dragon. So Glister—my agent—decided to cash in on the whole thing. If the Saint killed one dragon, hey, how about Jordan the Red kills a flock of dragons! And a disembodied burning head!"

He gave the fire a vicious poke. "Bloody stupid Thundersphere."

Cyral nodded sympathetically. "It ended up being all about the magic and the monsters. No character value."

"Yeah, the Thundersphere dragons were all way smaller than the one that ate Hopley," said Eliott. "So we can eliminate all of them."

"I'm not going to—"

"Eliminate them from the list," said Eliott. "If we had a list. We should have a list. Hey, Cyral, could you be writing this down? Not any of the Thundersphere dragons. And . . . it only had one head . . . It could fly . . . Did it have four legs or two?"

"Two, I think." The recollection came quickly, once Cyral forced himself to look past the memory of the massive jaws. "Yes, two legs and two wings, like a bird. It had a very long neck, if that helps."

"Making it sound like a big turkey," said Vaughn.

"The biggest," said Jordan. "We'll kill it by choking it to death on bread-and-onion stuffing."

"Here, it looked something like this . . ." Cyral scratched out a hasty cartoon of the dragon as he remembered it, wings spread wide and mouth gaping. "Sort of . . . yes, like that."

"And it was leathery," said Kess. "Not scaly."

Then, as if she had lost interest in the rest of the discussion, she folded her arms and walked away. Cyral watched her step out to the edge of the mountaintop, her hair and her cloak lashing wildly around her, and for one terrifying moment, he thought she was going to keep walking into the open sky. He started to stand, ready to run after her, but she turned away from the edge and went into the caves instead.

"That's it!" said Eliott. "I know which dragon it was that ate the white thread—Scoryx, the Blackflame Wyrm, from the 'Skarbolg Saga'!"

"Ah . . . that's terrific," said Cyral, who had never heard the ending of the 'Skarbolg Saga,' and was having a hard time at the moment remembering the parts he had heard. "Scoryx. Excellent. Now we know how it needs to be handled. Which would be . . . er, how, exactly?"

"We don't use any magic; that's for sure." Eliott grinned until it became obvious that no one else was getting the joke.

"We haven't got any magic," said Jordan, deadpan.

"Aw, come on. Don't you remember?"

"No."

"Okay, it's a Blackflame Wyrm. It was bred by the Shining Brethren of the Shadowed Dawn to be completely invulnerable to any sort of magic! That's how they were going to defeat the wizard cult of—"

"Jump to the part where I killed the damn thing, already," said Jordan. "I never paid attention to all the silly names of cults and wizards back then; I'm not going to start now."

Eliott looked disappointed, but rallied. "You pierced its left eye with an ordinary, completely nonmagical spear. Through its eye and straight into its brain."

"Yes, that would do it," said Cyral.

"I thought that was the dragon I killed outside Baddington," said Jordan. He frowned. "Through the eye? Are you sure?"

"The Blue Dragon of Baddington had three heads," said Eliott patiently. "And you never carried more than two spears. For that one, you used two crossbows and an axe."

"Oh. Yeah. Now I remember."

"So we'll need to get you a spear."

Cyral got up and wandered away, leaving them discussing the sharper points of dragon slaying. He had little to offer to the conversation, other than what he had learned from sagas, and in that regard, he was quite sure Eliott overshadowed him. So instead, he went into the caves.

The moment he stepped out of the wind, he realized how cold he had been, and how much better it felt to be surrounded by walls and a proper ceiling, even ones of earth and stone. The cave was deeper than he had expected, and drier, burrowing and twisting through the mountaintop. Small holes, worn away by the wind trying to escape, opened like windows to let in the lancing shafts of morning light. By it, Cyral saw and stepped around the stone table and the dusty skeletons of the riders at their card game. Farther in he found Kess, who glanced up at his arrival, then lay back down with her chin on her arms.

"Did they figure it out?" she asked, without much interest.

"The dragon? Yes, Eliott's sure it was Scoryx, from the 'Skarbolg Saga.' He seems quite excited about it."

"That's good."

Cyral found a passably comfortable rock and sat down opposite her. "There's another question that I'm more interested in finding the answer to at the moment. I wonder if you—"

"I'm fine."

"You're sure about that? Because you're not acting like yourself."

Kess rolled onto her side. "You've known me for two days. How do you know how I act?"

"I suppose I could be mistaken. Should I go and ask Eliott if he's noticed any difference? I know he's been distracted lately, but—"

"Don't be an ass."

"May I be a friend? A concerned friend?"

"If I say no—"

"Then I'll go listen to the discussion of dragon-evisceration techniques and leave you be."

She hesitated, then twisted herself around into a sitting position, cross-legged with her elbows on her knees. "You're good with words," she said softly. Cyral slid toward her, but she raised a warning hand. "This isn't that story. I'm not falling in love with you and I'm probably not sleeping with you. But I could use a friend right now."

Cyral regathered his abruptly fragmented composure and sat back on his rock. "We can talk, though?"

"We can talk." Kess smiled, from someplace far away.

A strand of hair, that until that moment had hung inoffensively down in front of her face, suddenly drew her anger, and she pushed it back with force. "Have you ever been drunk on fairy wine?"

"Er . . ."

She gave him an odd look. "Ever been drunk at all?"

"I haven't really had the opportunity. I'd like to, but it's always been a luxury, and, well . . . Sorry. Why?"

"The wine goes to your head," she explained, with forced patience. "Then your head goes away. I feel like I'm coming down from that. Like I'm off balance."

"Do you know why?"

"Because . . . because nothing is behaving like it should. Jordan, Hopley, me, the whole world. I've done things wrong. And he's not doing anything right! If he isn't going to go forth and do battle with his enemies, it isn't a story. If it isn't a story, then maybe there's no happy ending."

She quirked her head, staring at him with such intensity that he had to look away. He could feel her searching his mind for something, but whether she was looking for understanding or reassurance or for him to offer her a happy ending, he knew it was something he didn't have.

"This is about Eliott, isn't it? He's your friend, but you're not talking to him. Is that it?"

"He's part of it. Not all of it, but—it's complicated."

"Well, that's life," he said eventually. "It doesn't always end happily. I suppose that's why we tell stories, for the chance to make ourselves believe that things do end well, with justice and defeat for the wicked, and happily ever after for the rest of us. But that isn't always the way life goes."

"Humans have ugly lives," said Kess. She turned her face to the wall, and in the strange slant of the morning sun Cyral saw for the first time how alien she looked, with her large, almond eyes and long, pointed ears that could watch and hear so much more than any human ever could. He could scarcely see her beauty then, and wondered if he had ever really seen it.

"Not ugly—plain lives," said Cyral. "Boring lives. We just tell very pretty stories."

Head bent to avoid the low ceiling, he shifted himself and sat down beside her.

"What are you afraid of?"

"The end," she answered dully, without facing him. "What'll have to be done if we can't find the dragon. If Jordan's enemies win."

"Then we'll fight them. Not everyone's as apathetic as our Jordan—other heroes would rise up. They'd have to—"

"No. They wouldn't."

Cyral waited.

"Eliott," Kess continued. "He can end the wishes and put everything back to the way it was anytime. The white thread will break itself . . . when he dies."

"Does he know?"

"He should. I told him. I hope he's forgotten."

Cyral hesitated, choosing his next words carefully. "But . . . that wouldn't be such a terrible thing, would it? If everything goes back to the way it was, he'd be alive again, wouldn't he?"

"I don't know! He's not an elf; he's a stupid, mortal boy, and you—you people don't get to walk back on playing a different part after you die! You really die. And if he dies—" She grabbed Cyral's arm as if she could anchor him to the mortal world with her grip. "It'd be my fault."

Cyral nodded mutely, while his arm carried on with the vital work of forming bruises.

"If he dies," Kess repeated, "even if the white thread brings him back, he'll always be dead to me after that. I'll remember. And I will be done with humans. Forever."

She released her grip.

"You won't say anything," she told Cyral, with absolute certainty. "Not to Eliott, not to Jordan."

"No. No, of course not."

"If it has to happen—"

"But it won't. We'll get the white thread back and

break it the straightforward way. I promise you, even if Jordan isn't willing to be a hero, we'll kill the dragon. We'll do it ourselves if we have to." Cyral risked a smile. "I still think you could be a wonderful heroine."

"And you could be the famous bard who writes about me."

"I'd like that," said Cyral. "Very much."

He took out his notebook and, on the page where he had drawn the cartoon of the dragon, made a careful annotation: *Scoryx. Defeated by Kess, the mighty elf maiden.* Kess, reading over his shoulder, snorted and took the quill pen away from him, and crossed out the word "maiden."

"Better," she said, and handed him back the quill. Her fingers brushed against his.

"After the thread breaks," Cyral ventured, "things may go back to the way they were, but perhaps I can find you again? I mean, I'll be glad for a lot of this not to have happened, but—"

"You'll forget me. It'll all fade. You'll have a couple days. Maybe."

"—oh." He cleared his throat, where the remains of a beautifully romantic and poetical turn of phrase seemed to have died. "So everything we've done, everything we might have . . . simply gone?"

"No. I'll still have it all."

Cyral closed his notebook sharply. "You get to remember, but I don't."

"You're not an elf. Only wishers and elves get to remember things that didn't happen." Kess grinned, her ears twitching. "Life's not fair, is it?"

Before Cyral could answer, they heard a sudden rush of feet on stone and a shout of, "Horses! Horses coming back!"

Eliott's face appeared at the mouth of the cave. "They're on their way back—get out here!"

Kess and Cyral hurried from the cave, but the riders, when they saw them, were still far out on the horizon. The ghosts who had stayed behind on Shortfall were gathered once again on the edge of the mountaintop, like a crowd at the docks waiting for a ship to come in. There was a dockside sense of eagerness in the air, a hunger for news from faraway places from those who had been away, and it spread to Kess and Cyral as they joined Eliott and Vaughn.

"Do you think they've found it?" asked Cyral, keeping a hand below his eyes to avoid seeing the drop. "Do they look excited?"

"We'll see," said Vaughn. "They're coming on fast. Won't be long now."

And he was right. Soon, far sooner than Cyral would have thought, the ghost riders were reining in their horses and alighting on the mountain in twos and threes; but with each click of hooves on stone came another disappointment, another ghost shaking his head. They told of shooting stars, and monstrous eagles, and of strange armies crawling over the countryside, but there had been no sign of the dragon. Then, as Cyral was beginning to lose hope, the last pair of riders, returning with the moon rising at their backs, touched down. One, a tall and lanky ghost that Cyral thought might have been called Landry, leapt down and hurried up to Vaughn.

"We saw it!" he called out, and a general cheer went up among the ghosts. "East of here—going east and turning south. Followed it until it went to ground and waited to make sure it wasn't going to take off again, which didn't look likely. Reno and I figure it's down to rest for the night, so we came straight back."

"Good work, boys," said Vaughn. "You can find it again?"

"Yessir. There's a whole series of lakes along there we

can follow real easy. Be a fine place to put some spray under your hooves, too."

"Time enough for that later. I think Jordan here is itching to get off this hill and do some hunting for himself. Am I right?"

Jordan squinted toward the east. "Yeah. Yeah, may as well get on with it."

"Hah, then let's ride out! We'll hit the moon right in his eye tonight," said Vaughn. "Everybody coming?"

Jordan glanced at Eliott, who had the grace to look humble about it. "We're all coming," said Jordan.

There was a rush of activity as the riders rallied, remounting and grouping up. A horse crouched for Jordan to swing stiffly into the saddle, and others went over to Kess and Eliott. In short order, everyone on the mountain was in the saddle once more, except for Cyral.

"We, er, we have to fly?" he said awkwardly. "I suppose there wouldn't be a secret stairway in a tunnel or anything . . ."

"Only two ways off Shortfall," said Vaughn. "Flyin' or fallin'. But don't you worry—we won't let you fall!"

"Thank you. Very much."

"You can ride with me," said Vaughn, extending a sympathetic hand. "Old Atlas here is as sturdy and smooth a ride as you'll find among the living or the dead. Swing yourself up there, and I'll be right behind."

Reluctantly, Cyral obeyed. It was worse than being picked up and forcibly carried off; he was willingly choosing to climb onto something that would shortly be stepping off a very, very high cliff, with nothing to keep it airborne save for some spirit-world magic. Even Glister Starmacher's flying monkeys had wings. Neither horses nor skeletons were designed to fly.

The horse stepped to the very edge of the mountaintop. Cyral twisted in his saddle, forcing himself to keep his eyes open. It was too late to dismount now. He clung to the bony neck and tried not to look down.

"Are you okay?" Kess called over to him.

"Oh, yes! Just fine!" he lied.

"Then let's get you all out and aloft," said Vaughn, seated behind Cyral. "We've got a dragon to catch! Hyah!"

As the shout echoed from rider to rider, they took to the sky, the ghosts spurring their skeletal horses into a flying gallop. They rode out hard toward the dark blue east, and as they thundered through the clouds, their ghostly voices rang out in wild enthusiasm, "Yippee-kay-yoh! Yippee-kay-yay!"

"Mother—" whimpered Cyral.

THIRTEEN

THE VALLEY WAS littered with boulders of every size, ranging from the merely huge to the colossal. Monoliths pointed up to the darkened sky like raised fingers, remnants of an ancient ice age saying to the druids of Stonehenge, Anything you can do, I can do better. Jordan stood on the hillside above, watching one boulder in particular. It was roughly the shape of an egg lying on its side, but when the moonlight struck it at a certain angle, it looked vaguely like a dragon curled up under its own wings.

It was also breathing, slowly. Only someone paying close attention over several minutes would have noticed the slight rise and fall of its knobby spine. Someone who knew nothing of the habits of dragons would have put it down to a trick of the light or the low-hanging fog curling through the valley. Jordan had seen it from the air and, since landing, had focused his full attention on it. Now he was sure.

He said so.

"I still can't see it myself," said Cyral miserably. Flying through the night had been made worse for him by sudden squalls of rain, fog over the mountain lakes, and by Vaughn's impulsive decision to chase down an unsuspecting owl through an alpine forest. There were still pine needles in his hair. "Anyway, I would have thought we'd be looking for a cave."

"Good thing we weren't relying on you to find it," said Jordan. "Forget what you think you know, and use your brain for a minute. Dragons have wings. Being underground's as natural for a dragon as for a hawk."

Eliott frowned. Jordan could feel the question coming. "But what about—"

"Stories," said Jordan, a heartbeat late.

"But it's a classic," said Cyral. "The deep cavern, filled with hoarded gold. No one has ever heard of a dragon lying on a hoard of gold in the middle of a field."

"They don't. No caves, no hoards, no— Cyral, you should know this! It's a setting. Scenery. Central Casting trains its monsters to live in unnatural places, like you'd train a bird to a cage or one of those dogs—you know, the little yappy ones—to sleep on a cushion." Jordan squinted into the damp dark. "Glister gave me a tour of the Central Casting stables once. They had beds of gold, beds of human skulls, artificial caves, lakes . . . every damn thing. But none of it's real. That, out there, is a dragon doing what a dragon really does."

Cyral said nothing, but he looked unhappy in a different way. Jordan, who thought himself well versed in unhappiness, let the matter drop.

"I'll walk from here," he said.

"You sure?" said Vaughn, leaning down from his horse. "We can fly you closer. Close enough to spit, if you like."

Jordan shook his head. "I need to do this quietly. That'll be easier if I make the whole approach on foot."

"Are you finally going to do something heroic?"

He turned and gave Kess a perfunctory scowl. She was leaning against her horse with her arms folded as if he owed her something. "Don't make faces," she said. "Are you?"

"I'm going to kill a dragon," said Jordan. "Kill it, gut it, break your magic thread, and get on with my life."

"As easy as that?"

"As easy as that."

"How?"

"With my sword," he snapped. Patience was somewhere far to the south, waiting for him on the other side of a good night's sleep in his own bed.

"It's an enormous, man-eating, fire-breathing monster. You have a small piece of metal."

"That's the shape of it."

Not surprisingly, Kess persisted. "Do you have a plan?" she said. "Beyond walking down there and stabbing? I want to know that you're taking this seriously. That you'll do what you need to. I don't want to see you get eaten."

"Neither do I. And I'm going to be a lot closer to the mouth than you . . . so trust me. I have a plan." He kept his voice level. Eliott and the riders were already watching as if the argument was some sort of show. "Are you going to let me get on with it?"

"Tell me how you're going to do it."

Jordan shook his head. He had never had to explain the how of slaying monsters to anyone before. Most people were happy enough that someone else was doing it for them.

"Fine," he said, with a morbid sense of satisfaction.

"What I'm going to do won't be heroic. It won't be pretty. But it'll be what needs to be done. I'm going to kill it while it sleeps. A dragon puts its head down on the ground when it sleeps. Walk up quietly—really quietly, or you're dead—and stick a blade in behind the jaw, cutting the artery here." He tapped his own neck with the side of his hand. "And then run away while it bleeds to death. It's ugly and it's messy, but it's the only way I can think to do it with what we've got. Satisfied?"

"It sounds like a risk," said Kess coolly. Jordan wondered if she was more concerned for his safety or the dragon's death.

"Yeah, well, risky's as close to heroic as you're going to get. I'd call it stupid to the point of suicide, myself."

He looked back toward the valley, trying to remember if he had been afraid of dying when he had faced dragons before. Probably not. He'd been a cocky fool back then, believing his own press. Too many crowds cheering their invincible hero.

"Shame our dragon isn't one of the nice custom-made jobs Central Casting whips up," he said, as a distraction. "Every one with a patented press-here-to-kill-dragon vulnerable spot. I used to get little pamphlets from Glister, with diagrams."

"Jordan—" Kess began, but he shook her off.

"I'm going. I'll be back. Don't wait up."

He drew his sword, so there would be no rasp of metal when he got closer. Step by careful step, he descended into the valley, down a slope of bare stone. The moon was dim behind a gray weight of clouds, but there was still enough light for him to creep forward without stumbling. He tried to keep the dragon clear in his mind, where he had seen it and the shape of the landscape around it. Everything was different, up close. Time and distance distorted like a carnival mirror.

A drop of rain stung his hand. He looked up, hopefully, but no more came. The rain during the flight had been a welcome relief to his dry lips and the hot fever crawling under his skin.

The end was in sight. The end, and the dragon. At the other end of the valley, he could see it, the moonlight on the ridges of its wings and spine. No one would mistake it for a rock formation at this distance. If he ran at it now, he might barely be able to get one stab in before it woke, oriented on him, and ate him.

He continued forward at a silent crawl. Each step was its own thought, forcing out all others; even thinking about the attack had to wait. Concentrate on the here and now. Quiet and cautious. Hot and cold. Stiff and sore.

Bacon and cheese.

The thought snuck up on him, straight from his stomach, and made him stop halfway to the dragon. He ducked behind a boulder that was just a boulder, and cracked a manic smile. It was bad luck for an adventuring hero to get distracted by the reward he had yet to earn—that had been one of the first lessons Jordan had been taught—but he couldn't help it. When everything was done, when the wish was broken, he would get to enjoy a fried sandwich. Crisp bacon, runny cheese, crunchy bread . . . his jaws ached from thinking about it.

Do it for that. Be selfish.

He drew a long breath and let it out slowly. He rubbed his wrist until his sword sat more comfortably. He wished fervently that this could be someone else's job; but, of course, there were no other experienced dragon killers around, and since it had to be done, he had to be the one to do it.

Necessity really was a mother.

He glanced around the boulder.

The dragon stretched its wings and rolled its neck, on the edge of waking.

* * *

"I'VE LOST HIM," said Eliott, "between those rocks that look like rabbits and that one that looks like a nose. Or is that . . . No. Kess, can you see him?"

Kess put her chin on his shoulder and stretched out her arm, pointing silently to the distant figure creeping between the boulders. It was an old, familiar pose. She and Eliott might have been sitting on the back balcony at home, pointing out stars. Jordan the Red could have been a constellation.

"Got him. Thanks." Eliott resumed his vigil. "He should have let us go with him."

"Yes? What would we be doing?" Kess asked earnestly.

"I dunno. Something. Maybe distract the dragon if it wakes up early?"

"When this is over, I want to hear how you would have killed it," she said, and smiled. Eliott could feel it through his shoulder.

It would be over soon. Eliott lost sight of Jordan in the drifts of fog and shadow again, but it didn't matter if he could see. Soon enough, there would be a blood-chilling, monstrous scream, and then Jordan would come trudging back up the hill, bloody and stained with the gore of the mighty battle.

And Eliott would have missed out on the whole thing.

"At least you should have gone with him," he told Cyral, who took the news with bleary-eyed calm.

"Not on my life," said Cyral. "I'd sneeze and be eaten."

He buried a congested snort in his sleeve and huddled down deeper into his misery with his notebook pressed against his knees. There was a tiny pop as he uncorked another vial of ink, and then the scratching of his pen began again. He had been writing since Jordan left.

Whatever was going into the notebook, thought Eliott, there was no way it could compare to the epic battle between Jordan and the dragon that Cyral was failing to record.

"His bard should be with him," said Eliott. He glared at Cyral. "If you're not where the action is, you're useless."

"Leave him alone," said Kess.

"No. Jordan needs someone watching his back," said Eliott, his temper flaring. "He's gotten old, Kess! What if he falls? And what's the point of us coming along if we're not helping him? It's like we're just his audience, but he doesn't want us to see what he's doing. This is so stupid."

If there had been any place to go, he would have stormed off, leaving his frustrations to chase after him and eventually exhaust themselves. Instead, he sat down heavily on the nearest rock with his back to the others. He could feel the weight of the darkening sky pressing down on him.

"That was dramatic," said Vaughn. "Move over, or I'll have to sit through you."

Eliott squeezed over grudgingly. He hadn't realized the ghost was anywhere near. "You were eavesdropping."

"Yep," said Vaughn, unabashed. "Or, more listening in. Didn't take much dropping to hear you. Fair foul mood you've got going. Who did what when I wasn't looking?"

"Nothing," said Eliott.

"Nobody did nothing?"

"No, I did nothing! And now Kess and Cyral are doing nothing, and they're happy about it." Eliott forced his chin down through his hands until his fingers laced around the back of his head.

"Well, that's something."

"I spent a whole day tied up, like I was the damsel in distress."

"Yeah, that'd put anyone in a mood. Did they make you wear one of those dunce princess hats with the silk streamers coming down?"

Eliott gave the ghost what he imagined was a withering look. Vaughn, who had nothing to wither, chuckled and said, "There, at least you didn't get a hat."

"But I was useless," said Eliott. "I wanted to help, but I couldn't. And I can't help now. If I heard about me in a saga like this, I'd wonder why I was even in it."

"Don't judge yourself by that stick," said Vaughn. "I'm in a saga, for all of half a line, I'm told. Get killed in something like three words, and if you were going by that, I'd guess you'd say I didn't make much account of myself, either."

Eliott shrugged. A little of his inadequacy slid off his shoulders.

"One story won't be the end," said Vaughn. "You'll have a whole life to show yourself off. Afterlife, too, if you get lucky like me and mine. You could even end up with a horse. But focus on the life part for now. And let Jordan do this his way, whatever that way is. Man's got to do, right?"

"Yeah," said Eliott. "I guess he does."

"I meant you," said Vaughn.

Eliott hesitated. He had grown fond of his sullen mood in his short time with it, but if he was a man, then he could put it away for now. He stood up and walked back to Kess and Cyral. "Sorry," he said quietly. Then, before either of them could make a conversation of it, he focused his attention on the valley again. "So where's Jordan now? Oh, never mind. I see him—"

"Right there," said Kess, pointing.

Their arms crossed. Eliott turned his head slowly,

frowning. Where Kess was pointing, he could barely make out Jordan's broad-shouldered silhouette disappearing around a boulder—but off to the right, he had seen another figure moving through the fog. He stared, wondering if he had imagined it, mistaken a movement of the wind—except that there was no wind. Then, out of the corner of his eye, he saw it again: a pale specter, gliding toward Jordan.

"Is it a ghost?" he asked.

"Ain't a one of mine," said Vaughn.

"No," said Kess. "It's a woman. She looks human."

"The priestess," said Eliott, and he felt an eager thrill tighten every muscle. This was more like it! "I bet it's her—it's got to be! Vaughn, I have to warn Jordan. I need to get down there, right now. Can I have a fast horse?"

"Hell, if that's the priestess that did for Skilling Hayes, I'll take you myself." Vaughn raised his gloved fingers to his masked lips as if blowing a whistle. He made no sound, but his horse perked up and came to him obediently. Before Kess could stop them, before anyone could say another word, Vaughn leapt into the saddle and pulled Eliott up in front of him. Bones clicked, and the horse sprang into the sky, rushing down into the valley at a silent gallop.

JORDAN FROZE.

The dragon still had its back to him, the long slope of its tail curving up into the shadowed canopy of its wings. It beat the air once, wings swelling like sails, and the tendrils of mist woven through the valley went wild. Underneath its wings, the tight sinews of its legs stretched against the ground, ending in talons longer than his arm. Jordan could see its head twisting from side to side as its powerful, agile neck swung around; it was searching for something that had disturbed its sleep, sniffing the air it had set into turmoil. Its eyes were hooded, which Jordan took for a good sign. In the dark, the dragon was as blind as he was, and it was still waking up. He had the advantage.

At least, he reconsidered, he would have the advantage until it decided it could search more easily by firelight.

The dragon lowered its head to the ground and drew its wings back to its body. It gave a final snort and lay still. After a while, the ridges of its spine began to move in the slow, deep rhythms of sleep once again. Jordan gave silent thanks to the damp of the night for hiding his scent. The dragon had given him up for a splinter of a dream.

He waited, watching, until he was sure the dragon was going to stay asleep. Then he eased back against the cold rock and let out the breath he had been holding in. Stupid to the point of suicide was right. There was a reason dragon slayers either went through Central Casting or used large-scale weapons.

A ballista would come in really handy right now, he thought grimly. Or a volcano.

Another splash of rain struck his cheek, and he lifted his dry lips gratefully to the sky.

Eliott waved down at him and grinned.

When the shock and the urge to shout had passed, Jordan stood up and made a series of hand gestures that should have sent the boy back up the hill at speed. Eliott shook his head and gestured back. He slid from his horse and perched on the side of the boulder. Jordan could see his attention fix on the dragon, temporarily stalling whatever foolishness had brought him down here. The distraction gave Jordan enough time to brace himself to help the boy to the ground without making a fatal noise.

The moment Eliott's feet touched the ground, Jordan pressed a hand across his mouth.

Why the hell are you down here? Jordan mouthed.

Eliott gestured and pointed.

Charades, as a parlor game, was still an exclusive pastime of the highest circles of the nobility; neither Jordan nor Eliott had ever played it before. If they had, the next few minutes might have gone easier. Instead, they mutely fumbled through their own complex variation on the game, guessing at each other's meaning. Eventually, Jordan put up his hands in what he hoped was a clear sign of surrender and let Eliott stay.

Then, from somewhere far too close, Jordan heard a faint scraping sound, a loose stone sliding under an incautious foot. He picked up his sword.

In its dream, the dragon heard the sound, too. It let out a low, rumbling yawn. Its tail twitched. Jordan edged around the boulder, watching for the right moment to run. He might have one chance at getting a cut in, or he might have none at all.

He glanced back at Eliott, and caught the boy in the middle of making a face. He pressed a hand against his forehead as a ward against stupidity, and gave Eliott a short, fast gesture that anyone with half a brain would have recognized as "What are you thinking? Cut that out!" but somehow translated into the teenage mind as "What are you doing? Show me that again!"

With a frown, Eliott opened his mouth wide and huffed out a breath that hung frosty in the air. He pointed at the icy mist and gave a questioning shrug.

Jordan shivered. The night had gone suddenly, bitterly cold. The sweat soaking his shirt was freezing against his skin.

It was a familiar cold.

Not now, he thought. Not her.

And at that moment, a corpse lurched out of the dark and threw itself at him.

It was one of the quietest ambushes in the history of attacks by the reanimate dead. The frost-rimed corpse neither groaned nor growled as it strained to get its frozen hands around Jordan's throat, and as it dragged him, choking, to the ground, the thought flashed through his head that he might at least manage to die without waking the dragon. This gave him no comfort at all.

Then Eliott leapt into the struggle, and they all toppled over in a crash of bodies. With a battle cry that would have woken the dead, if they had not already been up and about, Eliott put both fists together and knocked the head of the corpse off its shoulders.

"Idiot," Jordan gasped, staggering free. He found his sword and pointed up at Vaughn. "Eliott—go!"

"I was trying to tell you—"

"Later! We're going to need cavalry."

A blast of wind nearly knocked him off his feet. When he looked, the dragon was fully awake, its giant wings unfurled. It belched a globe of flame into the rocks on the other side of the valley. Jordan barely had time to throw his arm up and avert his eyes. The last thing he needed now was to lose his night vision.

Then, seeing the line of walking corpses emerging from the mist, he changed his mind. There were many more painful last things he needed right now, most involving being dismembered by the risen dead.

"I'll be right back!" Eliott shouted, as Vaughn swooped down and carried him skyward. "We'll be back for you!"

The dragon's head whipped around. Another flare of fire lit the sky overhead, hot on the hooves of the skeletal horse, and the valley was filled with long, sharp shadows. The dead, illuminated, were dappled horrors in ancient furs and leather, blue skin pocked and mottled by slow decay. In the time it took for the flame to go out, Jordan recognized the dead. He knew for certain whose warriors they were.

And on the hillside beyond the advancing dead, he saw her.

What the hell; you only live once, he thought, in spite of current evidence to the contrary. He charged.

And broke through. The dead reached after him, grasping hands clawing at empty air, but Jordan ducked his head and kept running.

Weren't expecting me to do this, were you? he thought, as he pushed himself up the hill. His knees felt like they were on fire.

At the crest of the hill, the woman in white looked down at him with a cold, fierce smile and said, "Ah, my Red Warrior. At last, we meet a— Gmmph!"

Jordan never slowed down. He collided with her with his arms outstretched, knocking her off her feet. She grabbed at him, and they both fell, sliding and scrambling and twisting all the way down the hill until they landed in a gully in a muddy tangle. Jordan stood up, accepted the report from his knees that this was a bad decision, and sank back to the ground. Various factions of his body were currently at war over the right to claim the dominance of agony; the rest would have to settle for merely being brutally sore.

"That," he muttered, "could have gone better."

"Were you trying," said the woman in no-longer-white, "to get us both killed?"

She sat up, wiping the mud from her face and hair. She straightened the iron torc around her neck and spat out what might have been a shard of ice or a tooth.

"No, Your Majesty," said Jordan wearily. He caught his breath and watched it escape again in frozen clouds.

The first law of magic, he thought bitterly and not for

the first time, must be general unfairness. Chemi Two-Blades had been revived in the prime of his youth; Helga, Witch Queen of Hellsbrogdt, had been brought back at an age far past her chain-mail lingerie days, although Jordan had to admit that she still brought a certain presence to a full-length gown of goat's wool and arctic fox fur. He held out his hand, and they helped each other to their feet.

"Better," she said, pulling back her arm. "I know that's you, Jordan, but have you ever gotten old . . ."

Jordan grunted. The chill of touching her had left his fingers red. "And time's treated you with wine and roses. You planning on killing me tonight?"

She shook her head. "Capture. For old times' sake."

"Your bodyguard—"

"Would have strangled you to an inch of your life, then brought you to me, weak and helpless. They'll give us some privacy now." She looked over the edge of the gully. "But, since I've lost the Chains of Everlasting Servitude, I'm going to be improvising here. Sorry."

Jordan grunted. "Always fun with you. How'd you find me, Helga? And who else is on the hunt?"

"Business first? As you like." She leaned against the bank. "Everyone is after you. And I do mean everyone. There was a meeting, and we decided to deal with you before conquering the world—or destroying it; there's still some argument on that point. Most of the brute force is following General Sarod. Did you know he was just a floating head now?"

"Yeah. Not my fault."

"You should see him, being carried around in a bowl by four acolytes of the Crocodile God Zebek—who, by the way, are now secretly worshipping the Nether-God Czaal."

Jordan didn't have time for this. All villains loved to talk at length, but the Witch Queen of Hellsbrogdt could gossip like a fishwife. He interrupted her. "Am I likely to see him?"

"No. Fool that he is, he asked where you went after the battle at the mill. Anyone who knows you wouldn't expect you to stay in one place for long. I asked where you were going to be."

"Asked? Asked who?"

"Gorgos. Do you remember her, the Medusan Oracle?"

"Unfortunately. She was the one sacrificing babies in the caverns of Phorbis. I burned out her eyes."

"And now she's back, and performing divinations for anyone hunting you, in return for the promise that she gets to eat your eyes. She seems to think it's not an unreasonable request, given her history with you."

"Terrific. So the General's taken himself off the map, and you came here with your little bodyguard of dead snowmen—anybody else I should be expecting?"

"I didn't just bring my bodyguard," said the Witch Queen scornfully. "I had an army."

"Lose them, too? You're going to have to do like I do—start leaving yourself little notes."

"The dragon," said Helga, "complicated things. Five thousand ice demons. Who knew they'd melt so fast?"

"Yeah. I wish I'd had a dragon in Brok." Jordan shook his head. One old veteran of heroic sagas to another, he understood the annoyance of a rogue complication. "At least you can count on your walking corpses."

"Eternally. And I see you've begun consorting with ghosts."

Jordan shrugged, giving his injured arm a bit of a twinge. "The spirits were willing."

"I prefer the strength of the flesh," she answered, with a slow smile. "Damn. I've missed this, the banter. I never worked with anyone better after you, you know."

A renegade smirk twitched the corner of Jordan's mouth, unexpected and badly timed, but there. "You threw me some good lines while you were trying to make me a slave in your unholy army of winter. So you kept working?"

"They sent a few handsome young heroes at me, until my contract expired. You fought one of them tonight."

"Poor bastard," said Jordan, without much sympathy. Anyone going into the game knew the penalties for losing.

"It's good to see no one else got the pleasure of your death," Helga admitted. "I will have you myself one day."

"Yeah, over my cold, dead body."

"You're still a flirt." She slapped him lightly on the arm, sending an icy shiver through him. "So, now what? I call my warriors, and you try to escape?"

"May as well. You've told me what I needed." Jordan stretched his back and pulled his sword out of the mud. "Give me a head start?"

"Wait! I haven't told you everything."

"Is this a delaying—"

"No. Shut up and listen to your queen. General Sarod and I aren't the only ones hunting you. The Count and his Egyptian priestess saw the Oracle after me. He asked where he'd catch you if you slipped out of my hands. So think carefully about how fast you really want to run. Would you rather end up with me, or the bloodsucker?"

"I'll keep that in—"

A shadow swept over them, blacking out the watery moon. Giant wings thrummed heavily overhead in long, lazy beats. The dragon curved past and came circling around again. Jordan stood completely still, watching its trajectory.

Oh, right, he thought. The dragon.

"Do you think it can see us?" asked Helga quietly.

"No," said Jordan. "But if it really wants to . . ."

The dragon was nearly above them. Its mouth was open. They saw the glow in its cheeks.

"Run," agreed Helga, and they did, splitting in opposite directions a moment before a gout of searching fire swept up the hillside and into the gully. Flame splashed along the streambed, curling fiercely. By its light, Jordan had a glimpse of the dragon descending into the boulders, its long neck ducking and hunting among the rocks.

The fire went out.

Jordan stumbled on, through a night darker than before. His night vision was gone. He followed the gully until he found a spot where he could climb out. He dragged himself up, knees and elbows in the mud, and hid in the shadow of a boulder. Now all he needed to do was get out in the open and signal down a rider. The sky should be full of them by now.

Or it could be full of dragon, and the valley could be crawling with the Witch Queen's warriors. It was a toss-up.

Only one way to find out.

Jordan broke from the shadows, running toward the first open patch of ground he could see. He waved his arms toward the black and stormy sky. It was beginning to rain again, hard; the drops felt like ice striking his skin.

When he turned around, the dragon was there. For a creature the size of a small barn, it made unbelievably little noise when it moved. It slithered between the boulders with barely a whisper. It bent its neck and stared down at him, cocking its head curiously to one side, as if wondering why he wasn't running away.

Good question, thought Jordan. But, hell, I wasn't going to win by waiting for it to get tired of the chase.

The dragon snorted. Jordan felt its hot breath blow

over him, reeking like the bottom burning out of a pot. It was only a few yards away. One last charge would bring his sword to its neck, or send him down to join Hopley.

And then the dragon closed its left eye. It jerked its head back. It remembered him.

"Yeah," he growled. "That was me. And I'll give you a poke in the other one, too. Let's finish this."

But the dragon pulled back, retreating from him. It stood upright for a moment, and Jordan thought his world was about to end in fire; then the dragon leapt at the sky, its wings spreading wide. Higher it flew, and higher, until the rain and the black clouds swallowed it and it was gone.

"No! No, you get back here," Jordan screamed after it. "Damn you! You don't run away!"

He grabbed a stone out of the mud and flung it up into the dark, a furious, futile gesture.

And someone shouted back, "Watch it!"

Three riders swerved down from the storm, two with their bows drawn and arrows nocked. The third, with Eliott riding before him, was Vaughn, who gave Jordan a lazy salute.

"Been looking all over for you," he called down. "Climb up—there's still plenty of dead men walkin' out tonight, and they don't seem to mind our arrows much."

A horse dipped low, long enough for Jordan to haul himself into the saddle.

"Did you see the dragon?" he said, as they punched upward into the rain. "It's gone—it ran away from me!"

"Hell, the way you look, I'd run away, too," Vaughn called back agreeably. "Go, catch up with everyone else. Amos and I'll scout for it."

Eliott flashed a thumbs-up, and the two horses spurred away, leaving Jordan to ride back angry, soaked, and unsatisfied. The rest of the riders, with Kess and Cyral among them, were perched on the heel of a mountain safely above the valley and the Witch Queen's dead warriors. Jordan gave a quick, terse account of the fight, the whole time watching the sky for Vaughn's return.

It was a short wait. The horses tore out of the rain, water streaming off their bones.

"Any sign?" Jordan shouted, as they touched down. The leading ghost made a broad gesture—NO—and beckoned two more of the riders to follow him back out into the storm. They peeled away from the mountaintop and disappeared again into the churning sky.

"We've lost it," said Vaughn. "Jordan, I'm sorry, but we ain't gonna ride it down in this weather. We'll find a dry patch for you four that need it, and pick up the search in daylight."

"Oh, yes, please," said Cyral, a wet sack of misery.

"It knows we're after it," said Jordan, "and I've got at least two armies chasing after me. We need to keep flying."

"Where to? Blind? In circles? We could end up a hundred miles off in the wrong direction."

"It's okay," said Eliott brightly. "I know where it's going."

They looked at him expectantly.

"Or, I'm pretty sure I do, because if it isn't going after you, Jordan, then I think it's got to be trying to finish what it was planning to do when you killed it the first time— what the Brethren of the Shining Dawn ultimately wanted it to do!"

He paused to breathe. Jordan seized the opportunity. "Which was?"

"Kill wizards! All wizards." Eliott grinned. "Starting with the biggest gathering of wizards in the world—the Wizards' Conclave in the Central Casting building in Palace Hills!"

FOURTEEN

DAWN CAME TO Palace Hills in colors of pearl and crystal, another perfect day in the closest thing to paradise money could buy. There were laws against bad weather within the city limits, and because the city housed the largest body of wizards in the world, those laws were obeyed as rigidly as the laws of gravity. Some cities never sleep; Palace Hills was a city worth sleeping in, for the pleasure of having it be the first thing you saw when you woke up. It was a city for morning people.

Not surprisingly, it also had the best coffee in the world.

Glister Starmacher breezed into his office with a double-cream, double-foam wyvern-roast arabicano and a gleaming smile ready to make stories and influence people. He read his agenda, complimented his secretary, checked his hair in the mirror, and took the black cloth off his crystal ball.

A face was waiting for him inside it.

It said, "Starmacher. We need to talk. Do you know who we are?"

Glister, trying surreptitiously and frantically to dab hot coffee off his leg, looked deeper into the crystal ball. A second face was squeezing in beside the first, pale and gaunt as the first face was dark and round. The pale man said nothing, but drew back his lips in a feral sneer, revealing teeth that begged for a dentist, most likely as a snack. The dark woman pushed him out of sight again.

"Do you know who we are?" she repeated.

"Yes," said Glister unhappily.

"Good. Go out and hire a wizard to conjure us to you. One hour. Close your curtains."

A small part of his essential nature rebelled. "You know travel costs were never part of your contract," he managed.

"The terms are changing," said the dark woman. "And you will want to pick up the bill for this. We're going to bring you the greatest story you will ever get to sell."

IT WAS AN hour later. The curtains were closed. As an added courtesy, Glister had hung a black drape over the mirror behind his desk. In all, it made his office feel small, dark, and cramped, like the inside of a coffin. Even his similes were being redecorated to suit his visitors.

He focused on the business at hand.

"And you're absolutely certain he's coming back here? That's a big commitment you're asking for . . . a really, really big one . . ."

He swallowed uncomfortably, and immediately regretted it. Anything that called attention to his throat was, at this moment, a very bad idea.

"We are sufficiently confident," said the dark woman, smiling like a snake. Everything about her was serpentine, from the shape of her bangles to the golden scales of her priestly regalia to the sinuous way she shifted her weight from side to side as she leaned across the back of the chair in which her companion sat. She kept one hand on him all the time, as if her touch was the only thing restraining him. It quite possibly was.

High Priestess of the apocryphal Khol-Ra, the snake that consumes the sun. Glister had spent fifteen minutes digging through his old files to find her. The last of a long line of priestesses who had, in antiquity, provided Cleopatra with a pet asp. Jordan the Red had defeated her and destroyed her sisterhood in "The Burning Sky," a short saga Glister had forgotten about until his secretary reminded him that it was the one with the harem scene.

"Let me get this straight." Glister drummed his manicured fingers against his desk. "You want me to kill off Jordan the Red, effectively destroying any future equity I could make from a revival of his franchise. And you want me to fund the entire operation? Tell me why, exactly, would I be doing this? I mean, hey, you both gave a great effort your first time around, but it didn't go so well for you. Honestly. I'm not sold on doing it again."

Under the priestess's firm grip, the pale Count of Coldstone Castle growled quietly. If the rumor was true, that he could turn into a wolf, he had apparently forgotten to change his larynx back with the rest of him.

Glister held up his hands. "Okay, okay. Sell me on it. What's your pitch?"

"His enemies are back. All of his enemies. Sooner or later, they will catch up with him, and he will die. Do you want to let that happen somewhere out in the wilderness, where no one will ever hear about it? Or do you want to be in control, with your bards there to capture the pretty story of his death . . ." The priestess leaned forward. She gave him a hooded, smoldering look that could have lured any number of serpents out of baskets, and Glister had to admit, she made a compelling argument.

"We aren't alone this time, either," she continued, passing her hold on the Count from left hand to right. "Jordan is one man. He can defeat one army, or one enemy, or one plan at a time. But right now, he has a hundred reasons to watch his back. He'll be distracted when he faces us. Two contrasting strengths, working together. Night and Day. Sun and Moon. Does that fill you with confidence, Mr. Starmacher?"

"Very . . . filling. Yes."

"Then you can be the missing piece of the story. Don't wait to hear it from somebody else. You have the resources to give Jordan the Red the glorious ending he so richly deserves, the creatures to harass and weary him, the enchantments to make a spectacle of the event. We just need to know when he draws close. And we need a stage . . . for the execution."

Bards, thought Glister. Every bard I can hire. If that fool I sent out to trail Jordan ever makes it back, we can splice his side of this in afterward. Special effects. Pyrotechnics. This is going to be a crazy day for Central Casting.

"Now, tell me," said the priestess, "do we have a new contract? Or do you want us to wake you up when it's over?"

Glister shook his head hastily. "What are you going to need first?"

"Bats," growled the Count. "Lots of bats."

"To scout for us," said the priestess. She stroked the Count's white hair. "He's a traditionalist."

"That, I can do for you," said Glister, flipping through a drawer of index cards with a manic energy in his fingers. "The Central Casting catalogue. Never create something new if you can use something they have in stock. Bats . . . demon bats . . . Here we go. Used these for atmosphere in the Boneyard of D'loom, in Phorbis . . . a little saga called the 'Necromanticore.' Ever hear it? No, sorry; you'd have been dead by then . . . Winnie! A monkey to Central Casting, straight away—we'll need five, no, make it eight hundred of the *Chiroptera Osedax*, however you say that—Number 379—for immediate delivery."

As his secretary hurried to place the order, Glister Starmacher sat back in his chair and put his hands behind his head. "That's money invested. We're partners in this. Now, you're not going to let me down, are you? You'll make it look good; you'll do it with style. And you will follow through, right? At the end of the day, the payoff is going to be Jordan the Red, dead. Agreed?"

"Completely agreed," said the priestess.

Glister grinned. In his head, he was already casting the next rising young hero who would kill the unholy alliance of villains currently sitting on the other side of his desk. Kill them, save the city, and avenge the death of Jordan the Red. It was turning out to be a beautiful day.

FAR AWAY FROM Palace Hills, the promise of a beautiful day was a yellow light through the rainstorm, and the ghosts flew toward it at a full gallop. By Vaughn's best guess, they were still two days of hard riding away from the city, but with the storm finally easing and the rising sun to aim for, they swore horsemen's oaths not to slow down until they reached Palace Hills or intercepted the dragon.

"We'll take you up, soon's the sky warms," Vaughn

shouted cheerfully. "Get you above the clouds. Give y'all a real, proper view of the range!"

Cyral, huddled in front of Vaughn, made a noncommittal sound. Appreciating the view would mean opening his eyes. He was much happier with the flight as long as he didn't actually have to see it happening.

Palace Hills. The thought of it kept him going. Soon, he would be back in a proper city, where people behaved normally and nobody got attacked by goblins or eaten by dragons, and there was no danger of the municipal gardens suddenly springing to life and stealing hats. The stories would be just stories again.

"And here we go," said Vaughn.

Cyral tensed, digging his fingers into the old leather saddle. He had lost time, dozing off. The stinging rain scouring his face had stopped, and they were rising, up into the warmth of the sun on the other side of the clouds. He risked opening one eye.

Endless sky greeted him. Plains and pastures, rolling fields of clouds, gray and white and eggshell, stretching out to infinity. The sun was higher than he had expected, and rising, but still low enough that Cyral could imagine the horses changing the angle of their flight and riding up onto it. The thought made him shudder, and then laugh out loud in spite of himself. From here, he could fly into the sun. He could stroll around on the moon.

It was madness, but for the first time, it was a pleasant, calm madness.

"I fell asleep," he said, "and didn't wake up dead!"

He looked around, both eyes open now. Kess gave him a friendly wave, and he tried to remember how to smile back. In the shadowless light of day, the ghosts were practically invisible; she and Eliott and Jordan might have been wrangling the herd of skeletal horses on their own.

"Hey! Cyral!" Eliott called out. "Isn't this great? I bet you can see your house from here!"

And reality returned. Below the fantastical up, there was long, terrifying down. He pinched his eyes closed and screwed himself to the saddle.

"Eliott!" said Kess sharply. "What'd you do that for?"

"What?"

"You know he's . . ."

Their voices drifted away on the wind. Cyral let them go, shutting them out in favor of other, land-based thoughts. He tried to recall the rhyme schemes of different types of sonnets in his head—Oh, God, Oh, God, I am going to fall / A man's natural place is not the sky / A bird could live; I am going to die / I do not like this wild flying at all—but even classical poetics turned against him—

"You remember the 'Coldstone Castle Saga'?" said Jordan, suddenly close by.

"Of course," said Vaughn. "Bastard Count selling us out—"

"Not you," said Jordan. "Him. Cyral. You remember that one?"

Cyral let a small noise of agreement escape through his nose.

"Tell me about it."

"What?"

"Tell me," Jordan repeated, "about the saga. How I beat the Count. Helga says he's going to be waiting for me. You going to let me walk into that unprepared? Give me a refresher."

Cyral turned slowly, every movement risking a plummet. "Is this your way of—"

"Yes. Now, tell me the damn story."

He cracked one eye open. He had to be sure.

One corner of Jordan's mouth was turned up slightly.

"All right," said Cyral. "Well, er, you cut his head off and took a jar of pickled—"

"Not like that," said Jordan. "Give me the whole thing properly, prologue and verse. Do you know it or don't you?"

"Er . . . yes. But is this—"

"It's the perfect time. What else have we got to do? I've looked at clouds plenty of times before. From both sides. Now . . ."

Falteringly, dropping and repeating lines, Cyral began to tell the saga of Coldstone Castle, as he had heard and rehearsed it so many times before during his apprenticeship. Gradually, it all came back to him, the words spilling from his memory without needing to engage his brain. When he reached the part where Jordan was ambushed by the Count's marauding horsemen, and defeated them in a single line, a general cheer went up from the ghosts. When he described the death of the Count, the shouts and hollers came twice as loud.

"And we'll do it again!" one of the ghosts declared.

At the end, Cyral licked his parched lips and said nothing for a while. Eventually, he looked at Jordan and asked, "Was that good? Did that tell you what you wanted?"

Jordan grunted. "Yeah. Thought that was how it went."

"You did a way better job than the last bard I heard do it," said Eliott, on the other side of Cyral. "And you didn't cut out any of the blood."

Cyral frowned. He tried to read Jordan's face, which was rather like trying to decipher the financial markets of Byzantium by looking at the rings of a thousand-year-old tree stump. "Was that how it actually happened?"

"Something like that," said Jordan. "Less pretty. I was cold, wet, and tired most of the time, and things with sharp, pointy bits jumped out at me a lot. Sort of like this trip we're on now."

"But you did save the village."

"Oh, yeah. Just like it says. Someone needed to do it." Jordan shrugged. "Of course, by the time I got there, they'd been living under the shadow of that castle for eight years, saying to themselves, Someone needs to do it. They could have done it at any time without me."

"But you were the one who—"

"Had to. I was the hero, right? Passing through the neighborhood, everybody leaps on the idea I'm there to save them . . . which I probably was. Glister always set up my travel itinerary. One little village needing saving after the next, week after week. Year after year."

"No wonder they called you a hero, then," said Cyral. "That sounds unhuman. I'd have been exhausted."

"First thing you learn. Endurance. Get to the end." Jordan shook his head. "Yeah, I was pretty damn tired most of the time. But there was always someplace new to go, something that needed to be done. Good deeds, bad monsters. Someone looking to pick a fight, because they could. You know them all."

Years like this, thought Cyral. He had never counted the stories before; now he thought about it, he couldn't even remember them all. The long sagas and the short anecdotes, the comicals . . .

"I can't imagine how you could spend a lifetime doing it," he admitted.

"Me neither," said Jordan. "That's why I got out. Retired, remember? I got to the end, and I walked away. And soon as we kill this dragon, I'll do that again. Peace and quiet."

Cyral said nothing. He felt the lump of his notebook pressing into his stomach, full of experiences and observations about traveling with Jordan the Red, many of them unkind and unforgiving. He wondered if other bards had made the same notes, before taking their stories back to the city and turning them into sagas of high adventure.

"Vaughn! Right below us!"

A skeletal horse broke through the clouds, its rider briefly visible as a twist of the air. "Straight down, beside the bridge goin' over the big river," the rider shouted.

"The dragon? Have we found it?" said Eliott.

"Nope," said Vaughn. "We've found you a restaurant."

"About time," said Jordan.

They dropped out of the sky, and in a minute, they saw the restaurant, an inn on the bank of a broad river, under the sign of a willow tree. The smoke rising from its chimney carried the scent of baked apples and roasted meat. A dozen horses were already tied up in the innyard when the four skeletal ones bearing living riders touched the earth.

Eliott dismounted at once and ran up to the inn door, knocking loudly. "Service! Hey, can we get some service here—come on, open up; we're starving out here!"

The innkeeper came up to the door, grumbling right up to the moment when he needed to appear hospitable. He looked out at the four horsemen in his yard—a warrior with a sword, a skinny boy demanding to be fed, Kess hidden under her gray cloak and hood, and Cyral looking sickly green and ill—and screamed.

In case this was the local custom, Eliott screamed back. Then he shrugged. "So, yeah. How about some food?"

"It's the end of the world," said the innkeeper, and fainted cold.

When the panic and the running was over, they rode away with as much food as they could carry and four warm, quilted blankets, leaving a handful of coins in the innkeeper's apron at Jordan's insistence. Then they were off the ground and airborne once again.

"Got our bearings while you was down there," said a

ghost. "We're going to follow this road all the way to Palace Hills. If you see a coach, give a shout—we'll stop and ask 'em if we're goin' the right way."

"Plus," said another, "it's fun to skim over 'em."

But they saw no coaches, nor any sign of the dragon, through the rest of that day or the following night. They were glad of the road when the rain caught up with them again, in the middle of the night, and through the thick autumn fog that followed after. It was only when noon had burned away the fog on the second day of their ride that they began to find other travelers on the road, and by then, they could see Palace Hills sitting like an ivory crown on the eastern horizon.

"We'll be there before sundown," said Vaughn. "You ready to give this dragon-killing business another shot?"

"Yeah," said Jordan. "Think you can fly me close enough to drop me on its back?"

The ghost laughed. "Sure, why not. Ain't like it'll be the death of me to get too hot."

The city drew closer. The sprawling white palaces and villas decorating the five hills took shape among the forest of towers. Burnished copper and glass shone red in the echoed light of the setting sun. The fumes of a half million people living together, the rich and those who accommodated them, hung over everything, making it as hazy as a mirage.

But there was still no sign of the dragon.

"Did it already get there?" said Eliott. "Maybe it's already lying in the ruins of Central Casting. Are we too late?"

He looked around expectantly. "Well, somebody always says it, right?"

"Maybe they already killed it for us," said Kess, but she sounded unconvinced. "There's smoke. But I don't think it's from a dragon."

"There's always smoke," said Jordan. "Whole city'd be choking on it if they didn't magic it out to designated areas. Let's get in there."

"Wait," said Kess. "There's something rising. Black. Some black band around the city."

"More smoke," said Jordan.

"No. It's got . . . wings. Hundreds of wings. A swarm of . . ."

"Hey, yeah," said Eliott. "I can see it, too. I think it's coming toward us."

"We're gonna be ridin' through it anyway," said Vaughn. "You'll have a real good, up-close look."

". . . Bats," said Kess.

"Oh, no. No. Shit." Jordan twisted in the saddle, reaching for his sword, then changing his mind. "Bats. Really big bats? Freakishly, unnaturally big bats? Full moon, carry off small children, can't-stop-here big?"

They all stared at him, even the ghosts.

"They are big," Kess conceded.

"Phorbis," said Jordan. He spat the word like a profanity. "Vaughn, you need to put us down now. Before they—"

Something dark whirred past. It was indeed big. Cyral had a glimpse of red eyes and a mouth stretched out like a gargoyle with a dislocated jaw.

"They're bats," said Vaughn. "We can dodge 'em. Do it all the time, for sport. Swat 'em if they get too close."

"No, dammit! Down! For your own good. Every terrible thing I fought before, they all came back. These aren't normal bats. They're bats out of hell—demon bats from the Boneyard of— Look, they're bone-eating bats!"

And then they heard the screams.

The skeletal horses had nothing left in them to cry out their pain, but their riders had voices, and rider and horse were one spirit together. One and then another of the lead horses tumbled from the sky, black wings clinging to their ribs and skulls, white shards of bone splintering away. The ghosts fell howling.

"Down! Now!" yelled Vaughn.

"Bone-eating bats?" said Cyral, as they raced for the road. "Who comes up with these creatures!"

"Central Casting," Jordan shouted back. "They'll summon, mutate, or breed you any sort of monster you like—whatever your saga needs! Got a graveyard? Here's a freak hell-bat! Throw something new and different at your heroes today!"

"This would be the same Central Casting we're going to rescue right now?"

"Yeah. Fun business, ain't it?"

They hit the road. Jordan pushed himself out of the saddle at the first crunch of hooves on dirt, slapped the bony flank of his horse, and sent it skyward again. "Go! Go!"

"Good luck to you!" called Vaughn, as he rallied his riders. They wheeled and turned toward the setting sun, throwing arrows like slivers of starlight back into the swarming bats. In the last rays of daylight, he turned back and tipped his hat to Jordan; then he was gone, riding into the sunset with the bats of hell flying after him.

"Now what do we do?" said Cyral, dusting himself off.

"We get inside the city and under shelter," said Jordan. He strode toward the city gates, pushing through the carts and pedestrians brought to a halt by the spectacle in the sky. Some of them were applauding.

Kess hurried after him at a backward jog, her face still turned toward the departing riders. She called his name. He stopped. "What?"

"The dragon," said Kess. "We were faster."

He followed her pointing arm to a shape on the horizon. It might have been a bat returning, but it was growing larger far too swiftly.

"Faster, or it stopped for the night, or it got lost in the fog," she continued. "I don't know. But there it is."

Eliott scrunched up his face in thought. "Average airspeed of an unladen dragon . . ."

"Who cares," said Jordan. "We're ahead of it and we know where it's going. Let's get to Central Casting."

GLISTER TAPPED ON the dark surface of his crystal ball until he got the attention of the high priestess on the other end.

"Yes?" she said.

"We're getting the first reports back from the bats. You were right on the money—Jordan the Red has reached the city. He's coming in through the southwest gate."

"About time," said the priestess. "Send out the ghouls."

"Yes . . ." said Glister, stretching out the vowel uncomfortably. "About them . . . You wouldn't believe the hoops I had to jump through to get permission from the city for this stunt. We won't have any problems, will we? Tell me we're not going to be liable for anyone getting eaten—the Count will keep them under control."

"Send out the ghouls," the priestess repeated. "And I'll come up to your office to personally reassure you."

Her face disappeared from the crystal ball. Glister shivered.

"Winnie," he called to his secretary. "Tell Central Casting to release the ghouls. And cancel the rest of this evening's appointments."

THE STREETS WERE packed, in an untidy way befitting a city where the majority of its residents had a lot of luggage and someone else to iron things out for them. Jordan shouldered his way through the crowd, leaving the others to follow in his wake as best they could. It was an uphill battle.

"We aren't going to get there in time," said Jordan. "How does anyone get around in this city?"

"Transport," said Cyral, back in his element. "The carts never stop moving."

"Then find one we can point in the right direction and let's get on, before anyone sees the dragon and panics."

"I think what we're looking for," said Cyral, "is right over there."

"Oh, fantastic . . ."

The coach was long, white, and decorated with a desperate excess of fretwork and canopies. The two workhorses pulling it had feathery plumes on their halters. It was the most unheroic vehicle imaginable.

But the sign on the side said, TOUR BEAUTIFUL PALACE HILLS: SEE THE MAGIC AT CENTRAL CASTING.

A dozen people were already on board, and the coach was moving.

Jordan grabbed the coach rail and pulled himself on.

"Central Casting," he ordered the driver, "and don't spare the whip."

"Right you are, sir. Four of you? That'll be two and twenty, please, and take a seat to the rear."

"Kess, pay the man."

"I left what I had at that inn. Don't you have any money?"

"Not on me," said Jordan. "Cyral? Eliott?"

Cyral shook his head.

"Look, sweethearts, if you can't pay, you can't take the tour," said the driver. "Come on, you're holding everyone up."

"I've got . . . No, shoot, that's just chocolate," said Eliott, rummaging in his pockets. "Stone . . . string . . . Oh, huh, didn't know I still had that . . . I'm sorry, Jordan. But—hey, you've got your sword! You could threaten him and make him take us to Central Casting!"

"What? No—I'm not threatening some innocent coach driver," said Jordan, putting his hand on the driver's shoulder. "What sort of sagas are they telling kids these days?"

"You don't have to say you'll kill him," said Eliott. "But say, like, you'll cut his ear off if he doesn't cooperate. You wouldn't even have to really do it, just make the threat."

He gave the driver an encouraging grin. "That'd be good enough for you, right? Can we try it?"

Kess reached around and dropped a handful of gold coins into the fare box. "Here. I had some after all. Can we go?"

"As you say, ma'am."

The driver cracked his whip and the tour coach lurched forward. Jordan and Eliott stumbled into seats on one side, while Kess and Cyral took the other.

"I thought you had no money," said Cyral, under his breath.

"That was elf gold," Kess whispered back. "Fairy money. It'll disappear at sunrise. I hate doing that trick. It's gotten me thrown out of more bars . . ."

They sat back. The coach rumbled on. Jordan borrowed a handful of peanuts from one of the other passengers.

"Are we going to get there in time?" said Eliott, who seemed incapable of sitting still.

"Yes," said Jordan. "This is faster than walking, and we know we're going the right way."

"—and if you look over to the left, you'll see some of the very first houses built in this district of Palace Hills, before the Great Fire," said the driver. "You can tell by the very distinctive brickwork."

"Nothing more we can do right now," said Jordan, "so sit down, save your energy, and enjoy the tour."

"—coming up on the famous intersection of Fifth Street and Pie, where you may see the heroes of some of the very latest sagas being violently ejected from tavern brawls—"

"Lightweights," muttered Jordan.

"—and again, to the left, you can see the original Alec James Apothecary, where many of those same heroes buy the healing herbs and magical elixirs that get them back on their feet in time to slay the trolls and goblins that you know they slay so well—"

Kess leapt to her feet. "That could work!"

"What, a magic potion?" said Cyral.

"Yes! No—I'll see! I'll catch up to you."

"—and coming at us on the right, an impressive number of ghouls, obviously the product of Central Casting's Posthumous Creature Shop. You can recognize that they're ghouls by the manes of fetid hair, still matted with grave dirt. Don't they look fierce, folks? Let's give a round of applause to the wizards at Central Casting."

There was scattered clapping. Kess swung herself over the side of the coach and fell behind.

Eliott rushed to the back of the coach. "Kess! Wait!" he shouted. "You're going to miss the ghouls!"

"I'll catch up," she called back. "See you there!"

"—in fact, folks, it looks like we're going to get a very close view of those ghouls as they are, in fact, now chasing after us. This is a rare treat, as ghouls are not normally part of this tour. Again, please keep your heads, arms, and any other edible parts of your bodies safely inside the coach at all times—"

"Now can you give those horses some more whip?" Jordan growled at the driver.

"Hyah! Gee-up!"

"How fast can ghouls run?" said Cyral. "Aren't they all dead and rotting? We should be able to get away from them easily—"

"Oh, like that'd be exciting for an audience. Central Casting makes them extra fast. They can run—"

Something landed with a thump on the canopy roof of the coach. Jordan stabbed it. A ghoul tumbled off onto the street.

"—and they can jump."

"Hyah! Gee-up!"

The other passengers were beginning to realize there was something wrong with the horde of hairy, slavering corpses fighting its way through the street toward them. Only half the tour group applauded as a clawed hand hooked onto the running board; the other half made far more appropriate sounds of panic. The coach skidded past a lamppost, and the ghoul broke away.

"Jordan, we've got to do something," said Cryal urgently. "They're coming from every alley—we can't stay on this coach with all these people."

The coach lurched as something—Cyral prayed it was a ghoul—went under the wheels. Jordan grabbed onto him and kept him on his feet. "Think you can outrun them? No? Then hang on and be ready to hit anything that jumps us."

A ghoulish head appeared over the side of the coach. Jordan brought his fist down on it.

"Running water," said Eliott suddenly. "They can't cross it! Hey—driver guy! We need to go over some running water."

"Another one gets that close, I'll be providing it," said the driver, who was shaking. "Wattling Street Bridge, coming up."

"Are you sure about that?" asked Cyral, as Eliott returned to the back of the coach.

"Well, yeah. I read about it in a magazine."

Cyral looked back. "I hope the ghouls read it, too . . ."

"If we see a bookstore, I bet I could get them a copy." Eliott grinned. "They'd probably have to share it around, but that'd slow them down, too, right?"

"Eliott. I don't know if you're trying to be silly or helpful," said Jordan, "but stop it."

"Hold on!" screamed the driver.

The coach thundered across the bridge, barely avoiding a collision with a brewers' wagon coming the other way with an illegally large number of barrels strapped to it. There was a crash as the wagon hit the bridge railing. Barrels burst free, carts and pedestrians swerved to avoid them, and the whole of the Wattling Street Bridge twisted itself into a hopeless traffic jam. The tour coach shot out the other side, leaving the ghouls blocked off behind them.

"Woohoo!" Eliott punched the air. "See? Told you! They can't cross running water!"

"Not over that bridge, anyway," said Cyral. "Nor can anybody else, by the look of things. Well done."

"Folks, we're now coming up," said the driver, "on the Central Casting building. We are pleased to give you . . . a twenty-minute stop to look around . . . and have your picture sketched outside the famous arched gates . . . by one of the many local artists. Please tip generously . . ."

"Right," said Jordan. "This is our stop."

FIFTEEN

WALTER GAST, OF the Central Casting Elite Wizard Guard, fought back the terrible urge to chew at the hangnail on his thumb. It was the third straight week he'd been stuck on evening gate duty, meaning most of his night would be spent standing stiffly at attention for the benefit of no tourists at all. At least on the day shift, people came up and posed with him, getting their pictures sketched with the handsome young wizard in his fine red robe and black, pointy bearskin hat.

He started to feel a bit better when he saw the white tour coach come racing around the corner, until all the passengers jumped out and ran away. Even the driver ran off, which normally happened only when the tour inspectors were going around checking licenses.

The only ones who didn't run were a trio of filthy beggars who had obviously hitched a ride. Walter hoped they weren't going to come over.

They came over.

"Open the gate," said the oldest of the three. His clothes were torn and stained with mud, and his face was red and bruised from fighting. He had a sword. "We're here to see the wizards."

"Central Casting's not open to the public, Grandpa," said Walter. He knew he was supposed to respect war veterans and the elderly, but that was in general terms, not in the sense of having to deal with deranged old men carrying swords.

"Please," said one of the others, who wore the ragged remains of an old-fashioned bardic suit, "it really is an emergency. There's a dragon—"

"Not open to the public. Take a walk."

The beggars withdrew to the other side of the street. They held an animated conference of whispers. Walter watched them with bored curiosity, thinking that this would be the most interesting thing he'd have to deal with all night. As it would turn out, he was completely wrong.

The old beggar returned, looking unhappy. He stopped and glanced back at the other two. "You sure this is the only way?"

"Yes!"

He swore and muttered his way back to Walter. "Look," he began, leaning in confidentially. He smelled like he had forgone bathing for a week in favor of wrestling with pigs. Dead pigs. "I didn't want to bring this up, but I'm Jordan the Red. That's my bard back there, and my . . . apprentice. We need to get inside for a saga. If you don't let us through those gates, a lot of people are going to die. Got that?"

Walter blinked. "What, really? You're really Jordan the

Red? Gee. It's an honor to meet you—can I have your autograph?"

He cradled his Elite Wizard Guard fighting staff in one arm and dug in his robe for a pen and a bit of paper.

The old man took them grudgingly. "Fine. Now will you open the damn gates?"

Walter smirked. "Yeah, as soon as you sign it, 'Piss off and be crazy somewhere else.' Keep it; it's for you," he added, as the paper was thrown back at him.

"Idiot—pointy-headed—"

"Try it, 'Jordan,'" said Walter, raising his staff.

The old man retreated, still shouting, "Tell them there's a dragon coming! Get everyone out!"

Walter shook his head and smoothed out his robes. The day shift never had to deal with crazy beggars. They got to have all the fun.

JORDAN DRAGGED CYRAL and Eliott around the corner, still cursing all wizards, guards, and the general stupidity of the human race. They sat down on a bench carefully placed for the best possible view of the circular walls of Central Casting. The last light of the setting sun gleamed off the central glass dome and the forest of towers and statues around the roof. It was a marvel of architecture, breathtaking, awe-inspiring, and, at the moment, a complete pain in the rear.

"There's no other way in?" asked Eliott. "A back door or a secret passage through the sewers or something?"

"You've got a weird obsession with sewers, kid," said Jordan. "Did you know that? But, no. That gate's the only way in. Enchanted, too. Try to force your way in and you get turned into a frog."

"What about the windows? Some of them aren't even

glassed in—there's got to be some rope around, and I could throw a hook—"

"Those aren't windows. They're monkey holes."

"So?"

Jordan glared at the building. "So, only authorized courier monkeys can use 'em. I've heard about thieves trying to get in that way. It doesn't go well."

"More frogs?"

"And frog-eating snakes living in the stonework."

"Ew."

They sat in thoughtful silence as the shadows deepened around them. In the distance, the screaming and the snarling of the ghouls grew louder, slowly drowning out the normal sounds of the city.

"That came from this side of the river," said Cyral. "I guess they can cross water after all. We'll be running away soon?"

"Where to? We're here," said Jordan. He glared at the impenetrable walls of Central Casting. "And we can't get in."

"Then we fight," said Eliott, standing up and drawing an imaginary sword. "No more running—we stand our ground and fight the ghouls, and when the dragon gets here, they'll have to let us in."

"That's about what it looks like," said Jordan grimly. "Either that, or we get eaten by ghouls outside the gate while the wizards get cooked."

"That's not going to happen," said Eliott, with absolute confidence. For one brief moment, before he could repel the thought, Jordan wished he could be the boy's age again, immortal in his own mind.

"There's a lot of ghouls out there," he said, trying to chip away the optimism as gently as possible.

"But you're going to fight them. And then you're going to fight the dragon."

Jordan nodded. He dragged his thumb down the flat of his sword. There were more notches than he remembered. "Yeah. I am. And I'm probably going to die."

"You can't die," said Eliott dismissively. "You're a hero."

"I'm retired. I gave up the invulnerability with the rest of the benefits package."

"No, I mean, you're . . . you know. My hero. You saved me from that wizard, and you kept us all alive, and you never gave up . . . except, sort of, that one time on Shortfall . . . but you kept going the whole way. And, yeah, you're old, but that hasn't stopped you, either. You still kick some serious ass when we get attacked. I know you're going to do it again when that dragon gets here. I believe in you."

Eliott stopped, suddenly awkward and out of breath. "So, yeah. That dragon's totally dead."

Thirty-seven notches in the blade, thought Jordan. Weeds growing in the cracks between the cobblestones. Eight statues visible on the Central Casting roof. There were a million things he could look at besides the boy's face.

Damn his imagination.

"Still have to get inside first," said Jordan.

"Oh, right," said Eliott. He found a pebble and flicked it at the wall for lack of anything better to do. It bounced off the stonework and turned into a moth. "Stupid wizards."

"Monkeys," said Cyral.

"Stupid monkeys?"

"No . . . Monkey holes. That's how we could get in. I know someone who has flying monkeys we could use," Cyral continued, in the slow tones of a man chewing over an unpleasant-tasting idea. "Jordan . . . you know him too . . ."

"I do?"

"His office isn't far from here . . ."

"Who— Oh, no. No."

Eliott peered from one to the other. "Who're we talking about? Who's got monkeys?"

"Glister Starmacher," said Jordan. He got to his feet. "Oh, yes. He could help us. Or we could draw a nice magic circle right here and summon a demon to help us, instead! Because, yes, I would rather sell my soul than have to deal with that gold-toothed snake again."

There was a puff of smoke and a small, red imp appeared on the cobblestones in front of him. It waggled a cigar at him, held out a long contract, and said, "You got it, buddy—now buying souls at premium rates! Sign it away for cash now!"

Jordan swatted it away with the flat of his sword. It hit the side of the Central Casting building and turned into an angry red pigeon.

"Sarcasm," he said flatly. "Oh, hell with it. Come on, you two. Let's go see my agent."

ON THE OTHER side of the river, the bell rang inside the Alec James Old-Fashioned Apothecary Shoppe. When no one immediately answered, it rang again, loudly and violently, as if the ringer had pulled it down from above the door and was now ringing it by hand—which was in fact what Kess had done. She dropped it onto the counter as the apothecary shuffled out of the back room.

"Yes? What can I get you today, besides some patience? Tinctures, powders, healing herbs?"

Kess told him.

The apothecary looked sympathetic. "Of course. Important for a beauty like you to stay in the right shape in this town, isn't it? Be careful with how much you take; that's all I'll say. None of my business otherwise. How much will you want?"

He set a large bottle on the counter.

Kess worked out the math in her head. "All of it."

"All? What do you mean, all? That's four pints there."

Kess gave him a tight smile with exactly no patience in it. "Yes. And I'll take it all."

"Supplying an amazon army, are you? An ounce after meals is all you need—"

She grabbed his hand, and the apothecary suddenly found himself holding a small fortune in gold coins. She could feel guilty about it later, she decided. "Now, give me the bottle."

The apothecary slid it across to her. "Anything else?"

"Yes. What's the fastest way to get to Central Casting?"

"Traffic this time of day? Fly."

Kess gave him a searing look that would have made her grandmother proud. "I'll find it myself," she said, and left the shop.

"Sorry—sorry. Come back," said the apothecary, but she was gone. He leaned on the counter and took off his cap. His ears were suddenly feeling hot and itchy . . . and longer . . . and furrier. When he shouted after her again, he was braying.

THE CURTAINS WERE drawn across Glister's second-floor office windows, but to Jordan's disappointment, there was a light burning behind them. He steeled himself and pushed open the familiar doors. Everything looked the same as he remembered it. The awful yellow carpet on the stairs still crunched the same way; the waiting room

still had the same stale smell of hope. The tapestries on
the walls advertised different heroes, but they were still
essentially the same. There was even one with his smirk-
ing face on it, one fist raised under the rugged embroidery
of his jaw. He looked about forty years younger. Jordan
shivered.

Glister's secretary watched the three men suspiciously
as they crossed the waiting room. Jordan could see the
words "Can I help you?" which are never in fact an offer
of help, beginning to form on her lips. Then she glanced
at his tapestry. She rested her chin on her hand. "Oh," she
said, "it's you."

The same secretary.

"You know, you look just like your mother," said Jordan. He shook his head. "Winnie, right? I remember you
when you were crawling."

"That doesn't happen so much now," said Winnie.
"You here to see Mr. Starmacher?"

"Actually, maybe we don't need to bother him," said
Cyral suddenly. "Could you do us a favor, miss? We need
to borrow three flying monkeys to get into Central Casting. It's all part of the saga—and Mr. Starmacher did say
he'd take care of any transportation I needed."

"Sorry, hon. It's all enchanted. No flights without Mr.
Starmacher's personal voice authorization."

Jordan patted Cyral on the shoulder. "Nice try." Then,
to Winnie, he said, "Is he in his office?"

Winnie hesitated long enough to be sure the door to
Glister's office was shut. "Yeah. He's in a meeting right
now. But he's expecting you."

A warning prickle crept up Jordan's back and curled
around his neck. He could feel the shape of the trap,
the outline of its iron jaws. His enemies had an oracle
on their side, and the advantage of knowing where he

was going to be before he did. They knew he was coming here.

Through that door.

He smirked back at his face on the wall. If he was an inevitability, he was going to be a painful one.

"Thanks," he said, as he passed by Winnie's desk. "I owe you one."

She sniffed dismissively. "Mother said you told her that all the time, but you never gave her one."

"My loss."

He pushed open the door.

"Glister. I need your monkeys. Throw your sacrificial bad guys at me so we can get this over with and I can get on with never seeing you again."

He slammed the door closed again. He pressed his back to the wall beside it and slowly counted to ten. Cyral and Eliott stared at him.

"We're going to get attacked again? Here?" said Cyral.

"By who?" asked Eliott. Jordan had to catch him by the jacket to stop him opening the door again for a peek.

"The Count and some woman . . . seven, eight . . ."

"That'd be the High Priestess of Khol-Ra," said Winnie, reading out of Glister's appointment book.

"Whoever. Ten."

The door tried to open. Jordan grabbed the handle and pulled it shut. From the other side, he heard Glister trying to laugh the situation off. "Jordan? Was that you? You're such a joker—no, seriously, come in here and let's talk. You want something from me; I want a story from you; we've got room to negotiate the details. Details! That's all this is. Come on inside."

"Monkeys, Glister. Send for them. We can all walk away."

"Except that we'll be flying," said Eliott. "Not walking."

"Hey, you brought your apprentice? Fantastic. Kid's got a bright future ahead of him," said Glister, his voice weaseling its way under the door. "You don't want to take away his big break, do you? The showdown scene, heroes and villains? I know we had our arguments; maybe some bad calls were made—some wrong choices with your workload. I get that. But Jordan, baby, that's the past. You've got to let go of the past, start thinking about the future. Your future. The kid's future. The entire franchise. I promise you, everything will be different after today. Now let me out of my office?"

The door shook against Jordan's grip again.

"What're your partners saying about this?" said Jordan.

"They know I've got their best interests at heart."

"Same way you did the last time you threw them at me? How'd that work out for you two?"

"Contract revisions had to be made," said Glister. "One or two points. I've reassured them, they're not . . . What was your word? Sacrificial. There's a real market for misunderstood antihero types right now, and everybody loves a recurring villain—"

Jordan tightened his fists. "Give it up. We both know how this is really going to end. Big fight, they die, you make money off it. Call your damn monkeys before the Count figures out you're betraying him and eats you."

There was a pause, filled with the suggestion of a significant and wordless discussion on the other side of the door, before Glister answered, "So, hypothetically speaking, you'd kill him before that could happen?"

"Right now? Yes!"

"And this . . . very attractive . . . priestess, too?"

"Glister, I've got less than no time for your games—"

"Because, it's funny—I have this very clear memory of

receiving a letter from Jordan the Red saying he was finished with killing. There was all this really moving poetic language about blood on his hands . . . and when I say 'moving,' I mean bad. Unpublishably bad. So bad it could only be honest, straight-from-the-heart stuff. Am I losing my mind? Or are you being poetic again when you talk about killing these two living, feeling human beings I have sitting here with me? Because, if you did kill them . . . how would you sleep at night?"

A snappy answer jumped toward Jordan's mouth, but halfway there, it met a twinge of memory, a thing freed from the crypts of his soul. It choked his voice and slacked his grip, knocking down his battle-hardened survival instincts, just for one second.

One second too long.

The door moved again, wrenched inward off its hinges. The Count pulled it away from Jordan, then hit him with it. Festively colored pain exploded in his face and chest simultaneously, and in every other part of his body a moment later as the water barrel and the floor joined the party.

"Of course, one of them is living an alternative sort of lifestyle," said Glister, beaming. "Vampirism. But I don't judge."

"Oh, yeah?" shouted Eliott. "Hey, Count! Judge this!"

He tore down the curtains.

The dim light of evening spilled gently into the waiting room. Jordan groaned; he had been planning to anyway.

"You know, that window doesn't even face west," Glister pointed out. "But, hey, definite credit for effort. I like that."

He strolled over to Jordan, sad and sympathetic as a form rejection letter. "Oh, Jordan, my boy. You only were ever good at two things: killing monsters and spouting witty one-liners, and now it looks like you're all out of wit, too."

Jordan groaned again. He had heard something crack when he hit the water barrel. He didn't dare to touch his face. "You expect me to be witty?"

"No," said Glister, "I expect you to— What the hell is that!"

A huge, leathery shadow swept past the window, rattling the glass as it banked toward Central Casting. The tip of a tail scraped the building. A shower of plaster fell from the walls. A reverberant roar filled the street.

"That would be the dragon," said Cyral, who had taken advantage of the chaos to get behind the desk and cower.

"There's a dragon? Why didn't anyone tell me there was a dragon! Winnie—"

"Sit down and shut up, Starmacher," said the high priestess, pushing him into a chair. "We aren't finished with your Jordan the Red yet."

Jordan edged painfully onto one elbow. The Count loomed over him, hungry, angry, and more beast than human now. His burning gaze was fixated on the stream of blood pouring from Jordan's broken nose.

Which left him blind to the activity behind him, until Cyral and Winnie rushed at him and flung the torn curtains over his head. The Count staggered, spun, and entangled himself further as he tripped over the trailing ends. Jordan kicked out at his ankles for good measure.

"Don't just sit there," said the priestess, grabbing Glister by the collar and thrusting him at the Count. "Help him. I'll take care of Jordan myself."

She raised her arm, and the golden snake bangle around her wrist came alive, uncurling and stretching itself into a serpent-headed wand, glowing and spitting flame. She pointed it at Jordan's chest. Fire flared in the serpent's mouth.

Eliott crashed into her. He grabbed her arm with both hands, dragging her aim sideways. A tapestry showing the adventures of the Invisible Knight of Castile turned instantly to ash. The priestess swatted and struck at Eliott in a fury, but he held on. Her wand blazed like the sun. Ripples of heat distorted the air around them as they wrestled; through the haze, they looked like they were dancing a clumsy, brutal tango. Beside them, almost colliding, the Count dragged Cyral and Winnie around in a whirling tanoura, still trying to claw his way out of the curtains.

Jordan sat up against the water barrel. Every movement was another return trip to the wonderful old world of pain. "This really the story you want to sell, Glister? A farce? There's a dragon out there I could be fighting right now. Huge, fire-belching, wizard-eating nightmare of a thing. Forget these jokers, and it's all yours. Full rights. Three monkeys to Central Casting, and everybody walks out of here alive. We got a deal?"

At that moment, the priestess broke free, throwing Eliott into a corner. She leveled her wand at Jordan once again. "No deal," she spat. "Your soul will burn."

Jordan sighed. "What do you want, anyway?"

"To see you dead!"

"Yeah, fine. But after that. I mean, is this for the fame and the glory? The money? What are you after?"

The priestess hesitated. Behind her, the Count tripped over a chair, carrying Winnie and Cyral down with him. "Revenge," she said finally. "I want my Sisterhood back, you son of a—"

"Fine. Done."

"—what?"

Jordan shrugged, and winced as his shoulder clicked back into place. "I said, it's done. Wish granted. Same magic wish that brought you back to life must've brought them back. I'll help you find them again. Build you a new

temple—Glister can pay for it. Right, Glister? All the
money you'll make off the story of this dragon kill, you
can afford it."

"Hey, wait, now—"

"And new initiates," demanded the priestess. "We lost
decades of novices because of you."

"Winnie! Feel like a new job?"

From the tangle of bodies and curtains on the floor,
Winnie called back, "Sure. I could get religion."

"Oh, yeah, me, too," Eliott threw in, picking up on the
game.

The priestess regarded him coldly. "You would serve
as a eunuch." She turned back to Jordan. "All this, if we let
you go fight your dragon now?"

"That's the deal. Everything you could ask for." He
held out his hand.

She took it.

"I accept. And I'll hold you to it."

A wave of heat shot through him as she pulled him to
his feet, not unpleasant but intense, like diving into a hot
spring. Some of his pains decided to go sit quietly and
think about what they had done for a bit.

Glister scrambled over. He was sweating, and his hair
had slipped to one side. "But what about—"

Fabric ripped ominously. The Count lurched to his
feet, flinging Cyral and Winnie away, one with each hand.
He knocked Glister aside and thrust his teeth at Jordan's
throat.

"Ask him what he wants!" Eliott shouted.

"Blood," said the Count.

Jordan grunted. "Too bad."

He grabbed the snake wand out of the priestess's hand
and shoved it into the Count's mouth. They stared at each
other for a puzzled moment as the Count's cheeks lit up

from the inside like a jack-o'-lantern, before Jordan said, "How do you—"

"Here," said the priestess. "Like this."

She touched the end of the wand still protruding from the Count's bloodless lips. There was a sound like an oil lamp igniting, and then a flash of light so bright it left everyone in the room blind and blinking. When the light faded and they could see again, all that was left of the Count was an impeccably well-fashioned suit with a very charred neckline, and the lingering smell of burnt hair.

Glister was the first to find his voice. "Out of here. All of you—out! Out! Get out of this office," he ordered, his hand over his mouth as if he was about to be sick.

"What about the monkeys, Mr. Starmacher?" said Cyral.

"Yes, yes—take them! Winnie, three monkeys to Central Casting, right away. And I'll want that story on my desk ten minutes after the dragon's head leaves its neck, you hear me?"

He stormed into his office.

Then he stormed out again to pick up his door. "I'm slamming this on all of you."

Winnie got back behind her desk and performed some minor magic with a feather pen and enchanted paper. "Three monkeys up on the roof waiting for you. Break a leg out there." She winked at Cyral and added, "I'll see you later, hon."

"Good luck with your . . . religious experience," Cyral called back, as Jordan hauled him out of the waiting room and toward the stairs.

They climbed the stairs as quickly as they could, which was not very, and agonizingly slow compared to the speed of a dragon. Jordan could still feel the heat of the priestess's grip burning inside his blood, invigorating him, but he knew it would die out soon, just as he knew they were already too late to get to Central Casting before the dragon.

They reached the roof. Jordan stood disoriented; in every direction, the sky blazed sunset red and black. His hand shook as he picked out west, then turned away from it.

The city was on fire.

To the south, flames wreathed the Central Casting building, surrounding it but not touching it. Bursts of dragon fire, streaming out of the thick, black smoke, bent at right angles before they reached its roof, igniting the neighboring buildings. In the streets, people screamed and shouted as they watched the towers burn.

"We . . . we aren't flying into that, are we?" said Cyral.

The dragon circled into view, its wings spread wide and full as it rode the hot updraft. Flashes of blue and silver light exploded off the roof of Central Casting like fireworks and crackled along the dragon's hide like cheap special effects.

"They're throwing spells at it," said Jordan. "Can't they see they're not doing anything to it?"

"Well, yeah, of course they're not," said Eliott. "It can't be harmed by any sort of magic."

"Don't tell me; tell them . . ."

Another shock of flame erupted from the smoke. Jordan realized he was still staring at the burning buildings and shook himself out of it. On the edge of the roof, three monkeys sat, as still as statues, watching the city burn. Jordan waved Cyral and Eliott over to them.

"Come on," he said. "We're flying in."

"I don't suppose," said Cyral tremulously, "that you meant what you said, when you offered Glister the story of all this . . . did you? Because if you did, I would still like the chance to write it . . ."

"Doesn't matter, does it? We break that thread, everything goes away and gets forgotten, right?"

"Oh, right. Of course . . . I forgot— Ooh, nnn—"

The monkeys took hold of them. Feathery wings fanned out and tested the smokey air. They left the roof and plunged toward Central Casting.

SIXTEEN

WARNING BELLS CLAMORED through the white marble halls of Central Casting. Workshops and lecture halls stood empty and abandoned, their doors left open, experiments left bubbling and fizzing. Demons half-conjured into reality burbled within their chalk circles. Eliott ran from door to door, perpetually glancing back to make sure that he wasn't leaving Jordan and Cyral too far behind, or worse, that they weren't going in another direction and abandoning him.

"Nothing," he shouted, over the deep, iron hammering of the bells. "No sign of anyone—they must've all gone up to the roof to fight it."

"Then we'll meet them up there," said Jordan, catching up. "Stairs?"

"Not yet, but come check this out."

Eliott waved them through a deserted classroom to a

narrow, arched window set into the inner wall. Red light, angry and shifting, streamed through.

"You can see all the way up to the big glass dome in the middle," he said. "Look up there—see that flash? That must be the wizards fighting back. I bet if the smoke cleared, we could even see the dragon fly over."

Jordan squinted up. For the first time in more than a decade, his hair reflected his name as the firelight poured down on him. "Yeah . . . it hasn't landed yet. Why hasn't it landed?"

"Out here," called Cyral, and at the same moment they heard the tromp of many boots in perfect step echo down the hall. Eliott scrambled back through the rows of desks and benches, knocking ink bottles to the floor.

Six wizards in the red and black uniforms of the Elite Guard hurried past at a quick march, their staves crackling with raw, cosmic power, their beards trimmed with severe and threatening purpose. They spared no time to look left or right, and passed by the classroom with no notice taken of the intruders; they were fighting wizards with a mission galvanized into their minds.

Eliott shouted at them, and when that failed, he bounced a chalkboard eraser off the pointy hat of the last in line.

"Hey!" he demanded, as the wizard turned around. The rest of the guards carried on. "You're going up to fight the dragon, right? Which way is it to the roof?"

"Get back down with the others in the servants' hall, right now," the wizard ordered. "We've got the situation under control."

He pointed his staff back in the direction he had come from. A bolt of light pulsed out and down the hall, lighting a path. Then he spun sharply on his heel and quickened his pace to catch up with the other guards.

"Idiots!" Jordan shouted after them. "You can't fight it—you can't hurt it with magic!"

They chased after the guards, around the curve of the endless hall, but too slow, too late. The sound of boots had stopped. The wizards had teleported to the roof, where Eliott imagined them locked in a desperate but ultimately futile battle of sorcery and fire, their staves splitting the sky with bolts of impotent lightning. He stared up at the ceiling with no sympathy at all.

Jordan grabbed him by the hood of his jacket. "Come on. Let's do like they said."

"Leave it to them?"

"No. Find whoever else is here, and hope they'll listen to us before anyone else goes up."

In the opposite direction, the flash of light from the guard's staff still hung in the air, a fading afterimage but bright enough to follow. It led to a flight of stairs, tucked around a corner. Unlike the rest of the building they had seen so far, the stairwell was plain and unadorned; this was the servants' domain, not an area for wizards or their visiting clients.

Eliott hesitated. He felt like they were doing things backward, following stairs down when they should be going up, wasting time looking for someone to talk to when they should be fighting the dragon. It was so clear in his mind that, if it had been anyone other than Jordan the Red leading, he would have run off to find his own sword and his own way up to the roof.

But this was Jordan the Red, so this had to be the right way of doing things.

At the bottom of the stairs, they found a door, emblazoned with a complex mystical symbol that made Eliott want to turn back and rejoin his Central Casting official authorized tour group, possibly stopping at the gift shop on the way out. Jordan ignored it and pushed the door open.

A wall of sound pushed back.

At least a hundred people, sitting and standing, filled the room. Most had the dull, desperately clean look of maids and clerks, but there were wizards among them, too; formidably old men with their beards tucked into their belts, and younger men in white robes with equally pale complexions and frazzled expressions—Eliott guessed that the latter were the wizards who had been forced to abandon their workshops in midexperiment. Everyone was talking and everyone was moving in a slow, worried churn, the group embodiment of an upset stomach.

Jordan raised his voice. "Hey. Who's in charge here?"

One of the white-robed wizards pushed through the crowd. He had the rumpled, irritable look of a man called out of bed to deal with somebody else's problem. His bald head was bruised and cratered as if the problems he normally dealt with involved freak meteor storms. "Who're you?" he said. "How did you get in here? We're in the middle of—"

"You've got a dragon," said Jordan.

"He kills those," said Cyral.

"Glister Starmacher sent me. You in charge?"

"I'm the acting shift supervisor—"

"Good enough. Get your people off the roof, and tell me how to get up there."

"No. No! I'm sorry; roof access is strictly limited to authorized Central Casting staff and wizards, and who exactly do you think you are, anyway?"

"Someone who's got a better chance of killing that dragon than you do." Jordan looked around the room. People were beginning to take notice. "I'm a man with a sword and a lot of practice using it."

The Shift Supervisor cleared his throat. "The dragon situation," he managed, "is completely under control. We don't require any assistance, and we are in no significant danger."

"The city's burning down!" said Eliott.

". . . No significant danger within this building," the Shift Supervisor amended. "The city can look after itself. We have our own precautions in place, and our own guards will destroy the beast—they've already been sent into action, so I'm sorry, but you're too late for heroics today."

Eliott could see, behind Jordan's rigid expression, the urge to give the wizard a solid roundhouse kicking.

Instead, Jordan said, "Yeah? And what're your wizards throwing at it? Magic spells? They're not going to work. I'm trying to tell you, it can't be harmed by magic."

"Ridiculous. And immaterial. Central Casting is still one hundred percent secure and invulnerable."

"And the city can burn; is that it? Terrific. Call the fiddlers."

"Hang on," said Cyral. "What do you mean, you're invulnerable? I've seen this dragon eat a wizard, quite recently and quite effectively."

"We have defenses." The Shift Supervisor straightened his robes. He glanced at the crowd, which had stopped talking and started listening. Fresh anxieties flickered from face to face. "In fact, come with me. I'll show you."

He waved his hand in a complicated pattern, and another door opened, a door that led down a short corridor to the open courtyard in the center of Central Casting, the heart of the conclave, beneath the glass dome. The Shift Supervisor ushered Jordan through curtly, barely paying attention to Eliott or Cyral.

"There," he said, and pointed. "Behold."

They beheld. It was worth the formality.

A platform of polished wood and ornate metal railings floated three feet off the ground, perfectly circular and as wide around as any of the rooms they had seen. It spun gently, and as it did, it appeared to shift in place as though they were seeing it through turbulent water. Eliott squinted and rubbed at his eyes; looking at it for too long at once made his head hurt.

"Raw magic," said the Shift Supervisor smugly. "A natural spring being dutifully tapped and bottled by our magical craftsmen to provide everything we need."

Eliott looked again. Through watering eyes, he could make out the figures of at least a dozen wizards sitting in a circle on the platform, their hands held out in front of them.

"It doesn't look like they're doing anything," he pointed out, forcing himself to keep watching.

"Exactly," said the Shift Supervisor. "That's how good they are. Right now, those men are diverting the usual flow of magic from our regular outlets of business into a shield. All of our power is channeling through them, and all of it is protecting this building. Now, are you still concerned about the dragon?"

Jordan threw up his hands. "Yes! This dragon, it's the . . . wizard killer . . . from . . . that saga, the one . . . dammit, Eliott, help me out here."

"It's Scoryx, the Blackflame Wyrm, from Skarbolg."

The Shift Supervisor frowned, going through a mental catalogue of beasts and monsters. "Not one of ours. Skarbolg was done off contract. So?"

"Are you listening to me? These people, these . . ."

"Monks," Eliott supplied.

"These monks . . . they made this dragon specially for the purpose of killing wizards. It's immune to magic. While I'd like to believe your magic shield will stop it, I don't think it will. And I know you're not going to be able to kill it the way you're trying. You need ordinary, unenchanted weapons, and you need someone who knows how to use them to bring down a dragon. Here and now? That's me."

"Oh, yes? What are you, some kind of hero?"

Jordan pushed a hand stiffly through his hair. "Yeah," he said unhappily, as if he were admitting to an addiction. "I'm Jordan the Red. Can I kill your dragon now?"

The Shift Supervisor began to answer, his face shifting through disbelief into astonishment at an incredible speed, when a scream ripped through the courtyard. It came from the floating platform, but not from the wizards; it was an inhuman sound, a scream of air and magic being mutilated. Eliott shielded his eyes and stared into the heart of the conclave, in time to see a red flash of light lance down from the glass dome. There was another scream, this one entirely human and abruptly cut off. A wizard burst into flame. An instant later, all that remained of him was a small heap of ash.

"Wow," said Eliott. "That was so—"

"A man just died," said Jordan. "Show some respect." He pushed Eliott back, putting himself between the platform and the stunned witnesses. "Which way to the roof?"

"Through . . . through there," the Shift Supervisor said numbly. All the color had gone out of his face. He pointed to a door across the courtyard. "East tower. Goes all the way up."

"Right. Great. Now, look—last time when Glister brought me through here, you had a whole armory with a bunch of guys adding fancy enchantments to regular weapons, exploding-bladed daggers, that sort of thing. Got any that haven't been magicked up yet? I'll need a spear or a bow."

"We . . . might. But they won't be very good. We buy cheap, third-rate stock," the Shift Supervisor confessed. "All the added value comes from the applied spells—"

"I don't care. No magic. Go get one." Jordan looked at Cyral. "You up to this?"

Cyral nodded. "The grand climax? Wouldn't miss it."

"Then when he's found a weapon, you bring it up to

me. I don't need any more wizards getting in the way. Eliott—"

"Ready! What'm I doing?"

"You're going back to the servants' hall. Keep everyone calm, and if this all goes to hell, you get them out of here. Can you do that?"

Eliott stared. He could feel the building crashing down around him, the glass dome shattering, the stonework crumbling to dust, and his body sinking by the heels down into the pits of limbo at the center of the earth.

"Don't you want . . ." he tried, but he knew Jordan didn't.

"No. You'd just get yourself killed up there. I can't be worrying about you."

"Oh. Then, yeah, sure," he heard himself mumble. "I'll stay out of the way."

Jordan clapped him on the shoulder. "Good kid. Spread the word if I don't come back—gut it and break the thread. Right? Now, go on. Let's get through this."

Eliott nodded. His body was a hollow husk, doing what it was told. He didn't even turn to watch Jordan ascend the stairs. His adventure was over.

WAVES OF HEAT were already spilling from the roof down into the stairwell. Jordan waded upward, floor by floor, squinting and cursing all wizards, dragons, and architects. Stairs? Sure, build them steep and narrow as you like; no one important will ever use them. Everyone who matters can magically teleport wherever they want to go. Hand railings? Why bother?

Just once, Jordan wanted to fight the big, final battle at ground level.

He reached the roof and stopped. The stairs continued

on another turn up into the tower, which was his next destination, but he had to give the wizards one more warning to retreat.

The Elite Guard had fanned out around the roof. Through the smoke, Jordan could see them standing between the low hedges of the rooftop gardens, distinguishable from the bronze statues only by their gestures and the flashes of light from their staves. The dragon swept over them. A barrage of spells exploded impotently against its body. It struck back with a rush of flame that bent at a right angle above the wizards' heads and scorched a tower across the street.

Jordan grabbed the nearest wizard by the arm. "It's not working! Can't you see that? Fall back—let me handle this."

"Who're you?"

"Jordan the Red."

The wizard raised his staff and flung lightning into the smoke-blackened sky. "And I'm Merlin. Nice to meet you. Get back downstairs."

"Your shield is cracking! You're going to get killed!"

"Taking out a dragon—sounds like a good way to go to me," said the wizard, shaking him off.

Jordan gave up. A willingness to die had always been the one heroic trait he lacked. He had been ready to die plenty of times, but he had never been happy about it. Anyone whose battle cry was "Onward, to Glorious Death!" was, in Jordan's mind, somehow doing it wrong.

He returned to the tower in time to meet Cyral puffing up the stairs. The bard passed him a longbow and a bundle of fat arrows that were everything the Shift Supervisor had promised: cheap, bulk-produced junk. They would have to do.

"What now?" asked Cyral.

"I'm going up," said Jordan. "All the way up, to the top

of this tower. Need to get above this smoke for a clear shot. And then"—he held up an arrow—"I'm going to put out that dragon's other eye."

"Oh, excellent." Cyral hesitated. "Can I do anything?"

"No."

"Then, do you mind if I come with you? To watch?"

"Still trying to get your story?"

"No, I . . . I'd just like to see how you do it. After everything we've been through, I'd hate not to see the end."

"Fine. Keep your head down."

Step by step, Jordan pulled himself up the tower. The end, he thought. The end is when I can lie down and sleep for a few hundred years.

He climbed out onto the open top of the tower. He nocked an arrow, drew back, listened to the protests of muscles forced out of retirement, and waited for the dragon.

"Don't shoot until you see the whites of its eyes?" suggested Cyral.

Jordan grunted. "Lizard. No whites."

The dragon came out of the smoke, straight toward them, its attention fixed on the wizards below. Jordan looked past the fire-scarred jaws, into the eyes of the beast. Just like last time. He let the arrow fly.

And missed.

Damn, he thought, as the arrow glanced off the horned ridges of the dragon's head. Out of practice. He reached for another arrow.

The dragon twisted around, turning its vulnerable eyes away and putting its back to the tower. For a moment, Jordan thought it was going to run again, and swore. Then he realized what the dragon was about to do.

"Cyral! Down!"

The bard dropped into a crouch.

"No! Down the stairs—get down—"

He had just enough time to shove Cyral toward the

stairs before the dragon's tail smashed through the masonry beneath his feet. He had a last vision of an enormous reptilian rump adding insult to the injuries he was about to receive.

Then the top of the tower collapsed, and Jordan fell.

ELIOTT SLOUCHED TO the door of the servants' hall and leaned against it, unwilling to go in. If he went in, he would see people, who would want to know what was going on, who would make him explain that Jordan the Red was at that moment fighting a dragon amid an army of wizards while he, Eliott, was stuck sheltering with the peasants and missing the whole thing. He gave the door a kick and walked the other way.

He ended up in the Central Casting gift shop, not far from the gates. A labyrinthine path led him through a forest of plush golems and souvenir pointy hats, scrolls and boxes of magical fudge, enchanted rings and color-changing scarves. A floating sphere played obnoxious, tinkly music overhead.

At the end of the path, Eliott came to a counter, where a cashier would have been on a day without a dragon. A book sat on the counter, abandoned in the middle of being bought. It looked tacky, with slightly lavender pages and THOUGHTS written on the cover in a silver scrawl. For lack of anything better to do, Eliott sat down on the counter and flipped through it. The pages were blank, apart from a tiny, generic aphorism at the bottom of each one. *Virtue is its own reward. Hard work and patience are the keys to success.* Eliott smashed it shut.

"Useless." He pushed it onto the floor. "Like me."

He had tried. He had gone to warn Jordan about the ambush in the valley; he had pulled down the curtains to kill the vampire. Other things had interfered. Bad timing, misunderstandings. Jordan holding any of that against him was plain unfairness. Neither of them would have had an adventure at all if not for him.

He stared at THOUGHTS, trying to collect his own.

Maybe that was why Jordan sent him away: as a punishment for making that wish. Maybe Jordan really would have been happier if Eliott had never found him, if they had both carried on living their dull, separate lives.

"He'll get his wish real soon, then," said Eliott, as if the diary were trying to argue otherwise. "He'll kill the dragon and he'll break the thread, and he'll do it all without me. It's not fair! It was my birthday present—my three wishes!"

No, two. Two wishes. The memory came back to him in Kess's voice. Two wishes, because the white thread doesn't count. It only makes things go back to the way they were.

Eliott drummed his fingers on the countertop. If Kess were with him, she could tell him to quit whining and stop moping, and it would happen, because she could change his mood as easily as that. He tried to conjure her voice again.

The white thread puts the world back to how it would have been. It's the most powerful of all three. And if you die, it breaks itself.

If you die . . .

The horrible thought curled into Eliott's brain, terrifying in its seductiveness. He jumped down from the counter and kicked the diary away as if it were responsible, but the thought remained.

"If I . . ."

He could be useful. He could save the day.

His hands began to shake. This was his adventure, his story, and he could end it, the way so many stories ended, with a heroic sacrifice. Right now, he could do this, but only if he did it now, before he lost this moment of crystal clarity.

He needed to find Jordan. Doing what he was told no longer mattered. Only doing what he knew he needed to do.

Eliott ran back the way he came, his heart pounding. As he crossed the courtyard, he glanced at the platform at the heart of the conclave. There was only one wizard left.

COLD NUMBNESS ENGULFED Jordan. His fall stopped, leaving him hanging in midair above the heap of rubble that had been the crown of the tower.

Oh, hell, he thought. Life, if you're going to flash before me again, show me someone else's for a change. I've already seen mine.

Then he spotted the wizard pointing at him. The wizard lowered his arm, and Jordan descended slowly to the roof, landing out in the middle of the gardens on the marble statue of a lion. When Jordan looked around again, the wizard was already back among the ranks of the Elite Guard, pointlessly throwing spells at the dragon again.

"No worse than what I managed," Jordan admitted grudgingly. He dusted himself off and tried to think of a new plan.

The glass dome exploded.

The blast threw Jordan off his feet. The roof bucked, toppling statues and sending loose tiles flying. Jordan scrambled for cover as raw magic shot into the sky, uncontrolled, distorting the air into a helix of twisted light. Shards of glass hung suspended from it like hoarfrost. Then the magic faded out and the glass rained down.

The dragon roared. It swept low over the roof once more, blowing fire. This time, the gardens ignited like lamp

oil. An intricately wrought metal railing shriveled and collapsed. The dragon roared again, triumphant and enraged
by the destruction of the shield. Wizards leveled their
staves against it. They died. Jordan's rescuer vanished in a
sheet of flame.

Jordan picked himself up, carefully brushing shards of
glass off his skin and out of his hair. Blood trickled down
from a gash above his left ear, but it was the least of his
worries right now. He knew almost nothing about magic,
but enough about dramatics to understand that things were
about to get much, much worse. He looked back to the
tower.

"Oh," he muttered. "That was quick."

Out of the haze and smoke, Eliott came walking across
the roof. Even in the ruddy light, he looked strangely pale.
Jordan shouted at him, but he kept walking forward, as if
getting eaten by dragons or burned alive happened only to
other people. He found his way to Jordan.

"What the hell are you doing up here?" said Jordan. "I
told you—"

"I'd get killed. Yeah."

The flat, bloodless tone of his voice made Jordan falter.
Something was filling the boy's head, flickering behind
his eyes, blinding him to everything else. The timing
could hardly have been worse, but Jordan still pulled Eliott into the shelter of a fallen statue and spent the last
scraps of his patience to ask, "What's gone wrong now?"

Eliott shrugged weakly. "I know what we've got to do."

"Some trick to kill the dragon? Say it fast, because I
could really use—"

"No. No, Jordan . . . it's me. It's my wishes. I'm con-
nected to the white thread. If I die, it'll break, and
everything'll be fixed. Kess told me. And maybe I'll come
back, because it'll all be undone. She said it's like that for

elves. But—but even if I don't, it'd just be me who died. There's lots of other people who would come back, so that's not so bad, is it? So I figured—I figured I should come and tell you . . ."

Jordan stared. "You asking me to—?"

"Maybe. I . . . I can't do it myself, and I wanted it to be . . . good. I mean, something that'd be worth remembering? Something heroic? I dunno if I'll remember, but . . ." His voice broke. "It could be quick, right?"

One more time, thought Jordan. One life, against the weight of the world. Why did it always have to come down to this?

He clenched his fists. "Damn you. Not this time. Not by me."

"What? Seriously? You're saying no?"

"I'm saying no, you stupid, selfish— I'm not killing anyone else! Do it yourself—I've got a dragon to deal with."

"Fine! I will! I'll—"

Eliott froze. Smoke whipped past his face, driven by a harsh wind. He raised his face to the sky.

The dragon loomed over them, floating on the hot drafts of its own fire. It tilted its head thoughtfully, watching them.

"When I say, run," murmured Jordan, pushing Eliott away from him.

The boy shook his head. "No."

The dragon swept down toward them, almost lazily, as if roasting or eating them alive would merely be an afterthought.

Jordan drew his sword. "Pain in the ass . . ." He glanced sideways. "You sure about this?"

Eliott nodded, his jaw trembling. He got it under control. "Yeah. Are you going to stay with me?"

Jordan put his free arm across the boy's shoulders. He tried to think of some reassuring last words. "Right. Let's be heroes."

IN THE DOORWAY of the broken tower, Cyral watched in mute horror as the dragon plunged down, its wings beating the burning gardens into a frenzy. Jordan and Eliott stood together, directly in the dragon's path. They could see it coming—there was no way they could miss it—yet neither of them was moving.

Run, thought Cyral. Please run.

Jordan raised his sword defiantly.

The dragon stretched its jaws wide.

Someone pushed past Cyral, moving faster than anyone human should have been able. In the moment it took for him to recognize the flying limbs and hair, Kess had covered half the distance between him and Eliott. By the time he thought to shout her name, she was there. She vaulted a fallen statue and landed in a crouch. Her arm spun like a catapult.

The thing she was carrying arced away from her, into the gaping mouth of the dragon, deep into its throat. Cyral held his breath. He waited for it to explode.

The dragon, caught off guard by this sudden attack, veered away. Jordan and Eliott threw themselves to the ground as the dragon skimmed over them. Cyral kept waiting. Ten seconds . . . twenty . . . The dragon was gaining altitude. If it was going to explode, it would already have done so, he decided. He hurried across to join the others.

"What did you do?" he demanded.

Kess shook her head. She was clinging to Eliott, who appeared to be in shock. "Wait for it."

They all looked up at the dragon. While it was still not

turning into a simultaneous firework display and self-barbecue, it was clearly now in some distress. Its chest heaved and strained against its shoulders. Its long neck shrank and distended, while its tail lashed fitfully through the smoke.

"You . . . poisoned it?"

The dragon spread its jaws once more. It began to roar, then choked, wheezed, and made a sound which at that moment Cyral could only describe as the noise of a pig being deflated, but would from then on think of as the exact sound of a dragon vomiting out the entire contents of its vast stomach.

"Syrup of ipecac," said Kess, as the horrible mess landed on the roof. Cyral tried not to hear the splash.

"Like you gave me," said Eliott weakly, "when I found those mushrooms."

He began to laugh, and Kess laughed with him, until tears streamed down their ash-stained faces. Then Kess kissed his forehead, and Cyral suddenly felt like an intruder on the scene.

"I'll, er, I'll just go . . ."

"Watch out!"

Jordan pushed Cyral to the ground as the dragon dove at them. Its flight was still erratic, its head weaving and twisting as it shook the last of the bile from its mouth, but it was definitely recovering and coming back with a vengeance.

"Go find that thread," yelled Jordan, inches away from Cyral's face. "I'll give that monster something to chase. Go!"

"The thread? I— Oh."

They split apart, Jordan waving his arms and shouting, Cyral scrambling on all fours across the roof and through the burning gardens. Overhead, the dragon roared.

Ignore me, Cyral wished desperately. I wouldn't settle your stomach. Jordan looks much more like a salt cracker.

He pushed on, half-blind from the smoke, led by the reek of the dragon's vomit. When he found it, he nearly added his own to the steaming pool.

Do it, he willed himself. Everything will go back to the way it should be. A far, far grosser thing I do . . .

Cyral plunged in. Loops and strands of some unnamable slime clung to him, oozing around his hands and arms. He let them cling; trying to wipe them off would only make matters worse. He fought to keep his eyes open, his mouth shut, his mind from identifying the things he touched. Find the thread. Ignore everything else.

The dragon, designed not to be ignored, belched fire at the sky and circled around. This time, it kept its mouth closed and raised its talons.

A glint of white shone amid the muck. Cyral fumbled for it.

Another hand met his.

Cyral screamed and pulled away, dredging up Hopley's severed hand, fingers entangled with his. He almost flung it away, but twisted between the sticky, dead fingers was the last thread of the Braid, still white and gleaming.

Someone behind him was shouting. It could have been Kess; it could have been Eliott.

"Jordan! Run!"

"I am running!"

Cyral took hold of each end of the thread. He closed his eyes and made a wish. He broke the thread.

Nothing happened.

The first and most significant nothing was the absence of draconic fire roasting him alive, followed by the complete lack of giant talons impaling him. Cyral noticed those right away. Then, as nothing continued to happen, he opened his eyes.

The dragon was gone. So were Kess and Eliott and Jordan, and the charred remains of the Central Casting fighting wizards' Elite Guard. There was still a stain on the tile roof where the dragon's vomit and Hopley's remains had been, but only a stain; it might have been left by anything.

Cyral staggered up, finding his footing by process of elimination. The railings and gardens were back in place, but he was afraid to touch anything. In his mind, they were still smoldering slag, still gone. The glass dome wavered in and out of his mental picture of the world as sight and memory argued with each other. Eventually, he risked going to the edge of the roof to look out and see that, yes, the rest of the city had been restored as well. Everything was back to the way it had been. As if the wishes had never been made.

Except . . .

He took out his notebook and turned to a random page. There, in his own cramped, splotchy shorthand, was the story, still written down as he had left it. He flipped through a few more pages, half reading, half watching to see if the ink would magically fade away. It did not.

This, thought Cyral. I will remember you this way. And I will find you again.

Running feet on the roof made him look around, in time to see Glister Starmacher waving and hurrying toward him with several confused wizards in tow.

"Where is he? What did he do? Jordan the Red—he was back, wasn't he? I know he was back! And you, you, what's your name? Cyral! You were supposed to be writing about him! Weren't you?"

Cyral breathed out slowly. "I'm sorry, Mr. Starmacher. I think you're a bit confused."

"Nonsense! I remember . . . I can't remember now, but someone told me where Jordan the Red was, and he was here." Glister turned around, struggling with the same double vision as Cyral. "A dragon. I'm sure there was a dragon. It was laying waste to the city . . ."

"Doesn't look like it's been wasted," said a wizard.

"But I remember it! Vampires, dragons, the whole city under attack—my God, it'll be the biggest epic ever told! 'Jordan the Red Rides Again.'"

"It didn't happen," said Cyral distantly. "None of this happened. In a few days, you'll have forgotten all about it."

"What are you babbling about? Never mind; we've got work to do! Okay, so Jordan's gone. Jordan and the dragon are both gone." Glister clapped his hands together. "Hah, what have I always said—that man's the best in the business! Talk about setting up a sequel! Add a bit of flash, a bit of fire—Cyral, Cyral, my boy, tell me you got all this written down!"

Cyral looked at his notebook, and at the broken thread now fading from white to gray. He tucked the notebook into his shirt. "No, Mr. Starmacher," he said wearily. "I'm sorry. I'm afraid I wasn't able to write anything about Jordan the Red."

And with Glister's furious shouts chasing him, Cyral descended from the roof of Central Casting and headed for the city gates. Glister Starmacher was right. He would never work in that town again.

EPILOGUE

THE POND AT the bottom of the garden was covered with several inches of ice. Out in the middle, where no branches overhung and no weeds grew, it was also covered with two layers of thick, woolen blankets and, on top of them, two warmly dressed bodies. Eliott raised one fur-lined mitt and pointed straight upward.

"That one," he said thoughtfully, "looks like a giant chicken running out of a troll's mouth. It probably stole the troll's back teeth."

Kess snorted. "Why would it want a troll's teeth?"

"Dunno. Because hens don't have teeth of their own? Jealousy can make farm animals do weird stuff. Your turn. How about that one over there?"

Eliott looked sideways, waiting, while Kess considered

the pale, abstract shapes in the sky. He had given her an easy one—a boot, a hammerheaded turtle, a carnivorous stump—but she was in one of her strange, distant moods again. She always was, these days.

"A cloud," she said eventually, in a bored voice.

Eliott sighed. "We could be doing something else."

Kess's ears, in their long, rabbit-fur sleeves, twitched. "I've heard there's a new bard in town. We could go down there. Hear a saga?"

"I . . . I dunno." Eliott shrugged, scuffing his shoulders across the ice. "Sagas don't really seem the same, not since . . . well, you know."

They had agreed not to talk about it. The world had been fixed, and none of their adventures that autumn had really happened, so there was no reason to bring up false memories or unforgotten dreams. Eliott sighed again.

The doorbell clanged, up at the manor.

Eliott sat up and brushed the snow off his knees. "Who'd they forget to tell?"

His parents had decided to winter in the south of Spain, leaving him with the opportunity to prove his maturity as the master of the house while they were away. So far, it had meant signing three bills for firewood and being ignored by two fewer people than usual, but there was always the danger that he would be called on to entertain some passing nobleman who had missed the news of his parents' departure, which would undoubtedly lead to a letter regarding his shortcomings.

A figure was coming down the garden path. Unless the fashion at court had suddenly turned toward broadbrimmed hats with peacock feathers, it was no one from Eliott's parents' circle.

Eliott grabbed Kess's ankle and shook her leg. "Hey. Get up. I think . . . No. Whoa."

He scrambled to his feet, slipped, and got to shore on his second attempt. "Hey! Over here!"

The figure came bounding toward them. The feathered hat swept down in an elegant bow.

"You have no idea the trouble I've had to go to in order to find you," said Cyral. He straightened and smiled. "It's a good thing there have been very few Elvish babysitters in this part of the world, or I might never have been able to deliver this."

"You're really here," said Kess. She put a hand on Eliott's shoulder. "What are you doing here?"

Cyral held out a package wrapped in brown paper. "Open this."

Carefully, Eliott did so, half-afraid that he might suddenly find himself waking up back on the ice, cloud-blind and dreaming. He dropped the paper onto the snow and lifted out a leather-bound book. There was no title, but when he turned the first page and read the first lines, he knew exactly what it was.

"'Hear now, ye muses, of my experience / My journeys in distant and familiar lands / Hear, ye bored goddesses, of all these events / Of heroics unsung and stories unplanned / Old men who endure and young men who aspire / Of Childe Eliott and of Jordan (Retired)' . . ." He stopped reading, but his mouth refused to close. "You . . . you wrote it down. You remembered!"

Cyral looked embarrassed. He nodded. "There was wishing involved. I only made two copies, though—I don't intend to try to perform this. For one thing, most people would say I was making it up, and in a way, they'd be right. And for another," he added, glancing away at the distant mountains, "I don't think Jordan would be very happy with me if I did. So I'll leave his legend undisturbed."

"But this . . ."

He shrugged. "It's my story, too. And yours. Both of yours, I mean."

"Who's the hero?" said Kess.

"I believe I've left that open to interpretation," said Cyral. "Some things are better that way."

Their eyes met.

Eliott, paying no attention to their interpretive dance, flipped through the pages. "I have to see how it ends."

"You know how it ends," said Kess. "You were there."

Eliott ignored her. Being there wasn't the same as reading about it afterward, when he could see how he had looked through someone else's eyes.

"So. Two copies," said Kess, as Eliott tried to find the start of the last chapter. "Where's mine?"

"I . . . thought the two of you would share," said Cyral. "The other one, I'm saving to give to . . . well, to him. To Jordan."

Eliott stopped reading. "You know where to find him? We couldn't remember—I figured that was part of the wish fixing everything."

"I don't know, exactly, but there are clues. In the book, hints, that sort of thing. I expect it'll be another long journey. Which was, er, one of the reasons I tried to find the two of you first . . ." Cyral rolled his hat in his hands awkwardly. "I thought you might like to come with me?"

Eliott stayed focused on the book. If he looked up, he would catch Kess's eye, and she would grin, and then they would both fall into helpless laughter that would keep either of them from answering. So he let her speak for both of them.

"Will you tell me the story along the way?" she said, tapping the book.

Cyral bowed again. "Of course, milady."

Kess threw a snowball at him, and they were off, all three running across the white gardens to flee responsibility and the tedium of normal lives. Eliott could say he was being stolen away by elves, captured by a traveling minstrel show, but it was his life, and he would live it as he pleased; as an adventure story. As a fairy tale. As the stuff of legends.

Ian Gibson lives on Vancouver Island, in Canada. *Stuff of Legends*, his debut novel, was a finalist in the 2009 Amazon Breakthrough Novel Award contest.

**Explore the outer reaches
of imagination—don't miss these authors
of dark fantasy and urban noir that take you
to the edge and beyond.**

Patricia Briggs	Karen Chance	Anne Bishop
Simon R. Green	Caitlin R. Kiernan	Janine Cross
Jim Butcher	Rachel Caine	Sarah Monette
Kat Richardson	Glen Cook	Douglas Clegg